of Special Importance to our American Readers

The Case of the 24 MISSING TITLES ...

Over the years many of our American readers have been distressed that Harlequin Romances were published in Canada three months ahead of the United States release date.

We are pleased to announce that effective April 1972 Harlequin Romances will have simultaneous publication of new titles throughout North America.

To solve the problem of the 24 MISSING TITLES (No. 1553 to No. 1576) arrangements will be made with many Harlequin Romance retailers to have these missing titles available to you before the end of 1972.

Watch for your retailer's special display!

If, however, you have difficulty obtaining any of the missing titles, please write us.

Yours truly,

The Publisher
HARLEQUIN ROMANCES.

WELCOME

TO THE WONDERFUL WORLD

of Harlequin Romances!

Interesting, informative and entertaining,
each Harlequin Romance portrays an appealing
love story. Harlequin Romances take you
to faraway places — places with real people
facing real love situations — and
you become part of their story.

As publishers of Harlequin Romances, we're extremely
proud of our books (we've been publishing
them since 1954). We're proud also that Harlequin
Romances are North America's most-read
paperback romances.

Eight new titles are released every month and are
sold at nearly all book-selling stores across
Canada and the United States.

A free catalogue listing all available Harlequin Romances
can be yours by writing to the

HARLEQUIN READER SERVICE,
M.P.O. Box 707, Niagara Falls, N.Y. 14302.
Canadian address: Stratford, Ontario, Canada.

or use order coupon at back of book.

We sincerely hope you enjoy reading
this Harlequin Romance.

Yours truly,

THE PUBLISHERS
  Harlequin Romances

THE INN
BY THE LAKE

by

DOROTHY QUENTIN

HARLEQUIN BOOKS

TORONTO
WINNIPEG

This edition published in 1971
by Mills & Boon Limited, 17 - 19 Foley Street,
London WlA 1DR, England

This edition © Dorothy Quentin 1971

Harlequin edition published June, 1972

SBN 373-01596-8

Printed in Canada

1596

THE INN BY THE LAKE

CHPATER ONE

"*SIX heures moins vingt, monsieur. Nous arrivons à Basle pour le petit déieuner.*"

The *wagon-lit* attendant, a fat cheerful man with twinkling eyes, shook Jonathan Grant gently. "*Il faut passer les douanes, m'sieur,*" he added more urgently.

"*Merci*—" Jonathan roused himself from sleep that had been deeper, more peaceful, than any he had had for a long time. Once awake, his training made him instantly alert. They were arriving at Basle, where there would be breakfast at the station when they had been through Customs. They were almost in Switzerland—he tipped the attendant, bolted the scalding-hot coffee, and began to shave, humming softly that absurd but haunting song about the wild goose that one of the coloured G.I.s in the hospital had been perpetually crooning when Jonathan was recovering from his leg injury received during the bombing of Ming-dhu.

It was an old song, the G.I. said, perhaps twenty years old; he had learned it from his father. Somehow the plaintive melody in a minor key and the words of the song expressed all mankind's longing to be free—free of the lunacy of war, of the industrial rat-race, of a machine-dominated civilisation.

"*I must go where the wild goose goes, I must go where the wild goose cries . . .*"

Jonathan hummed in tune with the rhythm of the train wheels that were climbing steadily towards the frontier, surveying his lean, tanned face and dark unruly hair in the mirror above the washbasin with only cursory interest; but he was amused by the almost-boyish excitement in the grey eyes that stared steadily back at him, belying the fine lines of fatigue and strain that surrounded them.

Switzerland, with its clean beautiful mountains and lakes, lay ahead of him like some Shangri-la, an oasis of peace after the horrors of the torrid jungle warfare of Vietnam. He had never been to Switzerland and he found himself looking forward to it—to six glorious weeks of rest and holiday—with growing enthusiasm. He was sick of the whole beastliness of war, and of flying—that was why he had elected to travel in the old, slow, peaceful fashion by boat and train, unhurriedly making his way to the Promised

Land. He grinned at himself in the mirror and gave his thick hair a last disciplinary brush. Yesterday in France it had been grey and raining, a small disappointment; this morning was different; already the crisp, clean air was banishing the train-stuffiness and the pale golden sunshine was rimming the mountain-tops.

"Wild goose, brother goose, which is best . . . a wandering foot or a heart at rest . . . ?"

It was absurd, Jonathan thought ironically, the way that song had haunted him through the fever-ridden days and nights after Ming-dhu, throughout the flight back to London, and during his convalescence at home in the West Country. He was thirty-eight, almost middle-aged, not a boy from the American backwoods romantically turning himself into a wild goose to follow the spring migration . . . leaving a woman sleeping in his log cabin to awake and find her man gone, a shadow of wings sweeping across the sky, and a feather fluttering down on to her pillow . . .

Uncle Steve's gracious old house in the shadow of the cathedral of Combe Castleton that had been his home since the death of his parents in an air-crash years before was no log cabin . . . and since Fay's defection when he had been still a student there had been no woman in his heart. In fact, he thought drily, he had acquired a reputation for being ruthlessly woman-proof, which was sometimes useful to a busy surgeon fending off romantic nurses or neurotic women patients. There had been plenty of both during his years in the great London hospital, and probably there would be more when he took up his new appointment in August as consultant surgeon to the West Country regional group of hospitals in and around Combe Castleton. Women patients frequently fell in love with their surgeons after a successful operation . . . for a little while, and mostly out of gratitude. Jonathan was not a vain man, and he understood that adoration for the ephemeral thing it was.

After getting his F.R.C.S. and the termination of his Registrarship at St. Cuthbert's he had applied for and been granted the West Country appointment that would enable him to live at home and do some private practice as well in Combe Castleton, which he chose deliberately in preference to Harley Street. He had filled in six of the nine months intervening by volunteering to serve in an American field hospital in Vietnam, which cared for civilian as well as military casualties. It had been an experience he would never forget; increasing his skill and ingenuity in emergency surgery but shocking his humanity with the sight of women, children, old men and non-combatant villagers caught up in the savagery of modern warfare. The bombing of Ming-dhu had occurred a fortnight before he was due to leave Vietnam. They had patched him up in the field hospital and flown him back to London and St. Cuthbert's, where Sir James Hennessy had received his ex-Registrar back as a patient with kindly irony.

"This'll teach you not to go poking your scalpel into other people's wars! Should have put up your plate here, Jonathan, like I told you. Lucky it wasn't your right arm, though."

He was lucky to be alive, Jonathan thought grimly, trying not to remember the shambles they had made of Ming-dhu . . . probably by accident as there was no military installation there. He did not regret his six months in Vietnam; he was even obscurely glad that he had been injured, that in some small measure he had shared in the general suffering. He was also human enough to be glad his leg had healed properly; now it was just stiff and he walked with a slight limp that would gradually disappear with exercise.

The train drew to a standstill in the quietude of Basle station and disgorged its full load of yawning, grumbling humanity that after breakfast would proceed in a Swiss train. The Customs' examination was cursory; people who travelled by train these days were mostly having a cheap holiday and not smuggling—not going in this direction, anyway—and the officials were sleepy. Yet one of them stared alertly as Jonathan unlocked his instrument case.

"I'm a surgeon on holiday," he explained gruffly in French, almost apologetically. He had no right to be carrying that case; he had promised Dr. Cranford to be just a tourist; not to foregather with surgeons anywhere, not to talk shop, and in no circumstances to operate. Yet at the last moment he had included this case of instruments with his baggage; leaving it would be like leaving his right arm behind.

The Customs official shrugged, glanced again at Jonathan's passport, and drew a squiggle of blue chalk on the case. These Englishmen were peculiar always, and six in the morning is no time to argue with a man who chooses to take his tools of trade on holiday with him, but . . . !

The buffet was crowded with sleepy passengers off the French train. Jonathan thought the strong coffee, crisp rolls and butter and cherry jam delicious, but around him he heard the traveller's usual complaints.

"What I'd give for a good cup of tea! I never slept a wink all night."

"Those couchettes are a swindle."

"Next time we'll fly, Marge."

"Fancy cherry jam instead of marmalade for breakfast!"

"Oh, they're famous for their cherry jam, Hilda. We ought to get the recipe while we're here."

"They can't make decent tea, anyway."

Jonathan found himself wondering why people who liked English breakfasts so much endured the discomfort of travelling at all, if they came abroad only to criticise. Certainly there was no feeling among the majority of his fellow-passengers that they were drawn to follow the wild goose of imagination to lovely, unknown lands . . . then he remembered that not all of them had had the comfort of a *wagon-lit*; it was six o'clock in the morning and many of them had sat up for twelve hours in the rocking train.

The Swiss train, small and electrically driven and spotlessly clean, left punctually at seven-twenty. And there began for Jonathan and all the first-timers a journey of pure delight that banished such mundane thoughts as the relative value of jam or marmalade, coffee or tea for breakfast. For the little train ran smoothly down valleys between green hills scattered with wooden chalets so exactly like the toy ones that they looked unreal; the clear sunlight, growing warmer with every hour, shone down on window-boxes bright with flowers and trailing creepers, on fat cows whose bells tinkled as they turned and gazed placidly at the passing train, on men with peaked hats and *lederhosen* going about their farms, on streams crossed by little wooden bridges, on children who waved to the passing train as children wave all over the world. And everything was so incredibly bright in that clear atmosphere that it looked too good to be true. The electric train ran so quietly that the passengers could hear the cow bells and the chattering of the children in German as they walked to school.

Jonathan found himself travelling with a Swiss on his way to Florence, a man who spoke fluent French and explained much of the passing scenery to him. "If you're going to Lugano, it will be easy to see something of Italy

10

also," he said. "The coaches go almost every day to Florence and Rome, to Venice——"

Jonathan smiled. "But I am not trying to see Europe. I am going for a—a complete rest."

It was not the whole truth. He had chosen Lugano, of course, because of that fantastic story Uncle Steve had told him about old Mrs. Stannisford's granddaughter. Uncle Steve was the Stannisfords' solicitor; generations of legal Grants had looked after the Stannisford affairs; it was a family friendship of ancient origin as well as a business connection. And Uncle Steve had pounced on the news that Jonathan was to have a holiday in completely new surroundings. "For heaven's sake go to Lugano, lad, and try and knock some sense into Helen's granddaughter. The old lady is dying of curiosity, longing to see the girl and kill the fatted calf—and all she does is to return our letters unopened!"

"Isn't it a bit late to kill the fatted calf?" Jonathan had demanded dryly. He had been a schoolboy when Evelyn Stannisford had run away with Jean Berenger, a penniless French artist; but he could remember that he had liked Evelyn much better than her parents, those two wealthy old tyrants who lived in Osterley House and occasionally came to dine with his uncle and aunt. At fifteen, the fuss they had made about Evelyn's runaway marriage had seemed to Jonathan much ado about nothing ... Now old Henry Stannisford was dead. During the intervening years Jonathan had grown up, qualified, endured a war, and become a distinguished surgeon, and forgotten all about the almost legendary affair of Evelyn and her Frenchman. His uncle had mentioned that since her husband's death Helen Stannisford had started enquiries, trying to get in touch with her daughter through a Continental enquiry agent. Jonathan had been too preoccupied with his own work to take more than a passing interest in the Stannisford affair, but his uncle and aunt were excited when the news came from the enquiry agent. Jean Berenger had died in Paris ten years ago and Evelyn had died since, in Switzerland. But they had left one child, a daughter, who was twenty-two. There the work of the enquiry agent came to an abrupt full-stop. According to his reports, Nicole Berenger was not at all interested in meeting her English relations; she did not desire the reconciliation with her grandmother. She positively refused any further information and sent the enquiry agent about his business firmly. Letters from her

11

grandmother or from Stephen Grant, in fact any letters bearing the Combe Castleton postmark or the solicitor's address, were returned unopened.

"That child's as proud as Lucifer—she takes after old Henry!" Uncle Steve said ruefully. "A pity, though—with the old lady wanting to have her home, and all that money. It will go to Nigel if the girl won't play."

There was something in the legend of the young, proud Nicole Berenger that appealed to Jonathan. Rather than persuade her to come home he felt like encouraging her in her stand . . . yet after he had seen and talked with her grandmother he knew that his uncle and aunt were right.

Helen Stannisford was just what Aunt Bella had called her . . . a little old frail woman haunted by the loss of her only child, the victim for many years of her husband's temper; all the money in the bank, the good furniture that filled Osterley House, the depleted but still large and efficient staff, could not bring back her dead daughter.

"It was always thought Henry would relent," she said wistfully, and her faded eyes lighted up when she spoke of Evelyn, "otherwise I would have followed them to France. But young married folk don't want a mother-in-law tagging on. Jonathan—if you can bring Nicole home I shall die happy. Give her my love, tell her I will not keep her here if she does not want to stay; but I would so love to see Evelyn's daughter."

Jonathan had promised, unwillingly, to do his best. "But I'm not going to use any blackmail, emotional or financial, on the girl," he stipulated bluntly. He had been touched, in spite of his reluctance, by the old lady's frankness.

"Ah. You have been ill? You do not look like a convalescent!" The Swiss shrugged cheerfully. "It does not matter. You will find Lugano restful, and beautiful enough. It is in the canton of Ticino—that is the Italian part of Switzerland." He laughed, showing excellent teeth. "We are proud to call it Switzerland, but you will find everything Italian except the prices and the cleanliness! We are practically international here—French, Austrian, Italian. Perhaps after all you will see Europe very well by staying in Switzerland!"

Later, the man was engaged in German conversation by a newcomer, and later still he hailed a woman passing down the corridor in Italian. Jonathan envied him his command

12

of languages, but he was to find that a commonplace in this country.

By the time the train reached Lucerne it was hot, and he was glad of the big, wide-open window of the train. The lake glittered in the bright sunshine, and many of the parties got out at the station. The train climbed, seemingly effortlessly, towards the Alps; towards the St. Gotthard Pass. Round and round the little hamlet with the church spire it circled, each time higher up, and now there was still snow visible on the mountain tops. It halted to load up cars on the flat trucks at the rear, and the Swiss explained that the road across the pass was not yet open for motor traffic. "There are sometimes avalanches."

It was amusing, watching the cars being loaded on the train so effortlessly. People leaned from the windows to take photographs of the performance, of the little hamlet like a toy in the crystal air far below, of the snow-capped mountains. It was too late for winter sports, but the dazzling snow still dominated the scene.

"Now you will see—the houses, the farms, the vines—everything becomes Italian," the Swiss told Jonathan.

It was true. Though they were still travelling over the same land, a few miles after the St. Gotthard tunnel, the scene changed subtly to something more southern. The sun grew hotter, the farms and cottages were no longer like toys, neat and compact; the flowering vines straggled everywhere, and in every hamlet there was a church. The Swiss grinned. "Every three houses and you have a church! They are very old, these churches—medieval. The Ticinese are church-going people."

The train belled its way into Lugano station punctually at noon and Jonathan said good-bye to his travelling friend, and felt oddly alone as he stood on the platform and watched it going on its way to Italy. The capped and armleted couriers had already swept up their tourists; he was alone in the strong sunlight, at the end of a twenty-four-hour journey; at the beginning, he could not help feeling, of an adventure. He plunged into the subway that led to the station entrance, in the wake of his porter who showed him the funicular that would carry him down the steep hill into the town.

"What hotel?" the porter asked in careful English.

Jonathan shrugged. "Lunch first. Then I want to go here—an *albergo* is an inn, isn't it?" He showed the man the address of Nicole Berenger his uncle had given him. He

13

had intended to put up at a hotel in the town, but a sudden impulse made him look in his wallet for the girl's address. *Albergo Fionetti, Gandria, Lago di Lugano.*

The porter shrugged, tried a spate of German that Jonathan did not comprehend, and called to the American Express courier for help. The fair young man mopped his steaming face and grinned at Jonathan, after listening to a long explanation that made the traveller hungrier than ever. "He says the Albergo Fionetti is a poor place, not a hotel for tourists. A place for fishermen and artists. There are plenty of good hotels in the town."

"I want to go there—" Jonathan was becoming annoyed. His impulse to go and stay at the Albergo Fionetti strengthened into determination. He had seen brochures of the charming but conventional hotels scattered along the slopes of the town, and he felt suddenly that he did not want to stay with a crowd of English people, with the tourists on a hectic sightseeing holiday. He wanted to go somewhere peaceful, to live with the natives, to see for himself exactly how old Helen Stannisford's granddaughter was living and supporting herself.

The American Express courier shrugged again, amiably. "Me, I am from Paris. The Lugano hotels I know, and the expeditions to the other lakes—Morcoté and Gandria, I know. But I have not seen this *albergo.* You will have to hire a boat, if there is not an expedition to Gandria after your *déjeuner.*" He told Jonathan where to get a good lunch, how much to pay the porter, and where to find the *debarcadero centrale* from which boats—all kinds of boats—left for the various villages around the lake.

Jonathan thanked him for his helpfulness and went down in the little funicular to the town. Once away from the cluttered buildings surrounding the station it was delightful, and he ate an excellent lunch at a café overlooking the lake where the avenue of pollarded chestnut trees made a deep, shady promenade beside the glittering blue water.

It was a brilliant day, a day as different from the sad greyness of yesterday in England as could be imagined. Jonathan felt too hot in his lounge suit, he longed to relax in old clothes, to swim in that limpid blue water. Perhaps later he would swim . . . After lunch he hefted his two cases the few yards to the central jetties and looked about him interestedly. There was a steamer tied up, but with no obvious intention of sailing yet. There were plenty of row-

14

boats, empty, and two motor-boats whose captains were shouting out long itineraries for the afternoon trips. It was the siesta hour, hot in the noonday glare, and it seemed as if he was the only impatient passenger in the whole of Lugano.

A slim boy with fair, curly hair cropped short, and skin the colour of ripe, warm berries, and eyes that almost matched the incredible blueness of the lake, manoeuvred a clumsy row-boat up to the steps and accosted him. A fair Italian, Jonathan thought, taking in the thin, almost classical beauty of the boy and wondering at the strength in the thin arms. A spate of Italian made him shake his head, and suddenly he was shocked to hear perfect English from the laughing lips of the boy.

"Are you the Englishman who wants the Albergo Fionetti? Why do you want to come to us? There are plenty of hotels in the town—" the cropped, curly head gestured contemptuously towards the well-kept promenade —"and if you want luxury, go along to Paradiso!"

Jonathan grinned. He couldn't help himself. This ragged urchin had charm as well as impudence, and it was not a boy but a girl. Hardly more than a child. "I don't want luxury," he said firmly. "I want peace, and some fishing. I heard that you have both at the *albergo*. But how did you know about me?"

"Oh, Peppone told Emilio, who was collecting some people for Morcoté," the girl said as if people were parcels, to be distributed round the lake. She added dubiously: "We don't usually have people to stay. Only for odd meals."

She pointed up the lake. "Gandria's up there, very beautiful for artists. But you are not an artist, are you?"

"I paint a little."

For a moment under the hot noonday sun they surveyed each other, Jonathan amused, the girl slightly suspicious. She said childishly, "I said I would bring you over if I thought you were all right."

"And—am I all right?" he demanded gently, very tall above the jetty, looking down into the bluest eyes he had ever seen.

"I'll take you. But don't grumble when you get there," she answered obliquely. "Stow your things here, by my feet."

He felt suddenly as if he had been given some privilege. He offered to row up the lake, but the girl dismissed that with a casual "I'm used to it. It's easy." He sat where she told him to sit, looking at the child's thin shoulder-blades under the faded cotton shirt. The old boat moved slowly but steadily up the smooth, blue water. The girl did not make conversation but once she asked him his name.

"Oh—Johnson——" he answered vaguely. He wanted to get to know Nicole Berenger before she realised he had come from Combe Castleton. He would be just a stranger on holiday, a fellow who dabbled with painting as a hobby. "You're one of the Fionnettis, I suppose."

She turned her head to flash him a glance from those incredibly blue eyes. "I'm Nicole Berenger," she said proudly, simply: but it was as if she was announcing her title to an ignorant fool. Then, childish again, she grinned her wide, *gamine* grin. "But you can call me Nicki. Everyone does."

In a minute she turned again, pointing: "Gandria."

Jonathan turned obediently to look up the lake at the approaching coastline, with the big villas whose wrought-iron gates led down to private jetties, millionaires' homes; beyond the villas, to the stuccoed houses covered with flowering creepers that perched precariously on the bank, to the cottages whose stone steps were lapped by the blue water of the lake. But the beauty of it passed him by for that first moment; he was too stunned, looking at this wiry waif who handled a heavy row-boat like a fisherman, and thinking of Helen Stannisford and Osterley House. This was a pretty kettle of fish indeed.

It was a good thing, Jonathan thought, that Nicole had her back to him, or she would certainly have seen the dismay in his face. Lugano was a modern, civilised little town; during his brief walk through it he had noted the bright, clean shops, the well-dressed appearance of its inhabitants. Now the girl he had come to find proved to be a ragged waif—for Nicole's faded shirt and slacks were not casual clothes *pour le sport* which visitors indulge in; they looked like her everyday apparel, and seemingly she was not even conscious of her gypsy appearance. Jonathan recovered swiftly from his first shock, his brain reacted quickly to any emergency, but he was glad he had not given his real name to the child. To this girl, rather. He found it difficult to believe that she was twenty-two, and Helen Stannisford's granddaughter, and the possible heiress to Osterley House and a fortune. What a shock she would have given sleepy old Combe Castleton if she had answered Uncle Steve's letters in person!

Somewhere deep down in Jonathan a boy laughed. If Nicole Berenger had been dirty as well as shabby, cross-eyed or stupid, he would have given up his mission then and there; made some excuse to return to the town, and booked in at one of the very pleasant-looking hotels he could now see terracing the Bay of Lugano. But there was something undeniably attractive about Nicole's serious, sensitive little face and the *gamine* grin that lightened it occasionally. She certainly wasn't dirty; her hair and skin gleamed with health and cleanliness that owed nothing to cosmetics. When she was older she might very well be a beautiful woman. . . . Oh, hang it all, Jonathan thought whimsically in the midst of his catalogue, she's only a child, whatever her birth certificate might say.

There was a certain charm in her unselfconscious sex-lessness; she was neither a boy nor a girl; the same charm that one finds in intelligent children who have accepted life, children who have been brought up in a happy home. Yet Nicole's home life could not have been happy, in fact she *had* no real home. . . .

Compassion filled Jonathan as he looked at the slender back bowed with the weight of the clumsy oars, but already he knew better than to offer help. The tenderness in his face was banished instantly as she shipped an oar and kept the boat stationary, well out on the lake, so that he could get a fine sweeping view of Lugano and the immediate shores.

"San Salvatore." She indicated the mountain on their left, and the sharp peak on their right. "Monte Bré. Funiculars run right up to the hotels on the top; at night you can see their lights like a ladder going up, up"—her slim, brown fingers climbed vividly—"like a ladder of stars against the darkness of the night, and at the top the biggest star of all——"

She was not trying to impress him, he understood. She was simply doing her patter, being the guide for a stranger and a tourist. She pointed out Paradiso, with its luxury hotels and public gardens festooned with climbing roses; the Lido; the cathedral and several of the churches they could see from the water. The little town looked clean, charming, and a trifle conventional from out here. Jonathan found himself, unexpectedly, turning his eyes towards

17

the older, picturesque villages further away. "Lugano is pretty, but I think I shall prefer the old places," he heard himself saying, and was rewarded by that quick smile.

"Ah, but we have no bathroom or plumbing. There is a place down the garden that Emilio sees to," she answered prosaically.

Jonathan drew in a deep breath of the crystalline air, air purified by the vast expanse of water, by the mountains and the snows of winter. "I think I can manage without plumbing," he said gently, "and this is a big enough bath. I'd like to swim tonight."

"You'll find the water cold." She was matter-of-fact. "*We* don't swim yet, for a few weeks." She pointed out Bissone on the opposite shore, and told him he must see the seventeenth-century house of the painter Tencella Carpoforo, who had founded a school of art at the Imperial Court of Vienna and left his home to the nation. Again Nicole's brown hands came into play. "It's now a museum. Quite small, but very interesting—because it's still a *house*. Everything is kept just as it was used, the dining room and bedrooms and kitchen. All the paintings and *objets d'art* are the originals——"

He was amused by her competence, touched by it as he would have been touched by a child's skill; yet already he knew that both amusement and tenderness must be hidden from Nicole. The tilt of her head, the sculptured nose, the small aggressive chin, the fire that sparked now and then in her blue eyes, were signs of pride. He remembered, too, that her father had been an artist.

"I'll take you there, if you like," she offered, using one oar to keep the clumsy boat from drifting.

"Not today. I want to get home and change into some clothes more suitable for this sun——" Jonathan's crooked smile appealed to her and she nodded. Those were indeed silly clothes to wear in this place, but he looked distinguished in them. Not a bit like the usual tourists. She had promised Lucia not to bring him back if he looked stuffy, or likely to give them a lot of trouble. But she had liked him at once; it was as if they had been friends a long time. That was silly, she knew, but she was more homesick than she realised for her own kind; for the sound of an English voice that talked with her like a friend, not merely exclaiming over the beauties of the lake. As she began to row slowly and steadily towards Gandria he was asking,

"Do you take many tourists around?" and she laughed. It was the mischievous laugh of a child.

"In this old tub? Sometimes, but Emilio takes them in the motor-boat. She's called *Pegasus* and flies through the water. But she's not yet paid for and uses a lot of petrol. This one we use for fishing, and odd jobs like fetching you. And when I have to go shopping," she added casually. "But I detest shopping! Usually I get Bianca to do it on her way home from school. This is *my* boat. I use it very much."

"I can see you do. Surely"—Jonathan spoke lightly, gently, so as not to arouse that spark in her—"it's rather a heavy boat for a girl to manage?"

"Pff! I'm strong, stronger than I look." Nicole did not even pause to consider that. "And she only cost a hundred francs, because Stefano had finished with her. The motor-boat costs fourteen hundred francs and it will take Emilio a long time to pay for her."

Jonathan was doing sums with the unfamiliar Swiss francs. A hundred and twenty pounds. It did not sound much to him for a motor-boat. When he said so Nicole threw him one of her swift, curious glances.

"I suppose you're rich. If you are, we may make quite a lot of money from you while you stay at the Albergo Fionetti," she said with complete frankness.

Jonathan laughed. This was the girl who had turned down the chance of inheriting a fortune. He could not understand it, but he found himself suddenly curious, eager to know all about her background. He said dryly, "At least I've been warned. But who is this Emilio, and why is it important to have a motor-boat? You seem to manage very well in this one, and surely you're not tied for time in this place?"

She rested on her oars and swung round to look at him, with pity for his ignorance. "Don't you see"—she waved a hand round the shores of the lake—"all these places are far apart? Gandria up here, Melide down there where the bridge is, and beyond Melide the old, old village of Morcoté with its famous church—you have to climb up four hundred steps to that and the cemetery! And over there, Bissone and Campione—that's Italian, and they have a casino. Don't go there or they'll skin you of all your money. And Caprino—there's a *ristorante* there with a good wine, and dancing on a balcony over the lake, very romantic and not expensive!"

"It sounds delightful." Jonathan was still dry. He could not remember when he had last gone dancing. "But I still don't understand why you have to visit all these places in a hurry. You live here, don't you?"

Nicole's chuckle was both amused and impatient. "Naturally we live here," she answered with quaint dignity. "I live here with the Fionettis, with Emilio and Bianco and Pietro. The *albergo* belongs to them, but we should never make enough to live on from serving odd meals. Emilio takes tourists round to places of interest. I do it sometimes; it's rather fun—but a motor-boat makes all the difference. They're always in a hurry, the English and Germans and Americans! A few days here, then off to Florence and Rome or Venice. The French and Italians are not in such a hurry. They come to look, and to live with us for a while—not just to take photographs and say they've '*done*' Lugano!"

He found himself sympathising with her outlook. Even during his journey of twenty-four hours from London he had heard people discussing itineraries that sounded fantastic to him. He wondered just what Nicole's outlook was, all in all; she spoke perfect English without a trace of foreign accent—probably due to her mother's teaching. Remembering Evelyn, and looking at this fair child, he realised that there *was* a family resemblance. Probably Helen Stannisford, before her hair turned white, had looked like this girl. She was still *petite*. . . . Yet in spite of the perfect, easy English, Nicole was living with an Italian family, and obviously regarded the Albergo Fionetti as her home.

"And I haven't even brought a camera with me," he grinned boyishly, "only some fishing and painting tackle."

"Yes—you paint. That is good!" Nicole's approval strengthened. "A motor-boat makes *all* the difference. Emilio does three trips a day round the lake, morning, afternoon, evening. That way he earns the instalments. When *Pegasus* is paid for he'll be all right."

"And you?" Jonathan demanded, greatly daring. "What do you do with your time?"

"I paint too." She pulled a little grimace and startled him again with her honesty. "Very bad pictures. My father would have burned them. But all this"—again the slender, brown hand indicated the breathtaking beauty of still water reflecting mountains, of the rioting flowering creepers over old stone walls, the wrought-iron gates and poplars of the villa gardens, the huddled, picturesque cottages—"all this looks very nice in paintings. Tourists like to take back souvenirs, and most of them don't know that my pictures are very bad. I earn my living, and help Lucia to run the *albergo*, and look after the children when Lucia to run the *albergo*, and look after the children when they come home from school. Their parents are dead, you see."

"But——" Jonathan's eyes asked a question.

"My parents are dead, too," she answered briefly, and turned back to her rowing, and he knew that it would be unwise to ask any more questions yet. They had passed the villas set well up on their terraced gardens, and now reached one of the old stone steps in the bank. Nicole moored the boat to an iron ring in the wall and nodded upward, picking up Jonathan's cases with the casual ease of a porter. "The Albergo Fionetti," she said, and there was a hint of affectionate pride in her voice.

"I'll take those." He was determined, and with a faint surprised smile she surrendered the cases and led the way up the ancient, worn stone steps.

"Mind you don't fall back in the lake," she warned impulsively, and suddenly flushed deeply under her golden tan as she noticed his limp. "I'm sorry. I didn't see that you were lame, Mr. Johnson."

He grinned down at her suddenly.

"Only a temporary stiffness. It will go when I've done some climbing and swimming."

At first glance the Albergo Fionetti was a picturesque ruin, nothing more. They had left the attractive villas, standing in their own grounds, behind. This part of Gandria was a row of waterside cottages, their front doors at the top of worn stone steps to which small row-boats were moored, their windows barely above the water level. The *albergo* was larger than the cottages; it was raised up on the bank a little, and it stood in its own grounds. Jonathan stared at the little inn, fascinated; he had never seen anything quite like it. It rambled all over the place, an architect's nightmare; all the roof levels were different, covered with the old rose-red curly tiles that displayed moss and lichen so well. The lower windows and doors were supported by miniature Roman arches, none of the upper windows were straight, and every window seemed to possess its own rustic balcony over which wistaria and other creepers rioted. The garden, except for a few roses and a very neat vineyard, was ragged and unkempt and

21

possessed few flowers; but on every single balcony there were window-boxes blazing with colour—aglow with petunias, geraniums and pansies, and the vivid blue of the gentian. The walls had been washed in pale pink, and against this soft, glowing background the creepers rioted.

"It reminds me of Polperro a little," Jonathan said absentmindedly. His tidy surgeon's mind abhorred the peeling plaster, the lichened roof, the general untidiness of everything, the smell of damp; yet the artist in him stood transfixed. There was something undeniably beautiful in the place, and the windows must command a magnificent view over the lake. Just beyond, further up the coast, the hills rose sharply from the very edge of the limpid water.

"Polperro? Where is that—in Italy?" Poised like a brown nymph on the topmost step, Nicole asked the question idly. She was pleased because he stood still to look, instead of rushing indoors to see what kind of a bedroom they were offering him; Nicole had spent ten years here, and she loved the place. She had known the sadness of her mother's death here, but even that had been softened by the kindness of the Fionettis, by the beautiful peace of Lake Lugano. She had been twelve years old when they had come here after her father's tragic death in Paris, and the *albergo* had long since become her home. If this Englishman had stared at the *albergo* with supercilious eyes, if he had hesitated about the matter of plumbing, she would have made some excuse to dump him back in the town. Instead, he stood and looked at everything with a bright expression in his grey eyes, and the suspicion of affection already growing in his voice. He would do. If Lucia made a fuss or Pietro tried to be funny, she would deal with them. . . . She asked the question about Polperro idly, politely.

Jonathan smiled outright. "I suppose it does sound Italian. Actually it's in Cornwall."

Instantly Nicole's face closed up. The smiling pride left it, she stood straight and slim beside the stranger and demanded suspiciously, "That's in the West Country, isn't it?"

He realised he had blundered. Evelyn would have talked to her daughter, of course, about the West Country.

"Yes. . . ." He was elaborately casual, examining an old bronze statue in the wilderness of a garden. "I used to go there for my holidays when I was a boy. I'm very fond of the West Country."

"My mother came from there, she was English." Nicole relaxed again. That idiotic private detective with his impertinence had made her all on edge, unnecessarily suspicious. Lugano was full of English people at this time of the year; naturally, some of them came from the West Country. She added gently, "She said some of our villages reminded her of that, too . . . of the old fishing villages with the water coming right up to the doors of the cottages, like it does here. Sometimes I think she was very homesick, my mother."

Jonathan smiled down at her, relieved that the awkward moment had passed. That detective Helen had employed must have been an oaf. Just now the child—she looked such a child standing there in her shabby clothes—had looked both proud and frightened. He felt almost tempted to explain right away who he was, to seize this opportunity; the idea of gaining her confidence by a masquerade seemed suddenly the basest sort of trickery. Yet the child could be frightened so easily back into her shell, and he guessed that if she knew, now, that he was an emissary from her grandmother, she would have nothing more to do with him. Remembering the sadness in Helen Stannisford's faded eyes, Jonathan hardened his resolution. It was a ridiculous situation, a stupid misunderstanding; an old woman and a girl hurting each other through mistaken pride. It would be best to go slowly in the affair, and if he decided later not to interfere he could leave the Albergo Fionetti with no harm done.

"You speak English very well," he said gently, and the girl smiled.

"I speak French and Italian as well," she said indifferently, and pulled a childish face, "but German I hate! My father was French—perhaps that's why I can't get my tongue round the German gutturals. But come on inside, you're tired and hot——"

Leading the way past the shuttered windows of the ground floor she drew him into a big, dim kitchen with a red-tiled floor and a gigantic old stove. A carelessly fastened shutter let in a shaft of sunlight, but the room was cool and clean and smelled faintly of garlic and cheese and the wood used in the ancient stove.

"Ssh!" She halted on the threshold, smiling towards the old woman fast asleep on a rocker by the stove.

"Lucia—she didn't mean to have her siesta today because you were coming, but sleep has overtaken her!"

Sleep has overtaken her. . . . Jonathan savoured the poetry of the phrase together with the rich colouring of the scene in the quiet kitchen. Nicole spoke without a trace of accent, like any well-educated English girl—she had Evelyn to thank for that. He wondered whether she thought in English, or French, or Italian. One day, when he knew her better, he would ask her. Little Nicole Berenger—half boy, half girl; half English gentlewoman, half gypsy—intrigued him. There was something honest and brave and wholly enchanting about her.

"She has dressed up for you," Nicole whispered gently, and he looked again at the old sleeping woman before following her up a stone staircase. Lucia's face was lined with years, but strong and clean-featured still. Her beak of a nose and firm mouth might have been engraved on a coin, her breathing was deep and even. A black lace mantilla covered her iron-grey hair, a red woollen shawl was draped about her thin shoulders over her best alpaca frock; the thin, black-stockinged legs were thrust into red felt slippers. Her hands, folded in her lap, were brown and scarred with years of hard work, but there was in her whole pose an immense strength and dignity. She seemed part of the big, shadowed kitchen, with its red-tiled floor and the glow from the stove, the stone arches that served as door-ways to the larder and dining room, the deep green of the Chianti bottles suspended from hooks in a beam. It reminded Jonathan of the old Dutch masters.

"I would like to paint Lucia," he said quietly when they had reached the upper landing, which to his surprise was tiled like the kitchen. It ran from the back to the front of the house, up and down odd steps here and there, and turned a corner suddenly.

"Lucia has been painted many times, but not asleep," she told him seriously. "I don't think she would like to be painted asleep——"

"It does seem unfair—one is so unguarded, asleep," Jonathan agreed quietly. "Yet that old woman is very dignified and strong, even in her sleep. Not many of us could relax like that, without snoring, or gaping."

Nicole chuckled. "Do you snore? Emilio does, you can hear him all over the house. It's very quiet at night here."

"I hope not. I don't really know." He was amused.

"Then you're not married, if you don't know whether or not you snore," she announced matter-of-factly, and opened a door into a big, shadowy room at the corner of the inn. "But in here it doesn't matter. This room is over the stable—this used to be a farm—and you can make a noise like thunder if you wish!"

"Thank you!"

Jonathan put down the cases he carried, carefully because he could only see dimly a great four-poster bed, a table and a few odd chairs; until Nicole threw open the shutters suddenly and the octagonal-shaped room was flooded with clear light. Moving instinctively over to the windows, Jonathan uttered a small exclamation of delight. The room seemed to hang over the water, and across the lake the valleys between the mountains were beginning to take on the shadows of evening.

"In the morning you'll see the sun coming over the shoulder of Monte Caprino," Nicole told him, and turned back into the room with a small hostess-like gesture of her brown hands. "It's very—simple—here. No carpets, the tiles are cooler. And the small room through there is your bathroom." She smiled suddenly, mischievously. "If you decide to return to Lugano, you can go tomorrow."

"I shall stay here, if you and Lucia can put up with me, Nicki."

The diminutive slipped out so naturally that neither of them noticed it. Jonathan also used his hands to express something of his delight. "I like—simple—places. And with a view like this——" He chuckled suddenly, boyishly, "This room is fit for a millionaire! Now run along. I want to wash and get into something cooler."

Nicole was listening to the church clocks chiming in the clear quietness. She nodded gravely. "I should wear very old clothes here. If you want to paint we'll be using my boat—and your good clothes will get spoiled. That's half-past three. At four o'clock there will be tea, down in the loggia."

"Don't make it specially for me, I can last out until—until you have supper," Jonathan suggested, trying to save trouble, though the idea of tea was very welcome.

Nicole chuckled again, and he thought how pleasant her chuckle was, before a wistful expression crossed her small face. It was expressive like a child's face, with sunlight and shadows chasing across the fine features. "You think we can't make you good tea!" she accused directly. "But we

25

can. Every day at four o'clock I made it for my mother. In the town they charge you two francs extra for afternoon tea; English tea is very expensive; but here I won't charge you extra," she added, as he started to thank her dryly for the privilege. "It wouldn't be fair. Every day I make a pot of tea for myself. It's nice to share it with someone."

She whisked out of the door and closed it behind her, leaving Jonathan to unpack and explore his new domain. *Every day at four o'clock I made it for my mother. . . . Sometimes I think she was very homesick, my mother. . . .*

Gradually Jonathan, who could only remember Evelyn as a young girl, was building up a picture of this exile she had shared with her own daughter. It gave him an extraordinary feeling, remembering the gay, enchanted Evelyn, very much in love with her Frenchman; twenty-three years ago . . . almost a quarter of a century—and he had been fifteen. How old that should make him feel. But it did not. Today Jonathan felt young—younger than he had done for years. His boyish memories of Evelyn were merging with Nicole, who was so like and yet so different from her mother. And quite apart from his mission for his uncle and an old, lonely Englishwoman, Jonathan found himself enjoying a new experience. The rambling, dilapidated Italian inn on the shore of a Swiss lake, an old farm that was yet surprisingly solid inside; the extraordinary beauty of deep, still water lapping the feet of the mountains surrounding it; that ancient woman asleep in the kitchen; these things were so far removed from his recent experiences in Vietnam and the long years in hospital that he found himself looking forward to six weeks of freedom here as an adventure.

And that, he told himself dryly, is exactly what the doctor ordered! He grinned at his wet face in the spotted mirror above the deep stone sink in his 'bathroom'. The sink was fed by a single pipe and tap, presumably pumped from the lake, because the water was icy cold. In another corner of the tiled room was a concrete square with a drain, above it a shower. If it was going to be as hot as it was today for the whole of his holiday, that shower would be more than welcome. Nevertheless, he understood now Nicole's brusque references to plumbing. In the Lugano hotels there would be gleaming chromium taps, porcelain basins, hot and cold in every room. Yet already he would not have exchanged the Albergo Fionetti for a Hilton hotel. He hoped the family would accept his presence as easily as

Nicole had done, and wondered just what her position was in the household. She said she took tourists about the lake, and painted bad pictures to sell; did she pay the Fionettis for her board, then? And who was Lucia . . . the grandmother, or a domestic? Jonathan whistled as he put on a soft shirt and thin, ancient slacks and combed back his thick hair which had been liberally wetted during his ablutions. It occurred to him that he must not seem to take too personal an interest in Nicole Berenger, so when he joined her for tea he was content to sit and enjoy just looking about him.

The loggia was a sort of wooden verandah built in the middle of the house, slightly protruding over the lake, its three sides formed by the walls of the house itself. On the ground floor there were arched doorways but no doors, so that one could command cool-looking vistas from the loggia. Nicole had changed into a faded blue cotton frock and sandals to preside over the tea tray, but with her bare brown legs and arms she still looked a child. A child washed and brushed and on its best behaviour, copying the grown-ups, but still a child who would suddenly run off to its own world of make-believe where the grown-ups could not follow.

The loggia was open to the sky, though there were canvas blinds that could be drawn across it in bad weather, and as he sprawled comfortably in one of the swinging chairs he could see Monte Caprino across the lake, framed by the wistaria clambering over the rough log posts of the loggia. At their feet bark boxes were filled with petunias, pansies, gentians and lobelia, and on odd stools about the place stood pots with begonias and geraniums and ferns in them. There was a sweet tranquillity about the whole scene that arrested him on the threshold. He had followed his nose through the kitchen, where Lucia had vanished from her rocking chair, into the dining-room with its old refectory table and heavy carved chairs, into this courtyard.

Nicole looked up from her serious preoccupation with the tea tray, staring at him with a child's frank approval. "Now you dress sensibly," she said, "and you feel better?"

"Much better, thank you. What a nice place this is"—he accepted the swing chair she indicated—"in fact, I'm glad you took me in, Nicole. I much prefer this to any hotel in the town—and the bathroom will suit me perfectly!"

"Oh"—she bit her lip suddenly, flushing beneath her tan—"I forgot to offer you hot water! I am sorry. We always use the cold, but there are copper cans in the kitchen and the fire is always under the big kettles. Will you please take a can when you want hot water?"

"Of course I will. Don't worry, the cold was very refreshing."

Nicole soon forgot her embarrassment. They had never had an Englishman at the *albergo* for more than the odd meal, and the fishermen and artists who occasionally stayed were used to helping themselves to what they wanted.

"How do you like your tea?" she asked, so gravely that Jonathan wanted to laugh. This was an Englishwoman in exile . . . and afternoon tea a function. He thought of the tea he had drunk, hot and strong and sweet, from tin mugs during brief snatched intervals in the incessant work at Ming-dhu hospital.

"Oh—milk and a little sugar, please."

To his surprise—he had noticed the thick local pottery on the dresser in the kitchen—it was handed to him in an exquisite fluted cup of Sèvres china. Nicole saw him appreciating it and smiled suddenly. Not her *gamine* grin but a real smile, warm and tender and mischievous.

"My mother's. We're not complete savages here."

"I beg your pardon," Jonathan apologised gently, "I don't think you're savages at all—merely wonderfully—free."

He was just going to tell her that the tea was perfect when the Fionetti family descended on them, a sudden cascade of noise and rapid Italian and laughter, after the motor-boat had been tied up. Nicole's face brightened. "Emilio has brought the children from school."

"*Hola! Nicki—Nicki!*"

"*A'loggia——*"

A dark, good-looking boy with snapping brown eyes jumped the wooden steps to the balcony, his white shirt making his skin seem almost black; he was followed by two tall children, fighting for possession of a mysterious package which they deposited at Nicole's feet before turning to survey the stranger with curious, impudent eyes.

Emilio shouted in Italian. "Where is your precious Englishman, Nicki?" before he saw Jonathan and Nicki's warning frown. Immediately he smiled and held out his hand, "*Benvenuto, signore——*"

Almost amused by the sudden change of tone, though

he had not understood the previous sentence, Jonathan shook hands. And meeting Emilio's eyes he was suddenly shocked by the realisation that beneath the boy's courteous welcome as host there was an instant antagonism. Emilio might be glad of visitors to his inn, his living was earned through ministering to tourists, but as he took in the little domestic scene on the loggia he was not pleased that an Englishman was having tea with Nicole. Jonathan had no means of knowing that Emilio was scared that Nicole would one day leave the Albergo Fionetti, that she would return to her own people. But his instinct told him correctly that this Italian boy—a young man really—was jealous. Probably he was in love with Nicki.

Jonathan was troubled. And beneath his own pleasant manner as Nicole introduced the children there was a small undercurrent of doubt. If she was in love with Emilio it would explain her refusal of her English grandmother's overtures. It would also complicate his mission hopelessly.

CHAPTER TWO

JONATHAN liked the two younger Fionettis better than Emilio, that good-looking young guide who might have stepped straight from a romantic operetta instead of from a small motor-boat. Bianca at thirteen, small-boned and walking with the step of a dancer, was already a beauty, and she knew it. Beside her dark ringlets and brown eyes and glowing, olive skin, Nicole's fairness was almost Nordic; and suddenly, for no good reason at all, Jonathan was pleased because she looked so different from the Fionettis. He had no stupid prejudices against foreigners, but Helen Stannisford's granddaughter should not look like an Italian peasant. For a few seconds he amused himself by mentally dressing Nicole formally—as she would have dressed to dispense tea at Osterley House—instead of the faded cotton frock. But his imagination, ignorant about women's clothes, boggled at the job. Nicole was here in her old frock, radiantly alive and laughing up at the children, her bare, brown toes showing in her ancient sandals, and it was difficult, if not impossible, to imagine her wearing formal clothes, perhaps jewellery, and the mask-like-meaningless smile of a society girl . . .

Bianca curtseyed as she shook hands and said, "How do you do" demurely in English, as Nicole had taught her, but her dark eyes were shining mischievously as she assessed the newcomer. It would be fun having someone staying at the *albergo*, and she was already enough of a woman to show off to a good-looking man. She thought this Mr. Johnson distinguished-looking, far more interesting than the boys she knew in the village, and perhaps Nicki would let her off her homework tonight . . . Lessons, to Bianca, were a wicked waste of time. She knew all that was necessary to catch herself a husband; she could dance and sing, she could also shop and cook and make beds efficiently when she chose. One day she would have lots of *bambinos*, but before then she wanted to wear clothes like the girls who worked in the shops in Lugano, and have lots of fun. After her beloved *madre* died, Bianca thought she would leave school and preside over the *albergo*, but Nicki had persuaded Emilio to make her stay another two years. . . . It was absurd, and a foolish waste of time, because the things you learned from books were not at all useful for living.

Pietro, the youngest, a wiry little monkey of ten, also shook hands in the English fashion, and thinking carefully of his words demanded eagerly, "You go fishing? I take you. Pietro"—he banged his small, thin chest arrogantly "me, I'm the best guide for the Lago di Lugano!"

Emilio, who had been lounging against a pillar after refusing emphatically to share the tea party, boxed Pietro's ears gently and told him in Italian, "You won't be any sort of a guide at all unless you get on with your homework. History especially. The *inglesi* always want to know about the past . . . Now run along, both of you, *pronto*!"

Pietro went laughing, Bianca reluctantly, but both of them paused by Nicole's chair and she kissed them lightly on both cheeks, smiling. "Thank you for my lovely gift!" she cried, for the odd-shaped parcel contained a pure white begonia in a pot, a present for which the children had been saving for weeks.

Emilio stood resting, smoking, and surveying them lazily while they finished their tea. He thought tea drinking at this hour of the day absurd, though Nicki had always kept up the custom her mother had brought to the *albergo*. To his critical eyes she looked different today; there was something different about her, though she usually changed into a cotton frock at this hour. Naturally, he told himself, she was pleased and excited to have an Englishman here, someone with whom she could talk about things of which he and Bianca and Pietro and old Lucia knew nothing . . . the things Signora Berenger had talked about, day after day, at this hour, when he and Nicole had been children. Emilio was a fraction younger than Nicki in years, and he had loved her mother next to his own, they had been brought up like brother and sister . . . but now, today, he felt a queer unexpected pang of jealousy while he looked at the small, peaceful domestic scene on the loggia. They were always guiding English people, of course, but this was somehow different; this man looked as if he would be very much at home anywhere, he was not the ordinary tourist. Yet he did not look like an artist either. Emilio hoped he would not make Nicki homesick for the country she had never seen.

Gathering the words together carefully, because both Nicole and her mother had taught the Fionettis English, he said politely; "I must go and wash now, have a glass of wine and then—pff!—the last run to Morcoté. We dine early in Lugano, we are back by seven o'clock always. *A'riverderci, signore.*"

With a little graceful inclination towards the new guest he went away. Nicole gathered the tea things on the tray and looked up in surprise when Jonathan took it from her.

"I'll carry that for you." For the first time he was slightly embarrassed at her amusement.

"Here we wait on the men," she acknowledged mischievously, "and I go to help Lucia prepare supper. Will you help Lucia, also, then?"

"Certainly, if she will allow me in the kitchen!" Jonathan persevered and forgot his embarrassment. As they passed through the dining room they saw Bianca and Pietro doing their homework at the table by the window, arms sprawling and white teeth biting into pencils, and he smiled at them. He liked children much better than he liked most women, which was perhaps the instinctive reason behind his thinking of Nicole Berenger as an attractive child. One could never make that mistake with Bianca Fionetti, though she was years younger than Nicki.

Lucia was dealing with vegetables and steaks on the scrubbed wooden table in the kitchen. Now the best clothes had gone, the shawl replaced by an enormous and spotlessly white apron. She acknowledged Nicki's introduction of Jonathan with a brusque little nod and a shooing motion of her gnarled old hands, and a long, scolding spate of Italian to Nicole.

"She says we should have woken her when you came," Nicole translated smilingly as she washed up the tea things, "and now you must get out of her way, she is busy! Everyone comes into her kitchen, but she says Englishmen are no good at domestic work."

Jonathan laughed. "At least I can peel vegetables and cut up steak," he said quietly, picking up one of the old, thin, sharp knives from the table.

"*Dio mio*" Lucia stared at him, at the long, brown fingers wielding the knife so efficiently.

The old woman laughed suddenly, a dry cackle, and shrugged her shoulders tolerantly. "This one is different," she said to Nicole. "I have never seen a man so neat with his hands."

"I should know how to use a knife, at least," Jonathan said dryly, when Nicki translated his conquest. "I'm a surgeon." It was some sort of relief to be able to be honest about his work, anyway. Already the Albergo Fionetti was casting some sort of spell on him, so that he felt at home here and subtly guilty when anyone mentioned the name "Johnson."

"Oh. . . ." Nicole's small face was momentarily serious. "That is an important job. That is why you have a holiday?"

He knew she meant, that is why you wanted peace and quiet, not the conventional hotel holiday. He went on cutting up the meat into neat cubes, as Lucia indicated, and said briefly, "I was wounded working in a Vietnam hospital. I'm perfectly fit again, but my doctor ordered me to go away for six weeks, somewhere new—somewhere quite fresh where I could do no surgery."

Nicole nodded gravely, the tears running down her cheeks from the onions she was peeling. "Here you can rest, and paint, and fish—or just go to sleep. Here you can do what you like. If you get bored with us you can go to the town, or up the mountains—there are hotels everywhere."

Lucia, who would never bother herself to learn English, said, "You silly girl, crying over onions! I put them instead of garlic because this is an Englishman. Is he rich? Will he stay a long time?"

Nicki laughed through her tears, sniffed and blew her

32

nose on a large, masculine and none too clean handkerchief she took from her pocket.

"He can stay as long as he wants, and we are not going to skin him. He has been ill and wants a rest, and he is nice," she said firmly.

"I don't think I shall be bored here." Jonathan was washing his hands at the cold water over the sink, automatically looking for the brush to scrub his nails before he remembered the sort of sink he was using. He wondered what Sister Swanson, that austere martinet of the theatre, would think if she could see him now. Lucia was making the *pasta* that would eventually envelop the meat, and there was nothing more he could do in the kitchen. He asked permission from Nicole to explore the garden.

"But—of course! Go anywhere you like. After supper I will take you on the lake, it is pretty at night. *A'riverderci* "

"*A'riverderci.*" Old Lucia's carved face broke into a smile. "*Grazie, signore. Benvenuto.*"

It was a dark night, without stars or moonlight, and the lamps strung along the stone steps of the waterfront cottages looked attractive. Jonathan had witnessed a magnificent sunset after exploring the tangled garden of the *albergo*, and seen the mountains and the buildings reflected in the still water of the lake. It had been a full day after a night in the French train, but there was something infinitely peaceful and refreshing about the dark water with its shimmering reflection of the lamps. Jonathan was surprised that he was not tired, but now the sun had gone down the air was like wine—cool and revivifying—and he watched Nicole throwing old cushions and rugs into the row-boat with a whimsical expression on his face. Looking up and catching him unawares the girl smiled suddenly.

"You don't have to make love to me," she told him casually, in her usual sensible tone. "This is not Venice, and my boat is no gondola. But at night it is cold; I don't want you to be ill again."

"Thank you, Nicki," he answered gravely, touched by her thoughtfulness; secretly amused by the notion that he might have misconstrued her preparations. The girl had changed back to slacks after supper, and to him she was far too childish for romantic adventure ... yet he found himself wondering if some of the younger tourists tried to make love to Nicole. There was a lot he wanted to know about this strange life of Helen Stannisford's grand-daughter on the shore of a Swiss lake.

Supper had been an enjoyable meal. Lucia's *ravioli* and stewed vegetables had been delicious, and Jonathan discovered that he was hungry again. Salad, shredded and tossed in oil, was eaten with the meat, and crisp rolls that melted in the mouth, and the cherry *gâteau*, Gruyere cheese and coffee that followed completed a wonderfully satisfying repast. Emilio took more trouble to make the Englishman feel at home, and old Lucia presided at the other end of the long table. Nicole faced Jonathan across the soft electric candles, and kept a sisterly eye on the ravages of Bianca and Pietro. Now Emilio had gone off on some errand of his own, the children reluctantly shooed off to bed, the washing-up done, and Nicole preparing to take him for a short row on the lake. It had been, Jonathan thought, as he lighted his pipe, a very special sort of day. It seemed as if the ending was going to match the rest, as Nicole shipped her oars when they were well out on the dark water and said softly, "Now you can look. I wanted you to see the lights. When there is a moon or too many stars, they are not as good as this. This is a good night."

The town of Lugano wore her lights as a woman wears her diamonds, sparkling and glowing against the darker bulk of the hills behind; reflected in shimmering pillars on the dark waters of the lake. And, as Nicole had told him earlier, there were the star-studded "ladders" of the funiculars climbing Monte Brè and San Salvatore, and behind them, far down on the other shore—the highest ladder of all —the funicular climbing to the hotel on Monte Generoso.

"From the peak, on a fine day, you can see over three countries—Italy, Austria, Switzerland," Nicole told him proudly. "It is a very fine place, a grand hotel. Maybe you will want to stay there when you see it."

"I'm not in any hurry to explore far afield," Jonathan said with lazy contentment. It was very peaceful out here on the lake. Cool, but comfortable on the old cushions, and warm enough with the rug she had thrown over his knees. Nicole's small fair head was outlined by the lights of the town, and as she moved there was a nimbus about her hair. Her profile was dainty, clear-cut; her voice gentle to match the quiet of the lake, the only other sound the soft "lap-lap" of the water against the sides of the boat.

"This is very beautiful." Jonathan added gently,

"Thank you for bringing me to see it, Nicki. Now you'd better go back, you must be tired——"

She chuckled. "I'm never tired! All this is play for me—easy—not like rowing tourists all the way to Morcoté and back when it is very hot, and they want to stop and take photographs all the time—phew!"

So they sat for a while, watching the beauty of the lake and talking quietly, and Nicole was surprised to find that it was easy to talk with this Englishman. Usually, in spite of her childish outspokenness, she was reserved about her private affairs. Some of the tourists had poked and pried, amazed to find an English girl living with an Italian family, but she had not discussed the whys and wherefores with them. Somehow this one's quiet questions did not annoy her; perhaps because he was older. Old enough to be sensible, anyway. She had liked and trusted him at once.

Nicole said practically, "In a few minutes we will go back, the wind from the mountains gets very cold later. Tomorrow I will take you fishing, or painting; what you like——"

"I mustn't take up too much of your time—if you have a regular daily programme, like Emilio," he answered doubtfully, wondering if she would be offended if he offered to hire the row-boat.

Nicole smiled. "I work as I please, and we shall charge you for this as well. Would fifteen francs a day be too much? For that you will get full board, and I will take you everywhere—for fishing, or painting, or climbing, what you like——"

"That will be quite all right." Jonathan smiled, too, but he was careful to keep the amusement from his voice. "Are you sure it will be enough?"

She nodded vigorously, "Quite enough," and added honestly, "For thirty francs a day you could stay at a better hotel in Lugano, a good second-class hotel, with hot and cold water in your bedroom. But the trips would be extra . . . and, of course, with us, you can go in the motor-boat when you like, without paying. Emilio will be pleased——"

Jonathan laughed. "I doubt it. Somehow I think Emilio does not like Englishmen. But would you rather I went to Lugano, Nicki? It will make a lot of extra work for you and Lucia if I stay at the *albergo*."

Nicole made little waves with her hand in the lake and answered candidly, "We do not mind a little more work, and it is good for the *albergo* if you stay. Six weeks at fifteen francs a day is a lot of money; it will help Emilio to pay for *Pegasus*. We are very lucky to have you, and you must not mind Emilio—he is only afraid you will make me homesick for England, as my mother was homesick. . . ."

She had given him the opening he was seeking, yet Jonathan found himself oddly reluctant to ask the questions seething in his brain. This child trusted him; she might be—he guessed she would be—very angry if she thought he had come as a spy from her English grandmother.

He said diffidently, "These Fionettis—they are not relations of yours, are they? Yet you help run the inn, you look after the children——"

Nicole smiled again and there was warmth and pride in her voice as she spoke of the Fionetti family. "My father was French, but he had some Italian blood, too. They are my very dear cousins. Before my father died he begged Maman to bring me here if she could not take me to England—he knew Tia Maria would make us welcome . . . and she did. She had just lost her husband, too, you see, in an avalanche—she always said God had sent us for company, to console her. She and my mother were great friends—Pietro was born soon after we came——" Nicole laughed gently and now she did not sound at all childish; she was speaking with maturity, with the Continental woman's acceptance of the ups-and-downs of life. "He was my *bambino*, my little brother! There was not much money, but we were used to that. We missed my father so much—it was nice having brothers and a sister when we came here."

She added softly, as if she had momentarily forgotten she was talking to a stranger, telling him things she had never discussed with anyone, even Emilio. "She was a darling, Maria Fionetti—and almost a saint. She shared everything she had with us. Mother worked hard, helping with the *albergo*—we children had to go to school, of course, we could only help in the holidays—and she did exquisite embroidery to sell to the tourists. But she was not very strong even in Paris—my father's *atelier* was at the top of a very old house in Montmartre, and she used to sit and rest at the top of each flight of stairs." Nicole touched her chest briefly. "She had a weakness here, that was perhaps why Papa wanted her to come to Switzerland if she could not go home. But it didn't save her life. The doctors said she died of broncho-pneumonia. I think she died of a broken heart."

Nicole said it matter-of-factly, but with a conviction that startled Jonathan. He was finding this girl, with her odd mixture of common sense, basic simplicity, and deep religious feeling, extraordinarily interesting. An anachronism in the modern world; she must have met and mingled with hundreds of tourists every year, yet their casual permissiveness seemed to have made no impact on her. She seemed completely uninterested in sex or fashions.

He refilled and lighted his pipe, glad that she was talking to him of her own free will yet wishing that he had met her as a friendly stranger; he dreaded the day when she would find out—as she must—that he had come from the enemy camp.

"Why did you father die, Nicole?" he asked gently. "He must have been quite young."

"Yes, he was too young to die," she said brusquely, so brusquely that he realised she had loved her father passionately and bitterly resented his death, "there was a bad fire one night in the old house—the sculptor on the ground floor had sold something, and had a party to celebrate. I suppose they'd had too much to drink . . . when we woke up our place was full of smoke and the staircase was blazing—" She paused, staring at the distant lights of Lugano. Jonathan said quietly, "Don't talk about it if it hurts too much, Nicki."

"Of course it hurts!" she flared, turning to stare at him in the reflected lights angrily. "I was twelve years old, not a baby. I shall never forget—but sometimes it helps to talk, doesn't it? Now I am older . . . for a long time my mother and I—we could not talk about the fire, even to each other. Always we talked of the happy times, before—"

He nodded, smoking, waiting for her to unburden herself.

It was strange, Nicole thought, but she wanted to talk to this quiet man with a glint of humour in his grey eyes; perhaps because he was a surgeon there was a kind of strength in him, understanding . . . he must be used to human suffering. She didn't want anyone's pity, but she was only just realising how she had longed to talk over her affairs with someone older, preferably someone English;

37

she had been very much alone, boxed-up inside herself, lately.

"It was a very bad fire," she continued in a small, tight voice, "the house was very old and it was full of rotten wood—that was why it was cheap, it should have been pulled down long ago. It blazed like a bonfire. Papa got us out over the roofs—" she choked a little and plunged on almost aggressively, "then he had to go back to help the Duvals across the landing—they had three small children. He died in hospital three days later, of his burns."

"That was a brave death, Nicole." Jonathan wished that Helen Stannisford could have heard the story just as Nicole had told it. "If there is a war on, a soldier who behaves like that is decorated for heroism."

"Pph!" Nicki snapped her fingers contemptuously. "He was an artist, not a soldier! And a good one, too—but because he painted people and places as they are, and not women as triangles with currants for eyes and bananas for breasts, he did not sell many of his pictures."

He made a sympathetic grunt, disliking the Impressionist school as much as Jean Berenger had done. He liked the human anatomy to be dealt with faithfully, in life and art.

"What happened to Maria?" he asked after the boat had drifted a while on the quiet, dark water.

"She was very sad when my mother died, and four years ago—"

Nicole waved towards the other end of the lake. "They are buried side by side up there, in the cemetery on Morcoté; one day I will show you their graves."

"You poor child," Jonathan said gently, without patronage, seeing the glint of tears against the background of lights. He wanted to touch her hand, to comfort her, but she was somehow removed from the sympathy of a stranger. "You have suffered far too much for a girl of your age."

"I have not suffered at all," she said austerely, "it was the old ones who took all the burden. Me—I have been loved, and spoiled, and taken into the Fionetti family like one of themselves. It is right that now I should look after them. Tia Maria asked me when she was dying . . . she knew Emilio is headstrong, and Bianca a silly little thing, and Pietro——" Her voice softened again, but now there was laughter in it. "Pietro thinks he is a man! Always he is trying to do too much! Emilio need not worry that I will run away to England!"

No, Jonathan thought ruefully, Emilio need not worry . . . all her love and loyalty lay, naturally, with the Fionetti family. Nevertheless, it seemed an appalling burden for a girl of twenty-two to shoulder . . . and there was that other "old one," lonely and regretful for the past, in Osterley House. Old Henry's vindictive wilfulness had caused a nice tangle for his descendants to unravel.

Love and loyalty towards the family which had befriended her beloved mother were quite enough to keep Nicole here, especially when one remembered the way her father had been treated by her English grandfather. But Jonathan was somehow deeply pleased that the possibility of inheriting a fortune had not made Nicole swerve from her loyalties. That she was essentially practical about money was obvious—she was as open and honest as a child—but the bait offered by the private detective had not made her swerve a hair's breadth from her promise to Maria Fionetti. He wondered how long she would consider herself bound by that promise. . . . Bianca was thirteen, she would probably marry young. But Pietro was only ten . . . it would be long before he was grown up. Emilio . . . ? Emilio, who was actually a fraction younger than Nicole, but like most Italians, already a man at twenty . . . was Emilio in love with his cousin? If so, it would be an admirable arrangement for the Fionettis. That they all loved Nicole was obvious; she was their little mother. If she married Emilio she would continue to make a home for the younger ones, to run the inn, to share Emilio's tourist-conducting business. After ten years she belonged here, it was all natural enough, and Jonathan found himself more and more in sympathy with her attitude. Yet he could not help hoping that she would not marry Emilio; she was half English, more English than she realised, perhaps, and her rightful place was at Osterley House. Secret amusement shook him as he tried to imagine the attitude of the staff there if Nicole should ever appear as their future employer.

"Have you ever been to England, Nicki?"

She shook her head violently. "Never. I do not want to go. In England it is cold and grey and always raining, and the people are old and dull."

"Steady on!" Jonathan laughed, taking the pipe from his mouth. "Our climate is tricky, I admit, but there are compensations. And you would find some places very beautiful indeed—especially Devon and Cornwall. That was a sweeping statement, Nicole—and we are not all doddering in our dotage!"

"I know." Suddenly she was humble, contrite. "My father was very fond of the English, in spite of the way my grandfather treated him. It was my mother who was too proud to return . . . but of course you do not know that story. It happened a very long time ago and it was very silly. But my mother—she was too proud of my father to go and eat humble pie to my grandfather; he must have been a beast! I would have hated him. Yet she was very homesick sometimes. After we came here she would tell me stories of Combe Castleton. . . ."

She pronounced the familiar name with a slight rolling sound that Jonathan found endearing. "Tell me the story," he said, feeling a traitor yet anxious to hear Nicole's version.

The girl shrugged, unshipping the oars and beginning to row slowly back towards Gandria. "This is very deep here, the deepest part of the lake," she remarked conversationally, "and it is very cold. If you want to swim tomorrow, you'd better try the shallow water at the Lido, it will be warmer."

"All right. I'd like to wander round the town tomorrow morning, there are some things I want to buy." Jonathan did not press his question, but after a little silence Nicole said brusquely: "It is a stupid story. My father was an artist, a real artist. He would be ashamed of the way I paint pictures for the tourists. But like any artist, he was poor. . . . He went to England once, long ago—twenty-three years ago—after the war. He went to the West Country, because there are places there very good to paint —places like your Polperro?"

"Polperro attracts many artists, yes."

She said sombrely, "There were many of his English paintings in the Paris studio, but we lost them all, of course. . . . I think he fell in love with England a little, and very much with my mother. But her parents were rich, and stuffy, and stupid—her father did not understand about their being in love, he had no understanding of art, either. He said my father was trying to marry Maman because one day she would be rich, too—so they ran away." Nicole told the story simply, as if it was something from a book she had read. But suddenly her voice was strong and warm and vibrating with love and pride.

"We never had much money, but I never knew him do anything mean or dishonest. When he sold a picture he would treat the other artists in our house. When someone really liked a picture he could not afford to buy, my father would give it to him——" She smiled suddenly. "Often my mother would scold him for being so generous when he could not afford it, but she was just as generous. My grandfather must have been a fool not to know the sort of man my father was!"

Jonathan, remembering Henry Stannisford, could not help agreeing secretly with that outspoken verdict. He said gently, "I expect they were very different men, as you said, with no understanding of each other. But they were happy, your parents?"

"Very happy. You see, they were truly in love. They did not need anything else."

Jonathan was moved by that declaration of faith from a girl who was no romantic little sentimentalist; she had known family happiness and tragedy and enough hardship to make her a realist. For a moment the squeaking of the oars in the rowlocks was the only sound; there were no other boats this far up the lake.

"You believe in love, Nicole?" he said, not sceptically but a little wonderingly; almost enviously. This place, and this girl with her old-fashioned fairytale background, was having a strange effect on him.

"Oh, yes." She was mocking his wonderment a little but he could not doubt her sincerity. "When I marry, it will be for love, and for always. I do not believe in these casual arrangements—" She looked at him gravely, and in the soft lights along the approaching shore her face was suddenly beautiful. "How can a man and woman expect to make a good life together, to give their children happiness in this awful world, without love?" she demanded reasonably. "It is the *bêtise* otherwise! The first little storm will sink their boat!"

He laughed involuntarily. Nicole Berenger was full of surprises.

"Yet you believe in hate, too, I think. You said your mother wanted to go home—later, when you came here—"

"Of course she wanted to go home!" For a moment Nicole rested on her oars and the boat drifted gently. "She loved her mother, who was afraid of her father. After we

41

came here she told me much of the story I had not known before. Always Maman was hoping that there would be a reconciliation, an invitation for all of us—especially when she had written so many letters telling of her happiness! But my grandfather was too proud to admit he had been wrong and my mother would not beg!" the vivid blue eyes flashed fire. "Do you know, because Papa asked her to try again when he was dying in Paris, she wrote and told them . . . and they did not even answer *that* letter—and now, if you please, that that horrible old man is dead too, they think that I—Nicole Berenger—will come meekly back to the house that was refused my father!"

Jonathan felt in entire agreement with her. He wished again that he had not come as an emissary from Helen Stannisford, yet he could not forget the frail old lady's appeal. He wanted to tell Nicole the truth, but if he spoke too soon it might make the unhappy situation worse. He had certainly not expected Nicki to confide in him so soon.

"You think I am hard and unforgiving?" she demanded defensively when he did not speak. "Would you expect me to accept favours—*now*—to accept money that might have saved my mother's life . . .? Perhaps Papa's, too, if we had not had to live in that old cheap *atelier* house—"

"That we can never know," Jonathan answered quietly. "I imagine that your parents would have refused financial help while your grandfather was alive. But everything is different now."

"How—different?"

"Your grandmother must be getting old, and somehow I think your mother would wish you to forgive and forget the past," he said gently, "but it must be your own decision when the time comes, Nicole. These family-feud things are ridiculous in this day and age, but you will have to make up your own mind, child."

"I will," she laughed shakily, and began rowing again.

Nicole manoeuvred the clumsy boat alongside the iron ring neatly and tied her up. Handing up the rugs and cushions to Jonathan on the steps above she said shyly, "I am sorry to bore you with my family history. I do not usually talk so much to strangers."

He smiled down at her. "I'm glad you felt you could talk to me, Nicole. And I hope you'll think of me as a friend, not as a stranger, now——"

"*Grazie*" She allowed him to hand her up to the steps, and somehow the firm, warm little hand lying in his own made him feel suddenly that he had in truth made a friend.

That he could ever have thought of Nicole as a boy, even for a moment, astounded Jonathan during the days that followed. Slender and boyish, yes; active with some inner reserve of nervous energy; but nevertheless very much a woman. Not as young Bianca was a woman, all physical tricks and graces, but her spirit was feminine enough. Emilio, who loved her in a manner that Jonathan did not regard as brotherly; Pietro, even the wilful Bianca, all looked to Nicole as the woman of the house, the mistress of the *albergo*; she was their little mother, despite her gypsy boyishness. It was Nicole who arranged the meals with old Lucia, who saw to the comfort of the guests, who overlooked the children's homework and chased them off to bed at a reasonable hour, Nicole who did the small amount of book-keeping that was necessary for their tourist trade, and the running of *Pegasus* and the inn. Jonathan soon discovered that any money Emilio made and the sales of Nicole's paintings were all pooled in a common fund, from which she paid the running expenses and put aside each week a certain amount in Emilio's savings account.

"What about your future—don't you have a savings account also?" Jonathan asked cautiously one day when he found her wrestling with figures.

Nicole smiled absently. "I shall be all right. I can always earn my living. But Emilio has the *bambinos* to provide for, and one day he will want to get married."

She was completely practical, unsentimental; he dared not press her any more then with questions about her private affairs, but he found himself worrying about her future at times. If she was going to marry Emilio, then of course the problem would be simplified; she was working and planning for her own future as well. But if not, then all her hard work and planning would not benefit her at all in the end . . . Jonathan thought of Nigel, that amiable, feckless youth who would inherit the Stannisford fortune that belonged by right to this girl, and felt a surge of real anger at the twistings of fate. Yet Nicole was happy, in spite of her sad memories; when Jonathan tried to make her plan for herself she always smiled with a quaint wisdom that defeated his anxiety.

"Englishmen are always trying to plan ahead!" she

told him once, laughing. "*Ch' sara, sara* What will be, will be. It is no use looking too far ahead. Trust in God, He will look after us all, though naturally He expects us to work hard for ourselves, too."

"You still believe in God?" he asked curiously without mockery. "After all the suffering in your family, and the mess the world is in today?"

Nicole looked up at him, suddenly grave. She guessed that in his job Jonathan would see a lot of human suffering, and sometimes in repose his mouth was set in a grim line and there was a bitterness in his grey eyes that seemed to be remembering the savage devastation in the jungle villages of war-torn Vietnam. The things he had come here to Lugano to forget, the things he must forget if he was going to take up again his work of healing.

"Yes," she said quietly, almost maternally, as if for once their positions were reversed, "I believe in God. My parents and Tia Maria suffered—much. They died too young. Yet God was good to them."

"How do you make that out?" he demanded gently; in Nicole's position he thought he would have become embittered, but there wasn't an ounce of self-pity in the girl.

Her thin brown hands were clasped together almost as if she was praying. She smiled a little. "I told you, they had much happiness together, they loved God and each other . . . I think perhaps today that is a rare thing in your world, Jonathan?"

"Rare—people are so confused, mixed-up, in the Tower of Babel," he acknowledged drily, "with the scientists and the economists and the politicians all shouting their policies at us morning, noon and night."

Nicole nodded. "Perhaps they shout too much. If they left us in peace, to listen to God's voice, it would be easier. My father died bravely—did not Jesus say it is a good way to die, to lay down one's life for others? And you see, my mother and Tia Maria were allowed to join their loved ones quite soon . . . now nothing can separate them, ever again."

Jonathan was silent. It was a long time since he had heard death referred to as a blessing, in this way, except as an end to incurable disease. Nicole, for all her amusing childish ways, had the Latin philosophy of acceptance; of faith and wisdom that was beyond sophisticated cleverness. He felt oddly humbled in the realisation that this girl could perhaps teach him to recapture some of the ideals of his youth that had become somewhat tarnished along the road to success. Or at least they seemed tarnished to him in the clear light of Nicole's convictions.

"Nothing can spoil their happiness, ever again," she added gently, almost joyously.

An appeal for old Helen Stannisford's happiness trembled on Jonathan's tongue; he felt deeply that if he told Nicole the truth when she was in that serious, gentle mood, she could not fail to respond . . . yet he was afraid to put it to the test. She had emerged from an extraordinary tragedy with her faith and personality undamaged; he would have to walk with extreme delicacy in the matter of the grandmother. Above all, as the days slid past and Jonathan shed the last mental fatigue of war-strain and convalescence, he was determined not to cause Nicole any further suffering. Sometimes, smoking a last pipe by his bedroom window that jutted out over the lake, he felt reluctant to interfere at all. In spite of her sorrows, in spite of her practical responsibilities for the Fionettis, in spite of her wisdom, Nicole had retained the lovely, elusive independence of childhood; she could still escape to some magic world of her own, beyond everyday problems. Jonathan feared that life at Osterley House might change the girl too drastically, might even destroy her philosophy. He discovered, to his own amazement, that the idea of a civilised Nicole—chastened and tamed from her gypsy freedom—was beginning to appal him.

She was so very lovable just as she was.

That first morning Emilio had dropped him at the central wharf when he took *Pegasus* over to begin the day's trips round the lake. "Nicki will fetch you at noon; I have to take a party for luncheon at *La Romantica*," he explained.

Jonathan had enjoyed walking about the town, pleasant under bright sunshine and clear blue sky. The snatches of talk that swirled about him under the chestnut promenade by the lake made him realise that people from all over the world were here; English and Poles, Germans and French and American girls in every kind of way-out dress from the indestructible mini-skirt to hipster pants, that were masculine in a very different way from Nicole's shabby jeans and shirts. Having a drink in one of the open-air cafés he was in a completely cosmopolitan atmosphere. The English and Americans, discussing their itineraries for sightseeing, made him feel grateful that he was living over at the *albergo*, with no itinerary, no excited gaping and frantic photographing to do. In fact, the next six weeks stretched out very pleasantly before his tired eyes. For the first time in his adult life he was going to drift; to work to no schedule, but to do each day just whatever came into his head. The hospitals and the nursing homes of Combe Castleton seemed very far away; they might belong to another planet.

There's something in this complete change and rest idea, after all, he told himself. He was rediscovering the delight of small pleasures. To pass the Globus Coach Station on his way to Paradiso, to notice the seething activity of drivers, couriers and passengers on their way to Venice, to Florence, to Rome, or merely to Lake Maggiore, and to know that he need not do anything but wander round Lugano until Nicole came for him in her rowing boat was sheer delight. And when he turned back from the rose-garlanded terraces of Paradiso and the big luxury hotels he was glad he was not staying there, in a palace where formal clothes would be demanded and polite social intercourse . . . The children and Emilio took sandwiches, and he would probably share a picnic meal with Nicki and old Lucia. Already the *albergo* felt like home to Jonathan. He walked back to the town along the arcades of the Via Nassa, enjoying the bright and tasteful display of goods in the shop windows and the sensation of having a home in a place full of tourists in transit—hotel-birds. The *albergo* might be technically an inn, but by no stretch of the imagination could it be called a hotel, and Jonathan was glad. He hated hotels. Sometimes when he was called away to perform an operation he had to spend a night or two in a hotel, but he would never like them.

Already the sun was hot, and it was pleasant walking in the shade of the arcade. There were shops of every description—the most colourful, piled high with tourist goods; raffia baskets, straw hats, sandals, the small Chianti bottles in their straw holders, music-boxes like Swiss chalets, carved wooden toys and the prevailing bear of Switzerland. But there were besides many clothes shops of impeccable taste, shops displaying *objets d'art* of real value, chemists' and lingerie and stationery and book shops. Jonathan went into one of the chemists'; he had left his toothbrush on the train, and carefully uttered his first Italian phrase.

"*Uno spazzolino da denti——*"

"A toothbrush, yes, sir. Do you prefer hard, medium, or soft?" the elderly man behind the counter enquired suavely, and Jonathan felt himself colouring like a boy. Uncle Steve was right, all these people spoke English. But he was determined to learn at least some Italian while he was here.

He found the art shop Nicole had told him about, the shop that sold her paintings, the paintings that were so bad her father would have burned them. Here again the dealer spoke such fluent English that Jonathan had no chance to air his carefully rehearsed phrases. He bought some more materials and several etchings of the villages round Lake Lugano. They would hang nicely in his rooms at Uncle Steve's, he thought; they were excellent etchings, well enough executed for a consultant's rooms. The dealer was pleased with his selection, and a trifle reproachful when he asked to see some of Miss Berenger's paintings.

"They are a little bright, *signore*, to be hung with these good etchings——"

"I'd like to see them, all the same."

Nevertheless he flinched when the man strewed them over the counter. Nicole had been merely truthful when she said they were bad. The green of the lake, the violent magenta of petunias, the lavish purple wistaria, the Turneresque sunsets, hurt the eye. They disguised the soft and exquisite beauty of the ancient stone houses with a horrible garishness; yet Nicole said the tourists bought them. They were, he was thankful to see, unsigned.

"Ten francs each," the dealer said indifferently. "The *signorina* paints for the tourist, you understand. She can paint otherwise, if you want something better."

"I understand." Jonathan smiled faintly. "But I'll take these all the same."

"All six of them?" The dealer's respect for his client's knowledge was waning visibly.

"All six of them. I have some aunts who also like colour," Jonathan grinned.

"Ah, *si, si*—that is different!"

The purchases were beautifully wrapped for him between layers of tissue paper. Everywhere he went Jonathan noted this care, the scrupulously honest marking of prices, the giving of the correct change, so counted over that the foreigner could understand. That and the sparkling cleanliness of the town was due to the Swiss influence, but it was pleasant for the Englishman.

He went to the main post office and mailed a card to his aunt. A non-committal card merely saying that the journey had been good and that he liked Lugano exceedingly. "*I am going to fish and paint and laze in the sun,*" he scribbled, with a smile on his lips. That would please Aunt Bella no end, and it committed him to nothing with Uncle Steve. He felt oddly reluctant to write home properly, to tell them that he had already found Nicole Berenger; that he was living in the same house. Time enough for that when he had confessed to her and made his appeal.

The market, with its stalls piled high with gaily coloured fruit and souvenirs and sausages and cheeses, appealed to his artist's eye. Here the women shopped, dressed mostly in sombre black with shawls or mantillas over their heads; the real housewives and landladies of Lugano. They prodded and poked, chaffered and bargained, in the manner of housewives all over the world, and their sombre clothes only served to enhance the effect of bright sunlight and shadow, the colour in the fruit and vegetables and flowers.

Pausing by a flower shop, Jonathan thought it would please Nicole if he took her some flowers; it was she who kept the window boxes and plants at the *albergo*, and their healthy condition was proof enough that she loved growing things. He pondered over the begonias, but remembering the children's gift of the evening before, he did not want to compete with them and finally chose a gentian of the same vivid blue as Nicole's eyes.

Seeing him thus burdened, the old crones of the market place thought him a family man, not a tourist, and, grinning, cried their wares at him until he found his arms loaded with oranges and cherries and a melon, and a cheese of which he had never heard in his life. It was the smell of the cheese that drove him finally away from the fascinations of the market, back to the *debarcadero centrale* to search the lake for Nicole's shabby little boat.

Sitting there contentedly in the shade of the chestnut trees, Jonathan was well pleased with his morning. Now that he had parked the evil-smelling cheese well beyond the range of his nose he could enjoy the scene before him; the wide stretch of sunny water, to his right the cafés with their striped awnings and people enjoying their pre-luncheon aperitif, and the laughing couples pedalling the "beetle boats" about the lake, the larger boats bringing back tourists from the morning excursions. People of all nationalities, ages, colourings and taste in clothing passed continually beside his bench, and snatches of a dozen languages came to his ears. But what struck him most was the laughter that rang in the clear atmosphere, the expression of happiness on old faces as well as young. Perhaps because his work took him among the anxious, the unhappy, the sick, Jonathan was intrigued and delighted with this holiday spirit. Evidently people from all over the world came to Lugano to enjoy themselves, and did so in a way that was simple, healthy, joyous, very different from the hectic holiday programmes in the world's great cities.

I'm just a country bumpkin at heart, Jonathan told himself contentedly, and he was so absorbed in the busy yet tranquil scene that he failed to see Nicole mooring the row-boat just below his bench.

"*Hola*, Mr. Johnson! So you have been shopping!"

She stood before him, slim and laughing, her legs in their old slacks wide apart, her brown hands on her hips, her fair head on one side considering his heap of purchases. She demanded to know what he had paid for everything. "I expect they have cheated you, the old witches. A man shopping! For fifteen francs a day we will supply you with fruit; you don't have to buy it yourself!" she scolded. To appease her he held out the glowing gentian in its pot.

"For the loggia—you like flowers, don't you?"

"Thank you—you are very kind." Suddenly she was shy, soft and douce, as she stowed everything in the boat. "But you must not, please, buy food. How much was this melon? And the cheese?"

"I've forgotten," Jonathan assured her truthfully, helping to stow his purchases, "but you must not be cross with me, Nicki. I have not been shopping for years, except when I had to get new clothes." He grinned appealingly. "I have thoroughly enjoyed my morning! I began to feel I belonged here as soon as I had some parcels in my arms! I stopped feeling like a tourist."

She glanced up at him, shrugging. "All right. So you enjoy your morning, and spend too much money! Are you not still on the travel allowance?"

"No, not any more, thank goodness, so I have enough left to pay my bill; I'll pay in advance if you like—and no more shopping, if that will please you——"

A shadow crossed her small, sensitive face. She said with great dignity, "I was not thinking of the bill," and he apologised instantly.

"I know you weren't, Nicole. I was only teasing. I brought more than enough with me, and I don't want to spend much on trips, so I shall have plenty."

"*Bueno.*"

Now they had uncovered his last package, lying flat on the bench, and Nicole pounced on it. "You've been to Signor Castiglioni? This is his label. Let me see what you have bought—if the old devil has been cheating you I will make him give you some money back!"

"I—those are just some etchings. Well worth what I paid for them——" Jonathan was very conscious of the paintings in the parcel, very determined that Nicki should not see them. The boats had discharged all their passengers, the wharf was peaceful suddenly. Even the promenaders were dwindling away to their hotels and *pensions*. The girl had her hand on the string, sensing his reluctance.

"You saw my paintings? They're bad, aren't they? But you'd be surprised, people like them better than the quiet ones I used to paint."

Jonathan smiled, wishing he could not feel the colour mounting to his face. "They're pretty bad. But if that's what they want to buy—to take away as souvenirs——"

The church clocks were chiming the half-hour. Nicki looked at her lodger with the straightness he found disconcerting, the uncompromising honesty of a child. "You don't want me to see the etchings," she said slowly. "I think you know you've been swindled. Please, I would like to look—Castiglioni doesn't close until one o'clock, there's still time——"

"Very well." He supposed the dealer would be telling her, in any case, within the next few days that he had sold six of her paintings to one customer. He was prepared for her laughter, perhaps her mockery, when she saw the contents of his package; he was utterly unprepared for the tide of scarlet that swept into her face, for the dismay succeeded so swiftly by fury as she rewrapped the parcel and turned to him.

"You've bought six—*six*—of my things! You've paid sixty francs for that rubbish, knowing it was bad!" Nicole stamped her foot on the hard stones of the *quai*. "Do you think I sent you to Castiglioni for that?"

Now he could see the Stannisford pride. She stood there accusing him like a small fury and he knew he had blundered, blundered seriously. He held out his hand for the parcel, but she would not give it to him. "I'm sorry,

Nicki. I thought it would be a—a sort of present for you, like the flowers."

She clutched the parcel as if she wanted to throw it into the lake and he feared for his etchings. "The flowers were nothing—a nice present, yes—they cost a franc or two. But *sixty* francs! Do you think we want charity, when we're charging you for your board and lodging? These—these *things*—are worth ten francs to people who like them, who want them—but *you*—you know better!"

"My dear child, don't take it to heart so!" Jonathan took refuge in being avuncular, trying to tease her back to her usual good humour. To his utter dismay there were tears of fury in the blue eyes. "I'm sorry I was stupid, but you can paint me a real picture of the *albergo* to make up——"

"So you think I can paint 'real' pictures if I wish?" she demanded ironically, and swung on her heel. "Come, we'll make old Castiglioni disgorge your sixty francs. I couldn't bear to look at you another day otherwise!" And she marched before him through the streets of Lugano in her shabby shirt and trousers, seemingly oblivious of her appearance. Jonathan, following the slender, still scarlet neck in front of him, felt mingled shame and amusement. He had thought her practical enough to be glad of the sixty francs, or whatever she would get out of the deal; he had forgotten that her father had been an artist, that Nicole had both pride and integrity. And suddenly he liked her very much indeed for her anger.

She disappeared into the shadowy elegance of the art shop, and by the time Jonathan reached the doorway there was an altercation going on in rapid Italian. The suave Signor Castiglioni could also lose his temper, it seemed. Jonathan, feeling a fool, retreated down the arcade and hoped that she would not sell his etchings back to the dealer as well. But after a few minutes they were thrust into his hands by a smiling, triumphant Nicole, together with the sixty francs.

"He tried to give me forty, to keep the commission, the old devil! But in the end he paid up. Here are your etchings—they're quite good ones; you haven't been swindled over those."

"Thank you." He answered faintly, but an answering smile twitched the corners of his grim mouth. "You're very honest, Nicki. But won't this make it awkward for you with—future sales by Castiglioni?"

She laughed. Now that the battle was over and won she was happy again. "Oh, he knows he can sell my stuff all right; he won't make any awkwardness! And as for being honest—my father would never forgive me if I let anyone who didn't really want them buy my rubbish. Come, we must hurry, or Lucia will scold us for being late."

Rowing up the lake Nicole was quiet, Jonathan thoughtful. But when they had unloaded the boat at the stone steps she picked up the gentian and cradled it in her arms, as if to make amends for her temper.

"Thank you, *signore*—for the fruit and the flowers. The flowers I like very much, Mr. Johnson."

"Not Johnson—*Jonathan*," he answered quickly, "that is my Christian name."

"Jonathan . . . ?" She stared at him, puzzled. "I've never heard that name before. *Jonathan* . . . it is a nice name, but I could have sworn you said your name was Johnson!"

CHAPTER THREE

LUCIA consented to have her portrait painted, though she privately considered the *Inglesi* foolish to waste his time with an old woman when he could be painting someone young and luscious like Bianca or even Nicki—though how Nicki would ever catch a man's eye while she dressed in boy's clothing and did a boy's work old Lucia didn't know. . . . She was fond of the girl, especially because Nicole took good care of the children of her beloved Maria, God rest her soul, but in her young days girls had not rowed tourists about the lake wearing boy's garments. . . .

Jonathan sat Lucia in her rocking-chair out on the stone patio in the wilderness of the back garden, in the shade of a gnarled wistaria as old as Lucia herself. He had to accept her in her "best" clothes, but there was a tussle of wills when he wanted her to feign sleep.

"What use is a portrait of me with my eyes closed?" Lucia demanded crossly. "Does the man not know that a person's soul looks from the eyes? He might as well paint a death mask!"

Nicole, translating faithfully for both parties, smiled at the old cook, friend of the Fionettis down the years. "He says he first saw you asleep in the kitchen and fell in love with you, even if your eyes were closed!"

"Then he should not have looked!" Lucia argued. "No gentleman stares at a woman while she sleeps."

"Tell her," Jonathan said, arranging his brushes, "that I am in complete agreement. I did not stare, I only peeped . . . and for the present I am no gentleman but an artist. Tell her I have never seen a face I liked so much in sleep as hers."

Lucia chuckled harshly, shrugging, "*Dio mio, Inglesi!* All right, so be it."

While Jonathan, well pleased to have got his way, painted his portrait of Lucia in the mid-morning hour when the old woman's morning chores were completed—for they had a light luncheon and the main meal in the evening, when Emilio had finished his work and the children were back from school—Nicole made beds, dusted and swept, singing little French songs as she worked. Sometimes Jonathan could hear snatches of her singing, sometimes she glanced down into the patio when he was unaware and watched him working. He did not have to rest his model often, for as Lucia said, it was all resting for her, but between spells of furious painting they managed odd conversations in pidgin-English and dog-Italian, much to Nicki's amusement. The Englishman and the old Italian woman were a world apart, yet they shared some basic integrity and dry humour, and daily grew fonder of each other.

"He would make a good husband for you, that one," Lucia told Nicole one evening while they were preparing supper, and Jonathan was filling the big, burnished copper kettles that went on the wood stove. He wondered why the girl was blushing, but she laughed at Lucia as she replied crisply, "He probably has a girl in England. All the nice ones are caught before they grow old."

"He is not old." Lucia's black eyes sparkled with mischief. "He is thirty-eight. I asked him, and he counted on his fingers."

"You're an old gossip, and we'll have to get Emilio settled before I think of getting married. I think then I would like to go all over Europe, painting like my father did, before he met my mother. Maybe I shall never marry."

Lucia snorted. "It is every woman's duty to get married and have babies and make a good home for her husband;

why else do you think the good God made Eve? But you will never catch yourself a husband until you wear pretty clothes."

"I don't care a *centimo* about clothes, or about catching myself a husband; I'm far too busy," Nicole retorted crossly, "and please don't have any ideas about Jonathan. He is my good friend, the good friend of us all. Isn't that enough?"

Jonathan, hearing his own name, wanted an explanation of the argument, but Nicole said it was all nonsense, and time she helped Bianca set the table, anyway. But as she worked with the chattering schoolgirl a little frown etched itself on her forehead. Lucia was a very old woman with a single-track mind, living foolishly in the past, but Nicole wished she had not said that about Jonathan. She *liked* Jonathan so much.

Nicole was painting the *albergo* for Jonathan, the view of the old farmhouse jutting out over the water, with the sharp peak of Monte Bré in the background. Each afternoon, when they had had tea, she would row herself out into the lake, sitting there, a small solitary figure in the late afternoon sunlight; she would not allow Jonathan to accompany her, nor to see the result of her work.

"I will wrap it up and give it to you when you leave," she promised mischievously, "then you cannot tell me how bad it is! At least it will be a small souvenir of the Albergo Fionetti . . . a little bit of Gandria for you to take back to your cold, grey country!"

"England is not usually cold and grey in July," he argued mildly, but he did not want to think just now of the time when he would have to go home, when this strangely peaceful holiday would be over. He was beginning to think it was the best holiday he had ever had, to understand why Nicole was not anxious to leave Lugano. It would be easy, too easy, to make one's home among these mountains, beside this still yet smiling water.

The best time for fishing was in the evening, just before nightfall. Sometimes Jonathan went with the young Pietro, who, for all his size, was knowledgeable about the lake, a patient and skilful fisherman. Then Jonathan would insist on rowing up the lake, away from Lugano, away from the villages, until they reached the quiet stretch of the north-eastern tip, when Pietro would take charge of the boat.

"You make too much noise with the oars," he said once, grinning.

But when Pietro had homework to do, Jonathan went with Nicole. Returning from one of these expeditions, rather later than usual, she tied up the boat with her quiet deftness, making so little noise that a couple locked in each other's arms in the garden of the *albergo* did not hear their approach.

It was evening, an evening of blue dusk. Jonathan, embarrassed because they might startle the lovers, went swiftly into the loggia and switched on the lights. Plumbing they might not have, but at least there was plenty of cheap electricity here. He was troubled because the man outside was Emilio, and he was astonished to see Nicole laughing.

"I wonder who the girl is—*di notte, tutti i gatti sono bigi*." Seeing his expression, she translated lightly: "At night all cats are grey. I hope it is Francesca. It will be good if Emilio marries Francesca."

"You don't *mind*?" Jonathan was seething, ready to go and knock Emilio into the lake. He could not understand Nicole's perfectly genuine amusement. "I thought perhaps—that you and Emilio——" he said slowly.

Nicole stared at him before laughing outright. "You thought I would marry Emilio? But that is the *bêtise* It would be like marrying my little brother!"

"Come into the kitchen, we'll have coffee. Eugh! It's cold on the water, as late as this. We'll show Lucia the bass, she'll be pleased——"

Jonathan followed her willingly. The children were in bed. They had stayed later than usual for the fishing to-night, and the warmth from the big wood stove was welcome. It glowed and filled the big old kitchen with its pleasant resinous smell, mingling with the aroma of the coffee Lucia had left for them.

"She has gone to bed; it's later than I thought." Nicole gathered the fish and washed it in the scullery beyond, leaving it on the ice-cold slabs of rock in the pantry. This was a natural cave in the rock face behind the house, where the perishable food was kept; beyond it another cave served as a cellar. There was no need of a refrigerator at the *albergo*. On the hottest days these rock-caves were cool.

Jonathan enjoyed the steaming coffee by the kitchen stove; he was immensely relieved because Nicole was not in love with Emilio. It simplified the whole problem if she had no romantic ties in Lugano . . . and for the whole fortnight he had stayed there Nicole had had no meetings with other young men. She sat now in Lucia's chair, rocking herself to and fro gently, her blue eyes still curious and amused. They heard the soft phut-phutter of Emilio's motor-boat and Nicole chuckled suddenly.

"He takes her home now. I think Emilio is wasting petrol tonight! Why did you think we were *affiancés?* Did I not tell you Tia Maria brought us up, like brother and sister?"

"Yes, you did." Jonathan smiled across the glowing stove at the girl who regarded him with candid amusement. He made a small gesture with his hand. "Yet you're not too closely related. I find you here, running his home, looking after his family, sharing everything, even his business worries! Naturally I thought you might be engaged."

She shook her head vehemently, the short, fair curls like bells dancing in the firelight. "I told you about my promise to Tia Maria. When Emilio gets married—if he marries the right person—I can go away from here and do what I like . . . and the right person is Francesca. She would manage the *albergo* even better than I—her family has an inn across the lake and she knows everything. She would also be a good mother to Bianca and Pietro."

"You have everything planned out." Jonathan was amused, yet still relieved and a little curious. Nicole Berenger took her promise to a dying woman very seriously, in spite of her sudden lapses into childishness. "Supposing Emilio marries the wrong sort of girl?"

"Then I would have to stay here until the children were grown up, naturally," she answered calmly. "There is plenty of room here for one, two families—even three families."

He acknowledged that, thinking of the rambling old farmhouse, with its capacious storerooms and bedrooms scattered up and down the steps of the uneven corridors above. Yet the idea of Nicole staying here indefinitely did not appeal to Jonafthan. He said firmly, "I think you will have done enough or the Fionettis by the time that Emilio marries, Nicki. Has he any intention of settling down soon?"

She laughed, finishing her coffee and spreading her small brown hands in the gesture he was growing to know so well. "If anyone can make Emilio settle down it will be

Francesca—and your coming has made it sooner, I think. When he has paid for *Pegasus* he can think about marriage."

"Then I hope he chooses Francesca," Jonathan said dryly, his thoughts flying momentarily to Combe Castleton as he helped wash-up the coffee cups. At home Aunt Bella did not encourage her menfolk in her kitchen, the cook and parlour-maid did not like it. Yet it seemed the most natural thing in the world to help with the chores at the *albergo;* to peel vegetables for old Lucia, to carry the heavy kettles, to lay the table with the giggling Bianca, to help the children with their English and history homework, to dry dishes for Nicole, to help himself to hot soup or coffee from the stove whenever he felt like it, or to raid the larder when he felt hungry. For the first time since his mother's death Jonathan felt really at home, part of a family. Even Emilio had been very friendly lately.

He was fond of his uncle and aunt in Combe Castleton, of course, but he would spend most of his time up at the hospitals or in the nursing homes where he operated on private patients. Uncle Steve and Aunt Bella were in their seventies, after all, and most of Jonathan's friends were professional men, many of them married. As an eligible bachelor he received many invitations to dances, bridge and supper parties; most of them he refused, and when he did attend he was bored and cynical because invariably some unmarried woman had been paired off with him. He was sick and tired of being an eligible bachelor, caught as it were out of his generation . . . too young to really share his uncle and aunt's social round, too old for the trendy teenagers.

Jonathan realised suddenly, here in the warm kitchen of the old inn, that he was lonely in spite of the hard routine of his professional life. It was years since he had played. . . just for the fun of it. It was years since he had helped a woman dry dishes, or helped himself to a snack, or done anything homely, or enjoyed such simple pleasures as filled these days in Lugano so pleasantly . . .

Since Fay had deserted him, an ambitious, struggling young surgeon, to marry her American, he had not cared much about women; but during his illness he had been able to look back upon the episode of Fay without hurt, without even the cynical disillusionment that she had caused, that had armoured him against women ever since. Tonight he could remember how much he had been in love with her, and how he had dreamed of having a real home and children, and he could smile with a certain sympathy for that young idealist who had built up a dream-woman from very common fabric.

He had had compensations for his broken dream, great compensations. In his work, at least, he had succeeded beyond his wildest expectations, and he had given all his interest, heart and body and mind, to the task of becoming a great surgeon.

It was only lying in the Ming-Dhu hospital, listening to that coloured sergeant forever singing his plaintive song about freedom, that his feverish mind had grown restless, self-searching.

Was he missing something in life? The simple yet real pleasures of a home of his own . . . ? Some love greater than the foolish dream he had built around the worldly, fickle Fay? He knew he had given genuine pleasure to his aunt and uncle by his success; by coming to live with them; but after all, they belonged to a different generation; they had their own compact world in Combe Castleton.

And into that rare introspectiveness, the irritability and self-searching of convalescence, had come the haunting tune almost as an answer to his question.

'*I must go where the wild goose goes, I must go where the wild goose cries . . .*

'*Wild goose, brother goose, which is best . . . a wandering foot or a heart at rest . . . ?*'

Here at the Albergo Fionetti he had found happiness—a simple and homely happiness. He could tease the children, make love to old Lucia, talk for long hours with Nicole, and let the sun sink into his bones. Tonight he was suddenly aware of that happiness, as a lovely thing that would soon be only a memory, but something very well worth while. He looked at Nicole, her brown face in the firelight dreaming some dream of her own. Now that he knew for certain she was not in love with Emilio—and already he trusted Nicole's honesty absolutely—he wondered what she wanted to make of her life.

"If Emilio does marry Francesca," he said gently, with the hint of teasing in his voice that told Nicole he thought of her still as a child—a wise and sometimes clever child, but still not someone of his adult, responsible world, "what would you do, Nicki? Where will you go?"

She looked up at him, roused from her thoughts. "I told you—no, I didn't tell you." She smiled suddenly, spreading her hands wide, lifting her small, proud head, adding simply, "I would like to do what my father did, before he married my mother. . . . I would like to wander all over the world, painting. Painting real pictures for myself, painting enough silly things to buy my bread——"

"Man cannot live by bread alone," Jonathan said, and wondered why the quotation came into his head just then. She was so practical, Nicki, and yet such a dreamer. "You can't go all over the world by yourself, even nowadays . . . like a little gypsy. What would happen to you if you didn't sell enough 'silly' paintings?"

"But I would. There's always a market for rubbish." Nicole shrugged. "I don't think I would be lonely, or afraid, and I *want* to see everything!"

"That's rather a tall order." Jonathan did not know that his smile was full of amused tenderness as he imagined this gypsy child wandering over Europe like a troubadour. The wild goose song belonged to her, rather than to a staid, professional man like himself. *Little wild goose*, he thought, *with your quaint mixture of wisdom and childishness, don't you know that one day you will be a beautiful woman, and beautiful women cannot roam the world as gypsy artists . . . ?*

"I can take care of myself," she said quietly, as if she guessed some of his thoughts, "and I *can* paint, in spite of those things you bought from Castiglioni."

He wondered about that. His portrait of Lucia was coming alive very nicely, even the old woman was pleased with it, and he had promised to give it to her when it was finished. It would hang in this kitchen then, where it belonged, perhaps long after Lucia was dead. He was painting in oils, as befitted the strength of his subject; but painting with Jonathan was only a hobby, a complete change from his usual work. He was very curious to know what Nicole's 'real' painting was like; he could not forget the garish picture-postcard style of the ones he had bought.

"Nicki, please show me the one you're doing for me. Don't wrap it up so that I can't see it until I get home. Think of me burning with curiosity—perhaps the *douanes* at Basle will rip it open!"

"Oh, I hadn't thought of that!" She was dismayed, hesitant, almost shy. She wanted very much to shine before her new friend, now that she knew him better she cared for his opinion. She wanted to banish from his mind the memory of those awful tourist pictures . . . yet she had wanted, too, to give him a great surprise when he got home from his holiday. She had imagined to herself, many times, his surprised expression when at last he would unwrap her present. . . .

"Please, Nicki?" Jonathan smiled his lop-sided smile that had won him the undying allegiance of patients and his sorely tried staff at the hospital.

"All right—I'll get it." She was up from the rocking-chair and out of the room with swift grace, like a small wild animal, on noiseless feet. Little wild goose. . . . Now the phrase attached itself to Nicki for all time. Jonathan waited, half afraid that he would have to produce banal praise for something inferior, half excited. Nicole was so innately honest that she would not pretend to a talent she did not possess, but was her self-judgment to be relied upon?

"It's not yet finished," she said quietly, propping the water-colour on the kitchen table for him to see, switching on another, stronger light.

Jonathan stared, enchanted. Here was a delicacy of touch that far surpassed his own. Nicole had caught the charm of the rambling old inn leaning over the lake, the glimmering reflection of the soft afternoon shadows, the rosy glow behind Monte Bré, the quieter mauves and greens of the still water wherein everything was mirrored. A couple of small row-boats were moored to the stone wall, and at the head of the lake the hills rose sharply from the water. Even the peeling pink stucco was there, the sprawling grace of the wistaria. But the painting was more than a photographic reproduction of Gandria . . . it had caught the stillness, the peace of the place, yet withal there was a hint of life going on beneath the tranquillity.

Jonathan could say nothing for a long time. Nicole, watching his face, was satisfied. This absorbed silence was tribute enough, better than all her imaginings.

"This is lovely—and it is Gandria," he said at last, and turned to her. "And I thought I could paint! I owe you an apology Nicki. I shall always treasure this."

She smiled. "It is the Albergo Fionetti, for you to keep with you always," she acknowledged. "When one likes a place very well, it's good to take it with you always."

She added briskly, "It's not yet finished, of course. But now do you see why I want to go everywhere, paint everything?"

He shook his head, lighting his last pipe. "I see that you

love this place, Nicki. Surely you want to stay in your home?"

"Of course this will always be my home, if I need it——" The girl hesitated, looking away into the glowing embers of the stove. "Emilio and Bianca and Pietro would always let me come here. But you don't understand—I have no real home. When Emilio marries he will not want another woman helping here. Now I'm earning my keep, but Francesca can do all my work and do it better. I don't want anyone's charity! I can earn my living in my own way——"

"But——" Jonathan was troubled. If Helen Stannisford knew that her granddaughter proposed peddling her wares round Europe like a gypsy because she had no home, it would break her old heart. Now, at last, was his opportunity to plead with the child to return, in the name of common sense and humanity. Living here with the Fionettis, who were after all a sort of family for her, was one thing; this plan for her future was another; a very different and dangerous matter. Jonathan retracted his decision not to interfere. He said quietly, "But I understood you have a home, Nicki. Your English grandmother wants you, doesn't she?"

The small fair head went up, the blue eyes blazed suddenly. "My English grandmother," she said angrily, "employed an enquiry agent—a private detective—to come and spy on me! She couldn't send for my mother when she was sick, when she was longing to go home——"

"Perhaps she never got the letter. Letters do go astray sometimes," he argued quietly.

"Pph! She must have had the letter! How else did she know where to send her beastly detective to look for me?" Nicole contended furiously. "Oh, if you'd seen him! Such an imbecile, so impertinent! I sent him away with a face like that fire—and Emilio knocked him into the lake to cool off!"

Jonathan tried not to laugh. "Not exactly tactful. The poor chap was only doing his job." No wonder, he thought, that the agent's bill had been so enormous, that he had refused absolutely to revisit his client's granddaughter.

Nicole chuckled. "He was very important when he came, very patronising. He didn't look so important when we fished him out of the lake!"

"Nicki——" Jonathan began pleadingly, knowing that the time had come to tell her the truth about himself, yet

61

strangely reluctant to face the anger and disillusionment that would certainly follow.

"No——" She shook her head firmly. "Don't tell me I have committed the *bêtise*, that I should be nice to my so-rich grandmother! Would *you* go back and eat humble pie if they had treated your parents so?"

"Perhaps not. But——"

"If my grandmother wants me, she should take the trouble to come and see me herself," Nicole interrupted him.

"She may be too old—or ill——" It was extraordinarily difficult to tell Nicole about Helen.

"Then she should send someone—a relation or friend—*not* a paid agent," Nicki said proudly, and he thought, here we go, this is it . . . and gathered his breath to speak. But the tension was shattered dramatically by an appalling crashing noise in the back garden. Nicole and Jonathan were out of the inn before another word was spoken.

"*Dio mio.* It's the rotten brach—Pietro has been out again, up to his tricks!" Nicki cried, as she ran swiftly down the garden, Jonathan hard on her heels. Sure enough the big branch of the tree that normally reached to Pietro's bedroom window was lying on the ground, and beneath it the still form of the boy.

"*Carissimo mio*," the girl whispered, stooping over him, but the child was unconscious. She said with a little caught-back sob in her voice, "Sometimes he goes out at night, when he is supposed to be in bed, and climbs back along that branch. I begged Emilio to cut it down!"

The moonlight shone down clearly on the pathetic scene, the broken jagged branch, the still boy. Jonathan said quietly, "He fell on the stones—his head is cut," and picked him up very carefully, carrying him into the kitchen and laying him flat on the table. In the glare of the two electric bulbs the injury was very plainly seen, and Nicole gave a small gasp and turned green. Jonathan paid no attention to her, he was busy exploring the gash in the boy's scalp with sensitive, probing fingers, after a rapid scrubbing up.

His examination and the boy's breathing told their own story. There was a jagged fracture of the parietal, with the bone pressing on the brain. Very soon the boy would sink into a deep coma and die very quickly unless that pressure on the brain was removed.

62

Jonathan thought quickly, assembling the facts. The boy should go straight into hospital, but by the time a motor-boat could be found he might well be dead. Again, he weighed the probable risk of moving the boy, of carrying him down the stone steps, of holding him for perhaps half an hour in the open, before he could be got into the hospital theatre at Lugano. There was no telephone within a mile of the *albergo*, and Jonathan did not know whether there would be a specialist of the sort he needed in a small town like Lugano. This was definitely an emergency such as he had dealt with often enough in the bombed villages around Ming-Dhu, under much worse conditions than the kitchen of the Albergo Fionetti; he decided that the risk of performing an immediate trephine here was less than the risk of waiting for transport. The medical etiquette of the situation might criticise his action, but the boy's life was at stake.

He blessed himself suddenly for bringing his instruments with him, and Lucia for her everlasting kettles of boiling water.

He said crisply to Nicole, "He has a bad fracture which is pressing on the brain; it needs lifting immediately——"

"You will operate? Jonathan, you will do it yourself, quickly?" she beseeched him. Glancing at her, momentarily touched by the faith in her voice, he was pleased to see that the colour had returned to her face. His tone was grim, a trifle ironical, as he scrubbed-up again. So Lucia's kitchen sink was to be a theatre sink after all. Fortunately the table had a good surface, and was kept immaculately scrubbed; and the two electric lights were fairly bright.

"Yes, I'll operate. God knows what they'll say about it at the hospital, but we have to hurry——"

"*Dio mio! Il poverissimo e morto!*"

Lucia, hastily dressed, stood in the doorway wringing her hands. Bianca, in her nightgown, peeped over her shoulder, her brown eyes bright with excitement and curiosity.

"Take that child back to bed," Jonathan said harshly, and for once Lucia understood English, "and come and help Nicole. Pietro is not dead, but he has hurt himself badly. *Subito*, Lucia, *pronto*"

"*Si, si!*" The old woman, vastly relieved that her *bambino* was not dead and that the *signore* spoke with the voice of recognisable authority, bustled the staring Bianca away, and Jonathan turned to Nicole again.

63

"I shall need help," he said clearly, almost gently, wondering if he was asking too much of this untrained girl. "Can you help me, or do you faint at the sight of blood?"

Her face was pale but composed. "I can help you," she answered quietly.

"Good. Get my case down, will you? There are sterile gowns and masks, everything we shall need——" But she was gone, light of foot as a young deer, before he had finished. Good girl, he thought absently, as he moved a small table closer to the big one for his instruments and got his patient into a better position under the light. As long as she can obey orders without dithering or fainting, we may get through this. . . .

It *would* have to happen, he thought bitterly, on a night when Emilio was out with his lady-love. Emilio and his precious motor-boat should have been here; it was, strictly speaking, for Emilio to give authority for this emergency operation. But he had no intention of letting the boy die while they waited for any authority at all.

He showed Nicole the instruments he wanted sterilised in one of the big kettles while he gave Pietro the injection; there was no time now to think of anything but practical details. He supervised her scrubbing-up before and after she had gowned him and tied his mask, and after that he forgot her as a person altogether; she was simply a pair of hands holding a powerful torch where he wanted it, passing instruments to him as he asked for them. He did not look at the blue eyes, tragic and absorbed above the white mask, or notice that the torchlight wavered a little at first, then steadied. He did talk a little, explaining what he was doing, to help her keep going.

"This is a jagged fracture. I shall remove the pieces of bone that are pressing on the brain, but I shall have to make the opening a little larger—so. That is to make sure that no fragment of bone is left inside, and it will make the union of the new bone graft easier. Swab—swab——"

He preferred to work without gloves. Now he was so absorbed in the familiar task that he forgot Nicole altogether. There was the exposed brain pulsing beneath his gentle, probing fingers; a human life literally in his hands. The breathing of the girl standing so close to him became inaudible, her face as white as the gown she wore, and in the background old Lucia stoked the stove as she had been bidden—to make the kitchen warmer, to keep the water boiling—before dropping on her knees to say her

64

rosary. The tiny clatter of instruments and the gentle clicking of the rosary beads were the only sounds audible beside the difficult, changing breathing of the unconscious boy.

"Take his pulse-count, please."

Working against time, fighting his old enemy—death. It was a familiar race for Jonathan, and infinitely worth while, especially in the case of a child. Once the wound was clean and the boy's breathing easier, he straightened for a moment, the sweat running down his forehead, before beginning the difficult, delicate job of cutting the bone plate to fit the aperture exactly. Nicole, without being told, reached up and wiped his forehead, just as his theatre nurses did, but he was too busy to realise it. The small bone plate, though real bone, would be a foreign body in the boy's skull; it must be fitted exactly, neither too tight, so that it was pushed out, nor too loose for the living bone to knit with it.

He remembered Nicole suddenly. "Can't leave him with a hole in his head," he said cheerfully, "and his own bone will make calcerous matter, knit this up round the edges gradually, and he'll be as good as new."

It was a vague explanation to quiet the anxiety in her eyes, but she was grateful for it.

"He will live?" she whispered behind the mask, afraid even to ask the question after what she had just seen done to her poor Pietro.

"I hope so. Can't you hear his breathing? It's already more normal."

Jonathan did not talk for a long time after that. The job of inserting the new plate finished, he cleaned the scalp and stitched it neatly over the wound. Then, swabbed, there was only a bald patch where he had cut away the thick, black hair, and Pietro stirred a little.

"Another injection—the small hypodermic. He must stay absolutely quiet. Then we can put him to bed, carefully——"

Over at the sink again for scrubbing-up, Jonathan noticed Lucia still on her knees. He patted her shoulder, smiling, when he had dried his hands. "You prayed while I worked, and now the good God will do the rest. Pietro is young and strong and healthy, soon he will be running about again," he said slowly and carefully. To his embarrassment old Lucia seized his hand and kissed it, the tears running down her seamed face.

"Grazie, signore! Deo gratias!"

Jonathan had seen that look of love and gratitude on the faces of the parents of his child patients before. He smiled again and pressed the old hands holding his own. "We must get him into bed for a good long sleep now."

Nicole ran before him to turn on the lights, and he carried the boy very carefully up the uneven stairs, along the ups and downs of the winding passage, into his bedroom.

"Take the sheets and the pillow away; I'll lay him flat in blankets. Ah, Lucia has produced the hot water bottles, that's good."

In a few minutes Pietro was comfortably asleep, the colour returning to his olive skin, and only a small lamp left burning on the bedside table. In the stillness he heard the soft chug-chug of the motor-boat returning, and Jonathan's expression was grim. He took a pad and pencil from his pocket and scribbled rapidly.

"Tell young Lothario he can take this straight over to the hospital. He must give it to the resident surgeon personally—and I shall want a couple of nurses from tomorrow morning—no, this morning. I shall stay with Pietro until another doctor has seen him and the day-nurse installed."

"But you have done everything!" she whispered. "You're very tired——"

"Yes." Now he realised how deathly tired he was. It was late, after midnight, and the strain of working in poor conditions had been added to the tremendous responsibility. "But I shall stay with him, nevertheless. You don't understand, Nicole. Tonight I have operated without the consent of Emilio, without the approval of the doctors in Lugano. They may be very angry with me. It was an emergency and I had to do what I thought best, but it's all very unorthodox."

They were still in their gowns, though they had removed the masks. Nicole was standing very close to him, the note in her hand, and suddenly she reached up and drew his head down to her, kissing him soundly on the lips and holding him tight with both her arms. He found himself holding her, too, and for an instant his lips touched her fair hair.

"You have saved his life, so what does it matter what they think in Lugano?" she whispered passionately. "And I thank you, Jonathan! *Le bon Dieu* must have sent you to us!" and she turned and ran swiftly from the darkened

66

room, running to intercept Emilio and give him the message. Jonathan only glimpsed the brightness of tears in her eyes as she turned away from his arms. He sat down beside Pietro, holding the little boy's thin brown wrist lightly between his fingers, counting the steadier, stronger pulse beats with a great thankfulness in his heart.

"*I* could nurse Pietro," Nicole said, with the crossness of fatigue and reaction. Emilio, a strangely subdued and pale Emilio, had listened with bent head to Nicki's story of his young brother's accident. He had insisted on peeping at the unconscious boy before going on his errand to Lugano. He had wrung Jonathan's hand silently, when the surgeon indicated that no noise was to be made.

"Sleep is very important to him now," he said in a low voice.

"*Si, si*. . . . A thousand pardons, Jonathan, for not being here—and a thousand thanks for what you have done this night!" the young man had whispered emotionally, with the tears streaming down his handsome face. They were an emotional lot, these Italians, Jonathan thought; Nicole, with her half French, half English blood, was capable of great feeling, too, but she was much more useful in a crisis . . . He said firmly but not unkindly, "You get over to the hospital with that message, Emilio, or I shall get into trouble with the authorities."

"O.K., I fly!" Smiling now, Emilio gave one last look at his brother and sped away, wiping his handsome nose on the back of his brown hand. Nicole smiled at Jonathan in quick understanding of his feelings.

"Englishmen do not cry, *n'est-ce pas?*"

"Not very easily," he answered quietly, "but I have seen Englishmen weep, and it is a terrible thing."

She nodded, and he saw that there were great black smudges under her eyes. "All the same, Emilio loves his brother—he would die for him if necessary. It does not mean, because he shows his feelings easily, that he has no deep heart, too . . . and I think he is very ashamed because he was not here tonight."

"That's ridiculous. How could he know that the young monkey was going out? Where does he go, by the way?"

"Fishing." There was a tender, amused light in Nicole's blue eyes. "We wouldn't take him because we were going to stay out later last night, so he borrows Giovanni's boat and goes down the other way, by himself. . . . He's a great fisherman, Pietro, and he thinks he's a man . . ."

At the moment Pietro looked very much a small boy, lying there so still and defenceless. Jonathan looked across him to the girl who sat on the other side of the bed. He knew that ordinary low-toned conversation would not disturb the boy, but he had been afraid that Emilio would embrace him, disturb him emotionally. The surgeon said gently, "We will take him with us next time. No more fishing until Pietro can come as well."

"That will make him get well quicker than anything." Nicki thanked him with her eyes. Jonathan told her to go to bed, and she answered crossly, "*I* could nurse Pietro; there was no need to bring over women from the hospital."

"Of course you could." Jonathan rose and crossed the room to pull the tired girl gently to her feet. "You have done splendidly, Nicki! But I think you've done enough . . . and thank you, my dear, for your help." He saw the mutiny in her eyes and added quickly, "You don't understand the red tape, darling. I've done something very unorthodox tonight. From now on Pietro will be in the care of the local doctor and surgeon, and the trained nurses—"

"Pph! No doctor could do more for him than you have done, and these nurses will not do more for Pietro than I could do! I know he'll ask for me as soon as he wakes."

He was amused and touched to know that she could be jealous—but he kept his amusement well hidden. "Well, he will not wake for a long time, I hope, and his convalescence will be a slow, tedious business. There'll be plenty of time for you to help him, my dear child. Now go and tell Lucia to go to bed, and pop off yourself. Emilio will bring these people in and I'll sit with Pietro."

"I must clear up the kitchen first, and I will make us all some fresh coffee. If you are staying up you must have something to eat and drink——"

"Very well, *Maman!*" He could not help teasing her a little. "But please be very, very careful with my instruments—especially the sharp ones and the small ones."

"I haven't cut myself or dropped anything yet!" she retorted with a hint of her old spirit, and whisked out of the sick-room. In spite of her tiredness, her feet touched the old worn stairs very lightly and her heart was singing. Pietro, poor *bambino*, what a price he had nearly paid for his innocent mischief! Pietro was going to live. And she had not fainted down there, though once or twice she had felt very sick—and Jonathan had praised her. Just now he had even called her "darling," and that for an Englishman meant that he loved her a little . . . though she realised he still thought of her as a child and it had probably slipped out in the fatigue of the night . . . yet after tonight he would know that she was not entirely a child, to be petted and teased and soon forgotten . . .

She found Lucia scrubbing the kitchen table free of its sinister stains. "*Dio mio!*" she exclaimed. "How can such a little one lose that much blood and live?"

"He will live. Jonathan says he will live. But he will have to be good and quiet for a long time. He says also that you are to go to bed, my old one, and sleep soundly without fear." Nicole hugged the old woman's thin shoulders, taking the scrubbing brush from her. "Off with you, or no one will be up to give these nurses their breakfast later on!"

Lucia surrendered, grunting in her weariness. "Ah, well, it is late indeed for one my age to be about. The Good God must have sent this Englishman here at such a time."

For a moment Nicole's face was transfigured by tenderness. "Of course He did! Tomorrow you can see Père Angelo and have a Mass said in thanksgiving. Now go—"

The old woman patted the girl's cheek with a work-roughened, skinny hand. "You are a good child, Nicki. Maria will be looking down and blessing you for this night's work. Sleep well when you have finished here, little one."

"*Buona notte—cara Lucia.*"

The big kitchen seemed very empty and silent after the old woman had slowly climbed the stairs. Nicole flinched a little from the instruments she had promised to clean, and scolded herself for being squeamish now that it was all over. She cleansed and boiled and dried the instruments with scrupulous care, guessing that Jonathan would examine them later with critical eyes. These delicate knives and probes and forceps and saws were the tools of his trade, the magnificent trade of saving human life. Nicole made her work in the silent kitchen her own small prayer of gratitude, to God and to the good man God had sent them in their crisis.

When all was ship-shape she carried the tray of steaming coffee and crisp rolls and butter up to Jonathan. He was sitting very still with his eyes closed, but he was not asleep; he opened them at once when she came in.

She waited while he ate and drank ravenously. "I didn't realise I was so hungry. Lord—this tastes good!" he said simply by way of thanks. "You have some, Nicki—and then you must go to bed."

She did not want to leave him. Tonight they had shared so much; the peaceful hours of fishing, the quiet good talk afterwards by the kitchen stove; the little joke about Emilio and Francesca; the terrible operation to Pietro, and now this quiet vigil by the sleeping boy. But Nicki found her lashes sticking together over her tired eyes, and Jonathan's hands—warm, strong hands—pulling her to her feet again.

"Good night, bless you; go and sleep for ten hours. We'll manage," he said, and gave her forehead a light kiss. "You've been wonderfully brave, little one."

"Good night, Jonathan——"

This time she did not kiss him back, but as she went tiredly along to her own room she put her hand up to her forehead, as if his tender salute had left some imprint there, and she fell asleep with a tiny smile on her lips.

No one but Jonathan heard the arrival of *Pegasus* with the surgeon and nurses from Lugano, and they were installed without noise and fuss. Jonathan found that the coffee and rolls had worked wonders for him, in fact he was wide awake enough to discuss the operation at some length with the Swiss surgeon, who fortunately spoke excellent English.

"Congratulations, Mr. Grant. Of course I have heard of your work; we could not have had a better man. But if you agree I would like to send for Adler—he is at Zurich now—to have a look at your patient."

"By all means," Jonathan agreed affably, but he was thinking, now the circus will start. My holiday is over!

CHAPTER FOUR

"HE IS a famous man, your surgeon." Old Lucia smacked her lips with satisfaction, peering over Bianca's shoulder at the local paper. "Why did you not tell me we had such an honoured guest at our *albergo*?"

"Because I didn't know," Nicole almost snapped, stirring the custard she was making for Pietro. The child was on a special diet, very light; no Italian cooking with oils or wines, and Nicole had fought the nurses for the privilege of cooking for the invalid. "Lucia will leave the *albergo* if strangers come into her kitchen!" she had threatened, and the German-Swiss nurses—capable, stolid nurses—had succumbed to her ruling. It was Nicole who did all the cooking for the sick-room, Nicole who carried up and down the big copper cans of hot water for the bed-bathing, Nicole who sat quietly reading when he was allowed to have any visitors at all. As she had prophesied, Pietro had demanded her presence as soon as he was fully conscious, some days after his accident. And rather than frustrate the boy, Jonathan had decreed that she could sit with him by the hour, and read quietly to him when he was awake, to discourage him from moving at all.

"It's all here," Bianca cried excitedly. "All the papers are full of it! At school they are always talking about it. Look—there's a new photograph of Pietro, and a big, huge one of Jonathan!"

Nicole moved the custard to one side of the stove and looked, albeit reluctantly, at the severe studio portrait of Jonathan. She said angrily, "They must have sent to England for that! I heard him telling the reporter to go to . . . that he would not supply any details of the operation, or photographs for the press!"

"Oh, they can get these things of celebrities through the world press associations," Emilio said knowledgeably.

"I gave the reporter the one of Pietro, at school—it was one I took last summer," Bianca said smugly.

Nicole flicked her cheek with sharp fingers. "Then you had no business to interfere!" she cried furiously. "Did I not tell you—Jonathan asked that nothing, *nothing* should be said to the press? The doctors are the only people who have to know all the details, and they are satisfied."

"More than satisfied," Emilio added. "Listen to this: 'Jonathan Grant, the famous surgeon, recently returned from voluntary service with an American field hospital in Vietnam, was fortunately staying as a guest at the Albergo Fionetti last week when Pietro Fionetti suffered a severe fracture of the skull——'."

"Stop it!" Nicole shouted, banging the newspaper out of his hand. "You make me sick, all of you! As if it is not enough to save Pietro's life, without having to endure this *bêtise* from the press—and all of you, adding to it!"

She stopped abruptly, realising that they were all staring at her in various attitudes of perplexity—Lucia with a garlic in her hand, Emilio perched on a corner of the big table, Bianca with several papers spread above her homework books, her mouth hanging open.

Bianca recovered first. "I don't know why *you* are grumbling," she said petulantly. "They've put in all about you, too—you're quite a heroine!" The girl surveyed her friend with her dark head on one side, her eyes mischievous. "I think you would look wonderful in a nurse's uniform, Nicki!"

"Well, they have no photograph of me, with or without a uniform."

"I thought you were good friends, you and Jonathan," Lucia grumbled, as she rubbed her clove round the salad bowl.

"Yes."

Emilio slipped off the table and came over to Nicole, laughing and yet troubled. She shrugged off the arm he tried to put round her shoulders. "Why are you so angry? Surely all this story is good publicity for Jonathan? It says many good things of his work—during this Vietnam war, and at this place in England where he lives——"

"Combe Castleton," Nicole said stiffly.

"Combe Castleton," Emilio made heavy weather of the consonants, "and London, and Vienna, and Paris. And now our little emergency in Gandria. . . . Adler, the great brain surgeon, has praised his work so generously——"

"He doesn't need Mr. Adler's praise," Nicki said slowly, her face scarlet as she bent over the stove. "Can't you all see how he hates the newspaper stories? And people are coming every day up the lake to stare at us—not very close, because they know Pietro is being nursed here and must remain very quiet—but they come and stare at the *albergo* as if a murder had been committed here!"

"And very good for trade, too," Emilio grinned. "Later in the summer we shall be full up with visitors, and that is good for business. Your Mr. Grant has brought us luck."

"And ruined his own holiday," Nicole snapped, though under her brittle temper her heart ached with sadness for the happy, peaceful days that were gone for ever, before they had known anything about Jonathan. She added more quietly, "He came here for a rest, incognito. Now he can't step ashore without a reporter or a cameraman dogging his footsteps."

Emilio shrugged. "I shall never understand the English! They work so hard to get to the top of their profession, and then hate the publicity! Me, I am glad there are pictures of this house in the papers, I am glad many visitors will come to us later in the season. If the *albergo* is good enough for a famous surgeon's holiday, others will find their way here."

"Is that all you can think of, when Pietro is still so very ill?" Nicole asked sadly. She was realising these days that she was more English than she had thought . . . for in this matter her heart and mind were ranged wholly on Jonathan's side, though she still had a private battle to wage with him.

"Now that Pietro is going to get well—you yourself and Jonathan and Mr. Adler all say it is only a matter of rest and time—naturally I am glad we are going to do good business out of it!" Emilio argued good-temperedly. "It means I can get married sooner, and Pietro and Bianca will share everything I make! There will be a lot less work for you, Nicki."

There will be no work for me at all, for I shall have gone by then, the girl thought unhappily, but she made no further effort to stop the enthusiasm over the newspaper articles. A few nights ago it had been all tragedy, now it was all comedy; the Italians could be like children easily moved to the heights or cast down in the depths. Only Lucia, though she too grumbled about Nicole's temper these days, understood something of the cause.

Bianca had a sudden feminine inspiration. "I believe Nicki is jealous!" she cried triumphantly. "She has fallen in love with Jonathan, thinking he was just an ordinary man, and now he is much too rich and famous to marry her!"

Emilio, cuffing his sister soundly over the ears, saved the situation. "Shut up, you little beast! Remember we have to thank Nicki, too, for saving Pietro's life. And now get on with your homework or you will have to stay in all the afternoon!"

Nicole, feeling for the first time that she was not really a member of this family, prepared the invalid's tray with hands that were inexplicably shaking.

"Nicki, can you spare a moment? I want to talk to you."

Jonathan stood in the open doorway of his room, a pipe in his mouth after he had called to Nicki, his hands thrust suddenly into the pockets of his tweed jacket. Though the midday sun blazed down on the lake, making it a shimmering golden mirror, inside these thick stone walls it was cool; in most of the rooms the green shutters were closed and the glare shut out; only in Jonathan's room were they wide open at all hours of the day or night. He had been watching the girl walking down the long, irregular corridor with Pietro's luncheon tray in her hands, on her small face an abstracted look that was very unlike her usual alertness. She started when he called, and as she came closer he put one hand gently under her small, determined chin.

"What are you looking sad about, Nicki? Hasn't Pietro eaten his lunch?"

By way of answer she thrust the tray at him, and its empty dishes, and grinned. It was as if a mask dropped over her expression. So even this child could act, he thought ruefully.

"Pietro is doing fine; he wants to get up. I'm not sad any more, but I am very, very angry," she said defiantly.

"With me?"

"With you. If you hadn't saved Pietro's life I think I would like to kill you!" she said simply.

"That's frank, anyway." He took the tray from her unresisting hands and deposited it on a bench in the passage. "Come inside and talk, Nicki. Get it off your chest. This is siesta time and Pietro is resting, isn't he?"

"Pietro is resting," she acknowledged, "and that great cow of a nurse is knitting—always she is knitting! She must make enough socks to stock a shop!"

"Fraulein Weiger is not a cow, she is a very good nurse," Jonathan smiled down at the girl with a twinkle in his grey eyes, "and it is me, not the poor nurse, with whom you are angry. Come and scold me—you've been avoiding me all the week, haven't you?"

"I have been busy, looking after your—nurses," she retorted with immense dignity, "and telling lies to the reporters, saying I know nothing."

"Very kind of you. I'm grateful." Jonathan was dry.

"And it would not be proper for me to come and talk in the bedroom of the great Jonathan Grant!" Nicole added fiercely.

"Oh, oh! Since when have you become so anxious about the proprieties?" he demanded, unable to stop the laughter that rumbled in his chest. This fierce yet demure child was so unlike the Nicki he knew, yet beneath his amusement there was a great tenderness for the hurt he knew she had sustained. He drew her inside firmly and over to the broad, shallow window seat. "We will leave the door wide open, child, and not even the proper Fraulein Weiger can complain!"

He felt her arms trembling in his gentle grip, and her face was averted from him as she stared over the lake. He sat down close to her, and suddenly he was not amused any more.

"Nicki, look at me. Tell me I'm every sort of scab for coming here—knowing all about your family history—and not telling you at once——"

"Jonathan *Grant*," she whispered fiercely, but she kept her face averted. She might have been addressing someone across the lake. "Mr. Johnson, a nice English surgeon on holiday! The same name as my grandmother's solicitor, living in Combe Castleton—I suppose you are his son! I suppose he sent you here to make your report on me—like that horrible detective! And I—like a fool, I trusted you and told you everything! How you must have laughed inside yourself!"

Jonathan felt the slow colour mounting to his own face. He answered soberly, "I've never laughed at you, Nicki—in that way. Stephen Grant—your grandmother's solicitor—is my uncle. I live with him and Aunt Bella. The Grants and the Stannisfords have been friends for generations..."

"So they sent you to find out about me," she said stonily.

"In a way, yes. I want you to try and understand how it happened, Nicki. It's true that I'd been ill, that my doctor ordered me away for a complete rest and change—preferably to some place I hadn't visited before. My uncle, who is very friendly with your grandmother and anxious about her health, asked me to come to Lugano—"

Nicole got up restlessly and stood with her back to him, staring out of the side window. "You could have told me who you were," she said in a muffled voice.

"And been sent away immediately with a flea in my ear like the enquiry agent?" Jonathan asked dryly. "Have some sense, Nicki! All their letters were coming back unopened; there seemed no way of reaching you, to tell you what conditions in Combe Castleton were really like, to plead with you for mercy to an old and frail woman——"

"Who had no mercy on my mother!" Nicole answered quietly.

Jonathan came and stood behind her shoulder. "You have every right to be angry with me for deceiving you child, but now I want you to give me a fair hearing."

"Well, I'm listening," she said stonily.

He told her of his great reluctance to interfere at all in a family dispute that did not, after all, concern him at all; of his visit to Helen Stannisford, and how it had changed his opinion . . . that, and the sidelight thrown on Henry Stannisford's character by his uncle.

"So you agreed to come and spy on the wicked, wilful granddaughter," she said dully.

"I did nothing of the sort." Jonathan was stung to self-defence. "I agreed merely to take my holiday in Lugano, to try and meet you and put your grandmother's point of view before you. I warned them all that I would not attempt to persuade you unfairly—if you were happy here."

"So you gave me a false name, pretended to be my friend, and let me tell you all my history!" she cried angrily, and suddenly turned to beat her small fists against his chest in a desolation of weeping that she could not control. "Oh, Jonathan, how could you, how could you! And I thought I'd found a friend!"

"And so you have, my darling." He held her close, until the first paroxysm of grief was over, knowing that she was temporarily deaf and dumb and blind to reasoning. But his arms holding her securely, his hand smoothing the small fair head, gave their own message of loving kindness to the stricken girl.

"There, blow. It'll do you good to get that out of your system. And now will you listen to me carefully, Nicole— because I do want to be truly your friend, and I'm bitterly sorry to have deceived you at all. But you must admit you would never have allowed me to come here if you'd known who I was from the start."

She used the large, clean hankie vigorously. Her small ravaged face hurt Jonathan, but he did not want to weaken her further by too much sympathy. "I would have sent *you* away with a flea in your ear!" she admitted shakily, with a faint echo of her usual dry humour.

"Right, now we're getting somewhere. I was 'Mr. Johnson' because you would never have had any dealing with anyone called Grant. But as soon as I got to know you, Nicole, I felt a mean scab—several times I nearly told you the truth, because you had convinced me that you knew your own business best and I was not prepared to interfere in any way, except just to tell you about your grandmother and let you make the final decision."

"But you never did tell me—even that night in the kitchen," she said faintly. She wanted so much to go on believing in Jonathan, believing every word he said, but her heart was aching and sore with the discoveries of the past week, and she was still too tired to reason properly.

He smiled suddenly. "Dear Nicki, have you forgotten —we heard the branch breaking, just after you'd said something—something about your grandmother sending a friend if she couldn't travel herself. I was just going to tell you that I was that friend——"

"It would have been better if you had told me in the beginning," she said sombrely, "then I would have saved you a lot of bother, wasting your holiday! I shall *not* come and eat humble-pie in the house closed against my father. Never, never will I be such a traitor to his memory! You can write and tell my grandmother so, and your precious uncle!"

"I haven't wasted my holiday." Jonathan put an arm lightly about her slim shoulders, and both of them stood looking out over the lake, very peaceful in the golden afternoon. "You're not stupid enough to think I haven't enjoyed every moment of my stay here, Nicki."

"Except this last week," she murmured.

"Perhaps not this last week," he acknowledged ruefully, "though even that has been infinitely worth while in another way." He looked down at his free hand, flexing the fingers thoughtfully. "I know now that I'm strong again, that I shall go back to my work refreshed. And apart from anything else, I want to thank you for that, Nicki. You have given me a wonderful rest."

Her gentian-blue eyes were still misted with tears. She said, with a faint echo of her old insouciance, "And you have saved my little cousin's life, so we're quits. I couldn't be really angry with you, Jonathan, after that."

"That was pure chance." For a moment his voice sounded crisp, impersonal, as it had done while he was operating. "Let's not have any emotional blackmail,

Nicki, on either side. I want us to be real friends from now on, with no more lies—if you can trust me?''

"I want to. Oh, Jonathan, I want to!" For the first time she turned and faced him, and her eyes held his with the old frankness. "I think—I think it hurt most to find that you had lied to me!" She added doubtfully, "But I suppose you thought you were doing me a kindness—''

"You—and an old lady who has led a wretched life under the thumb of a bad-tempered tyrant." He thought for a while about Helen Stannisford, adding suddenly, almost harshly, "But I gave them no promises to try and influence you. And I did not even write at once and say that we had met. . . . I only wrote last week, after Pietro's accident, and I want you to read my uncle's reply."

She took it from him reluctantly. It was a typed letter on the headed paper that she hated so much, *Grant, Noble, Grant and Grant, Solicitors* . . .

For the past week Nicole's head and her heart had been in bitter conflict. She had liked Jonathan so much, trusted him absolutely; on the night of Pietro's accident she had almost worshipped him. This was a man she could love and respect, a man doing a wonderful job with high skill and courage—enough courage even to defy medical etiquette —and the sureness born of experience and good training. To discover from the press reports, from the visiting doctors and specialists and the nurses, that Jonathan was an emissary from what she always thought of as the enemy camp, had been devastating. Against the personal anger that flared in her was the gratitude she felt for what he had done for Pietro, and the instincts of her own heart that he was, in spite of everything, still trustworthy. Now he had dragged all her misery out of her; now she had to read this letter from her grandmother's solicitor. But the wording of it soon banished every other thought from her head.

It was not a dictated letter couched in legal phrases, it was, in fact, rather badly typed, obviously by the uncle himself.

My dear Jonathan, it ran,

Your aunt and I are delighted to know that you are having such a splendid holiday, and that you feel quite fit again. At first we were so pleased, too, that you have found Nicole Berenger such a charming girl, and happy with her adopted Italian family . . . also that she is so like Evelyn as you re-

*membered her. Yet, following on that good news, your decision
not to try and influence her one way or the other came as a
grievous disappointment to us both.*

*I dared not read more than the first part of your letter to
Helen when I visited her yesterday. The doctor says her
heart is in very poor condition and he emphasises the effect
of further disappointments on her health. She was utterly
delighted to hear some personal news of Nicole, and is living
for the day when she will see her granddaughter. I do beg
of you, dear boy, to reconsider your decision and ask Nicole
again to come home, if only for a visit. Otherwise I fear
Helen will travel to Lugano herself, against all her doctor's
advice.*

With love from your aunt and myself,

S. Grant.

For a long moment Nicole stared again over the water,
her mind a tumult of conflicting emotions. She remembered her mother's unchanging love for *her* mother, her
father's generous lack of resentment. Just now, down in
the kitchen, she had realised that the time was coming
when she must leave the *albergo.* Everything was against
her stubborn pride. She sighed as at last she turned and
handed the letter back to Jonathan.

"Very well. When Pietro is well again I will come and
visit my grandmother. But I want no charity from her, and
I don't promise to stay."

"Dear Nicki!" Jonathan smiled at her suddenly,
tenderly. "That's generous of you. I don't think you will
regret it. And you can always come and weep on my
shoulder when you want to."

Nicole laughed shakily as she picked up the tray and
went away.

"She must be rich, your grandmother." Emilio and
Nicole were sitting on the stone steps in front of the *albergo.*
It was early morning and almost time to take *Pegasus*
across to be fuelled for her day's trips. Emilio had been
cleaning her out just now, until he intercepted the postman
in his launch. Sometimes the mail came by the coast road
from the village, sometimes by water. Today there was a
fairly big packet for the *albergo.*

"Getting quite famous, with your broken-down old inn,
aren't you?" the postman greeted his friend cheerily in
Italian. "My, but some folk are lucky!"

Emilio grinned and whistled for Nicole, who came running to fetch Jonathan's letters. Always their English guest had the letters. But today there was one for her, and when she had given Lucia the rest to put on Jonathan's breakfast tray she returned to the steps to open it. Since the house had been invaded with visitors and nurses, Lucia was getting flustered by so many strangers, and Nicki had persuaded Jonathan that he was doing them all a kindness by taking his breakfast in his own room. Actually she knew that he preferred to be alone. The old happy, growing familiarity with the Fionettis had been disrupted since Pietro's accident, and though she could not prevent Bianca's pestering adoration and Emilio's curiosity at supper, she could at least let him eat his breakfast in peace.

"Of course she is rich, we have always known that," Nicole answered impatiently. She was more interested in the letter she was reading than in the bank draft on the Bank of Switzerland for six hundred francs that Emilio was holding so respectfully.

The delicate, spidery handwriting was not easy to read, but Nicole persevered with mixed feelings. This reaching out towards reconciliation between herself and her English grandmother was contrary to all her pride, to her loyalty towards her dead parents, to her own instincts to preserve her freedom . . . yet it was what her parents had wanted. Above all, it was what Jonathan wanted, and Nicole hardly realised how much she had come to rely on his advice.

"Six hundred *Swiss* francs, not French francs, Nicki— that is quite a nice amount," Emilio said.

"Most of it is for the fare, the rest—she says here, it is the most they would allow her to send out of England, and I can use it how I like; we can buy clothes or anything I need when I arrive." She looked up, flushing with annoyance at Emilio's grinning face.

"How you have changed!" she accused scornfully. "Only a few months ago you enjoyed kicking that detective down the steps! When Jonathan arrived you were afraid he would tell me stories of England and make me want to go there—now you can't get rid of me fast enough!"

The expressive young face sobered instantly, and the boy took her free hand in both his own, giving it a little squeeze. "Silly one!" he said affectionately. "You know I love you like a sister, Nicki. You know that you will always, always have a home here with us, whenever you choose to come. But things have altered since Jonathan came—yes, that is true. I have almost paid for *Pegasus*, and we shall have much trade here in a few weeks, and Francesca's parents look upon our marriage much more favourably."

"So——" Nicki looked as cross as she felt. "So now you can do without me, you will send me to my rich grandmother with your blessing, eh? Two months ago it was different—what would the *albergo* have done without me? And the children——?" She caught her breath, thinking of the children. "You were not so pleased to think of me going away to England then!"

Emilio caught her small head between his brown hands and kissed her soundly. "It was *you* who said you would not stay here when I married," he reminded her gently, "and it was you who helped to make my marriage come closer. We love you dearly, *carissima*; even Francesca loves you dearly; she will never mind you living with us if you wish it——" He could not tell her that other things had altered besides his financial position. He had offered Jonathan every franc he could lay hands on, he had even offered to sell *Pegasus*, but the surgeon had refused to take any fee for the operation.

"Call it a busman's holiday; I am only too pleased young Pietro got out of his scrape so lightly," he had said, smiling.

"He will never play truant again, the villain," Emilio had promised, his gratitude bubbling out of him like champagne, until Jonathan sent him about his business briskly.

Now Emilio liked and trusted the Englishman, and he thought Nicole had a good friend in Jonathan, one who would see that her English relatives did not impose on the girl. It was all very different from sending her out to an unknown country, to unknown relations, at a time when it would have been most awkward to manage the *albergo* and the children without her. Emilio, for all his Latin impulsiveness, was a realist; he was frank enough with his adopted cousin.

"Never, never will we forget what you have done for us," he said at last, emphatically, releasing her, "so shut up and do not talk any more silliness, it is not like Nicki."

She smiled in spite of her temper. "If I have done anything for you it was only paying a debt," she said slowly, "a debt to Tia Maria that can never be properly repaid."

"O.K., so you know my mother would want you to look upon this as your home, always," Emilio answered promptly, and got up to shout for the lagging Bianca. "Meanwhile, you can go and enjoy a holiday with your rich grandmama. Why not?"

When the motor-boat had sputtered away with the boy and the schoolgirl, who had submitted unwillingly to a last-minute inspection of her hair and fingernails, Nicole resumed the reading of her letter.

My Dear Nicole, the spidery handwriting ran,
It gives me such joy to be writing you a letter which you will actually read, at last. I cannot put into words the sadness I have felt for many years at the estrangement from your mother—you must take my word for that, and then we will try and forget the sad past. I am so pleased that you have agreed to visit what is really your own home, and hope that you will be happy here. I am looking forward so much to seeing you—Jonathan says you are very like my dearest Evelyn—and can hardly believe that a cherished dream will soon come true. . . . Forgive the ramblings of an old, tired woman, my dear, and believe me——
Your loving Grandmother.

There was a P.S. about the bank draft, and a request that Nicki should draw upon Jonathan for anything more she might need, and it would be repaid as soon as they arrived in Combe Castleton. *For, of course, you will travel with Mr. Grant. I would not like to think of you undertaking such a long, tiresome journey unescorted,* the old lady had concluded.

Nicki sat for a long time with the letter in her hand, her blue eyes clouded with perplexity. It was written on stiff, good quality paper, and the Osterley House address was engraved. A flicker of ironical amusement crossed the girl's face at the final postcript, as she remembered her plan to paint her way round Europe—round the world—unescorted. . . .

Unescorted! What an old-fashioned word! Had this elderly, rich, sheltered Englishwoman any idea at all of what had happened to her daughter after she had run away from the sheltered tyranny of her home twenty-two years ago?

But Helen Stannisford had a weak heart, she must be

kept wrapped in cotton-wool, though her daughter Evelyn had died in her forties from a broken heart.

Nicole put her head down on her knees in a sudden paroxysm of weeping and fear. Already she was the grand-daughter of an old, rich, respectable woman . . . a woman with a great big house that could hold six families comfort-ably, a staff of servants, and plans were being made for Nicole's entertainment as if she were of the blood royal.

"*Maman! Maman!*" Nicki whispered desolately, "why did not this happen to you, instead of me!"

It seemed to the girl the cruellest of ironies that the invitation, the letter full of affection, the bank draft, should have come years too late. . . .

"What's the matter now, Nicki?" Jonathan, looking out of his window, had seen the small figure huddled on the steps. The abject misery of her attitude was in such startling contrast to the beauty of the June day that he had come down swiftly to find out the cause. "Dear Nicki, do you want a shoulder?" he demanded gently.

By way of reply she thrust the wet letter into his hands, and the envelope and the bank draft. "It's no good!" she cried desolately, childishly, wiping her tear-stained face roughly. "I shall never be able to live up to it! I shall give my grandmother heart attacks, I shall be rude to the ser-vants, and if they treat me like a child I shall spit in their eye!"

"Aren't you behaving rather childishly now?" Jonathan said casually. "There's nothing wrong with this—we can travel together at the end of next week. Pietro can be safely left to convalesce then; the nurses will stay on until Emilio gets married, of course."

She stared at him, trying to recover her poise, her in-dependence. "You will not want to be bothered with me," she said, with an attempt at dignity. "I am a gypsy. I do not know how to behave! In the dining car I shall em-barrass you, and my clothes will be all wrong. I shouldn't have said I would go—I shall feel like a wild animal shut up in a cage!"

"A very small wild animal."

He was laughing at her, and it was infuriating. He added dryly, "And the *wagon-lits* make very comfortable cages. Stop being a little idiot, Nicki—go wash your face, and we will go to the bank and cash this draft."

She looked doubtfully at the draft. "I've never had that much money in my life," she said suddenly, "and I

83

know nothing of banks. Will you really come with me?"

She added quickly, "The papers say you are very famous, very rich, so you'll know all about money."

Jonathan grinned. "I'm not very famous, and certainly not rich by your grandmother's standards," he said dryly. "I have only what I've earned, no inherited capital."

"But that's so much better!" Nicole brightened at once. "I *hate* the idea of waiting for people to die, so that you can have their money! What you have earned yourself, with hard work, that is good money."

"Good or bad, it melts away pretty quickly. But I think I know enough about banks to help you cash that draft, Nicki; then we'll buy your ticket and reservations. After that, if you are worried about clothes, something to wear on the journey—and don't forget, you can call on me for more money if you need it. My uncle will pay me back."

He was so comforting, sitting there on the steps, smoking his pipe. Nicole had been looking over her beloved lake, wondering how on earth she could ever bear to leave it. Her grandmother's letter had left her unmoved, her heart was still too full of the bitter past; she had consented to go because she knew her parents would have wished it, because Jonathan advised it. But already she was full of foreboding.

"Will you help me choose the clothes?" she demanded childishly. "I'm no good at clothes. They don't interest me——" She glanced down at her small boat anchored by the steps, the boat she loved so much; the boat that had given her, with the addition of her own young strength, the freedom of the lake; a whole world to live in. "In a rowboat one does not need to look *chic*," she said sadly.

"I'm afraid I won't be much help in choosing clothes." Jonathan looked doubtful at last. "Wouldn't it be better to go with Bianca or some—some girl friend in the town?"

Nicole shook her head emphatically. "I have no girl friends in the town—they are all chic young ladies there, and I am a gypsy! And Bianca would make me look like a——" She used an Italian word whose meaning was very clear. Jonathan threw back his head and laughed.

"All right, only the sales ladies won't like it. I'll help you choose something that won't shock your grandmother out of her wits——"

"Thank you, Jonathan." Nicole jumped up, her tears forgotten, her small face alight with mischief. "I hate shopping, too! I think you are my very good friend, we will suffer together."

"Get a move on, then, or we shall be late for lunch," he retorted good humouredly. He wondered if his whole life would have been different if he had had a young sister like Nicki. . . . She was perpetually interesting to him, with her changes of mood, her extraordinary mixture of age-old wisdom and tragic experience with childish fears, childish dreams, childish honesty.

I hope to goodness they don't make her into a *chic* young lady, all the same! he thought vehemently. For an instant his heart misgave him that he had, after all, influenced her towards this great change in her life. He could understand her love of this place, and there was in her a freedom of mind and body and soul that was very appealing . . . she was not a wild animal, but she was his little wild goose. . . . Somehow he could imagine Nicki, flying free and unfettered, above the ordinary world. It would be a thousand pities if Osterley House changed her too much, transformed her into the conventional Miss with a round of provincial social engagements, dinners and dances and bridge parties . . . with regular appointments with her hairdresser, her dressmaker, her manicurist . . .

He heard her light step on the stone and looked up, and was immediately comforted. Nicki had washed her face and lightly powdered it, and because she was going to buy clothes she had put on one of her three cotton frocks. By now he knew them all—the faded blue, the green, and the russet. Nothing that they could do to her in Combe Castleton would ever transform this girl, with her small, proud head poised firmly on her slender neck, into a conventional society girl—she had far too much character, he realised thankfully.

"It's only about fifty pounds, you know. We'd better get your ticket and clothes first, darling."

Nicole was practically dancing out of the bank. She had no handbag, only the shabby little purse she usually stuffed into the pocket of her slacks, and she had passed the bundle of stiff, new notes over to Jonathan for safe keeping. Already she was spending her windfall in imagination as they passed the windows of shops—sports shops, stores, seedsmen. She made Jonathan feel very tall as she walked by his side through the sunlit town, so lightly that her feet hardly seemed to touch the ground.

She made him feel very old, she was so light-hearted in her planning, as if the tears and rebellion of an hour ago had never been.

"Pietro can have the fishing-rod he has been after for so long—there, in Caeno's. Bianca says going to school each morning and coming back each afternoon he stands and stares at it. I'm giving him my boat, of course, but I shan't tell him until it's time to go; it will make parting less hard for him, poor *bambino*." She rattled on gaily, more talkative than Jonathan had ever known her, choosing gifts as they walked. "A wrist watch for Emilio—he never knows the time without listening for the church bells—and a blouse for Bianca. She is growing so fast! Oh, this morning I feel like a millionaire, Jonathan!"

It was then he made the remark about fifty pounds. Nicole would have none of his prudence. He had no means of guessing that her joy in spending, in buying presents, the novelty of being able to give lavishly, was compensating her for her coming grief. Beneath her gaiety she knew very well she would soon feel the parting from Emilio and Bianca and Pietro and old Lucia terribly. Probably before the train got to Basle she would be bitterly homesick. . . .

She kept reminding herself that she was only going to England on a visit; that had been clearly stipulated, her grandmother and Mr. Grant and Jonathan had all agreed to it. Yet deep within her heart she had the feeling that once she had crossed the threshold of Osterley House it would not easily relinquish its hold on her.

"Lucia must have a new shawl, it is cold here in winter." She smiled up sideways at Jonathan, using her hands. "Does one not always give gifts at parting? They're going to miss me, those four, even if they don't think so now, and to use my gifts will bring me back to them."

Jonathan did not argue any more. Going up to the station in the crowded funicular he noticed people smiling at Nicki—young men and old women alike. She chatted in rapid Italian with the housewives in their sombre black, discussing the bargains in their loaded baskets, and played with a very sticky baby. There were all sorts of people in the crowded car—travellers catching trains, town-people taking a short cut to the Via Basilica, workers going home for early lunch; and Nicki seemed at home with them all, and quite oblivious of her faded cotton frock and shabby sandals. He wondered why she had suddenly worried this morning about appearances and manners. Hanging on to the strap, watching her unobtrusively, Jonathan felt a warm affection for his young protégée. Whatever clothes she had on, however empty her purse, Nicole Berenger—unconventional and impulsive little wild goose—would always be what her blood and upbringing had made her, a gentlewoman—in the proper meaning of that old-fashioned word.

How Helen would love her, when she had got over the first shock of meeting, the first shyness caused by the shadows of the past!

At the station, while Nicole was absorbed in the travel posters, he managed to pay for her ticket and sleeping reservation without touching the six hundred francs. Judging by the shopping programme ahead, that would be needed for other things. After making his own reservation, Jonathan found that he would have to go carefully with the remainder of his own allowance, and for the first time he cursed the stringency of the currency regulations. It would have been fun to let Nicole have a real orgy of spending. . . .

She was tugging at his elbow with sparkling eyes, drawing him over to a brilliant poster of the Grand Canal. "Jonathan! You haven't even seen Venice! You must go—the buses go there twice a week. One day going, one day coming back; a whole day and a night in Venice—there's still time!"

"Have you ever been there?" he asked curiously.

Nicole grinned. "Once. The lady courier was taken ill, and a driver who is a friend of mine got me the job. They knew I could speak three languages, but I had to sit up half the night before learning all the patter! There's much to see on that trip; it's quite cheap and very worth while. There's the Basilica of St. Antony at Padua, and Milan—Lake Como—and Venice is wonderful, though I should hate to live there!"

"Why?" He was amused by her eagerness, and curious. "I should have thought Venice would appeal to an artist."

Her eyes acknowledged the tribute, but she shrugged. "It's too much of everything! The buildings are huge—enormous slabs of marble and stone. It must have taken years and years to make the mosaics for the walls, and the paintings—— And it's too full of tourists always; the canals are dirty, full of paper and orange peel, and the air is too hot. In summer it's like trying to breathe in front of an oven door!"

"You're not a very good publicity agent!" Jonathan laughed. "I think we'll give Venice a miss this time." He did not want her to know that there was not enough money left for a trip to Venice.

She looked up at him searchingly. She almost whispered, "This time . . . ? Do you think, then, that one day you will return to Lugano?"

They had walked slowly out of the station, and he looked down the steep hill, past the cathedral, to the sunlit town on the shore of the smiling lake. "I think it very likely that I shall come back to Lugano, one day," he answered quietly. And he knew that he was speaking the truth. This place drew him, inexplicably, with its peace and sunshine and cleanliness and its cheerful people. "Perhaps many times," he added.

"Oh, it's good to hear you say that!" For a moment Nicole was very happy. "It makes me feel I'm not going away for ever——"

"You silly child! Travelling is easy now, and I think your grandmother will do anything to make you happy."

Nicole nodded doubtfully. "If she likes me. She may not like me at all, and I may hate her."

"I don't think you will, but if you do there's no harm done. You can start off on your world tour from England just as well as from Lugano," he teased her.

She glanced back over her shoulder regretfully at the gay poster. "All the same, I'm sorry you haven't seen Venice—it is very beautiful at night. And coming back there's the Roman amphitheatre at Verona, and the houses of Romeo and Juliet, and Napoleon's chapel at Bergamo . . . and, all the way, the Italian farms and vineyards. At this time there would be whole fields of scarlet poppies——" She laughed suddenly at the sound of her own voice. "You see, I was not such a poor courier! All the people in the bus gave me presents at the end, anyway."

They were walking down the steep hill past the cathedral, which she made him visit. When they came out he said thoughtfully, "You're a mystery to me, Nicki. You don't mind taking tips from tourists, or selling them bad paintings; you don't mind spending this money from your grandmother on Emilio and the others—yet you refused even to answer my uncle's letters offering you a comfortable home, a good allowance from your grand-mother——"

She stopped walking and withdrew the arm she had slipped companionably inside his, to look at his face; to make clear to him the difference that was so plain to her eyes. "But I *earned* those tips! I worked very hard for them! And at the bad paintings. It is much more work to paint what people want than what *you* want to paint."

"Whoa—let me get that tongue-twister straightened out!"

Nicole shrugged impatiently. "You're not usually stupid. Can't you see, I will sell my work . . . but myself I will not sell! If my grandmother thinks she can buy *me*—with her so-comfortable home, her clothes, her big allow-ance of money—she is being very foolish and I shall run away, like my mother did."

"I see."

"This money she has sent now—it is to please herself. I didn't ask her for anything. I shall have to work very hard for that, too, for I don't want to go at all. It's only just that I should share it with my family."

"Come on, then, let's get the shopping done," Jonathan agreed good-temperedly. The presents were bought first, he observed, and for someone who said she hated shopping Nicole seemed to be enjoying herself tremendously. She borrowed a pencil and an old envelope from him, and did laborious sums as they went along. To his surprise she knew what the fare was, and deducted that from the six hundred francs, so his little ruse went for nothing.

"I will borrow from you for the *wagon-lit* only," she said with dignity, "for that is a luxury. I would sit up all night, myself."

"All right. Now what about this shop for your clothes?" Jonathan stopped by a corner shop in the Via Nassa, a shop displaying good-quality travel clothes and sports-wear. "We can get everything here; they seem to have shoes and handbags, everything."

"Oh, but it's much too expensive here!" Nicole looked really shocked. "And the assistants would laugh at me. We must go to one of the stores near the market. There, too, they have everything."

Jonathan gave in reluctantly. This particular shop appealed to him; the goods displayed so elegantly in the double windows seemed to promise good taste. But he bowed to Nicole's good sense about money. She was keeping her sum very accurately.

But in the dress department of the store she grew suddenly panicky, confronted by a very smart young assistant and the rows and rows of dresses on their stands. "Help me!" she whispered, keeping very close to Jonathan, so that the assistant thought they were father and daughter.

"Will you please show us something—er—something suitable for travelling in?" he said quickly, and gave Nicki a little push as the girl smiled and sped off to one of the glass cases. "Go with her, you dope, and choose something you like the look of——"

Still the girl seemed rooted to the ground. She was pale beneath her golden tan, and the hand still holding his arm trembled. He felt an upsurge of loving sympathy for her. Here, indeed, her faded cotton frock and shabby sandals looked conspicuous, among all the glossy frocks. She whispered, "When we go into the fitting room, will you call her out, Jonathan? I don't want her staring at my underwear." She added with great dignity, "It's quite clean, but it's not new."

"Then we'll buy you some of those, too," Jonathan grinned down at her, "on our way out. Now—over the top with you, little one. Don't let all this nonsense get you down."

He sat on a chair by the big plate-glass window, looking down a busy side street and feeling very masculine and out of his depth in this perfumed, soft-carpeted place, and all too conscious of the chattering group of assistants at the other side of the room, of their subdued laughter and sidelong glances. Good lord, what did they take him for? Nicole's fond papa or something worse? Certainly, among these sophisticated young women, Nicole looked like a schoolgirl getting her first grown-up outfit, and he smiled inwardly at the thought.

He had to screw up his courage, as out of a corner of his eye he saw the assistant—a pile of clothes over her arm—ushering Nicki into one of the velvet-curtained cubicles. He waited a few seconds and called out, "Er—mademoiselle!" and was intensely amused to see that Nicki practically pushed the girl out to him.

"*Signore?*"

She stood before him, dark-haired and provocative, her brown eyes smiling. He was rather nice, this *papa*, and she wanted to please him. It was almost lunch time and business had been slack this morning.

"Do you speak English?" he asked, more to gain time than anything, hoping that Nicki could change quickly.

"Yais, a leetle. Please, what would you like?" The girl showed dazzling white teeth.

"Oh, that's good. Wonderful place, Lugano; everyone seems to speak about four languages." Jonathan smiled back at her, feeling a fatuous ass and racking his brain for any excuse to keep her away from the cubicle. Rejecting the weather as a topic for conversation with the pretty Italian, he said at last in desperation, "My—er—my niece wishes to buy some shoes and a handbag and—a—a hat to go with her travelling outfit. Do you sell those things here?"

"Si, si. The 'at you will find over there, on this floor— the ozzer things downstairs. . . ." Obviously, she thought, she had made a hit with the Englishman. The other girls were watching from across the big room, though they pretended to be busy tidying the cupboards. "Ah—'ere is your niece, signore."

Jonathan turned his head with a tremendous sensation of release, and found himself staring at a transformed Nicole. He hardly heard the approving little murmurs from the sales girl behind him. Nicki stood there, still and slender and demure, in a black linen suit with a crisp white blouse. The blouse had a tiny ruff at the neck and cuffs, the only touch of decoration anywhere, and the suit fitted as if it had been made for her.

"Yes," Jonathan said deeply, oblivious of the Italian chatter behind him; amazed that, in spite of her fright, Nicole had gone unerringly to the right garment. She looked cool and elegant, her fairness set off by the narrow white ruff; no one would have guessed she had been a panic-stricken child a few minutes before.

Nicki's eyes seemed pleased with his approval, and she turned to the girl and said she would take the suit. "The price is a little high," she added for Jonathan's ear, "but not too bad for this thing. A hundred and twenty francs. I could buy six frocks for that!"

"You buy a frock as well," he ordered, suddenly very pleased with her and with himself. The assistant wasted no time but produced a crisp dress in gentian blue that matched Nicole's eyes and held it up under her chin.

"*Si, si*, it is the *signorina*'s size," she chanted affably. Jonathan paid for the things, telling Nicole to keep on the suit so that she could choose accessories to go with it, and steering her towards the hat department.

"Oh, Jonathan, *not* a hat!" she cried, her new-found poise deserting her suddenly. "I never wear a hat, even in church I put a scarf over my head!"

"For Combe Castleton—when you arrive, anyway— you must wear a hat," he retorted firmly, "but you can make it a very small hat." He was beginning to enjoy himself hugely. The tiny white hat that Nicki finally chose altered her appearance still more.

"Now you do look like your mother," he said thoughtfully, as they went in search of handbag and shoes.

"You really knew my mother well?" she asked eagerly.

"Only during the holidays. I was a kid—a boy of fifteen—but she was very nice, Evelyn—"

Nicole chuckled suddenly. "She was more than 'nice', she was adorable, my *maman*! And—if you were only fifteen—you aren't old enough to be my father, not even my uncle!"

"You see, you haven't embarrassed me, in fact you look very charming, Nicole, and not at all like a wild animal!" Not even like my little wild goose any more, Jonathan's mind added privately.

They were enjoying an excellent dinner in the dining-car of the Basle Express. And Nicole, though her face took on a sadness in repose, was behaving as if she travelled first-class every day of her life. The little hat, though she had hated the idea of a hat, seemed to have worked a small miracle for her. Though she still looked enchantingly young she did not look a child any more.

"The last time Maman and I came from Paris with all our possessions in a paper bag," she said wistfully. "We had lost everything in the fire."

"Try and forget it, Nicki." For a moment his big hand rested over hers on the table. "This is the beginning of a new adventure for you, and your mother would be very happy to know—"

"I think she *does* know, and she *is* very happy," Nicole answered with complete faith, "because she is with my father, and they would wish me to be polite to my *grand'mère*."

92

The train climbed effortlessly through the endless mountains. A summer sunset dyed the valleys to gold and red against the softer greys and purples of the dusk, and lights began to twinkle from the chalets perched on the hillsides. It was warm and still, the electrically-driven train made little noise, and now and then they could hear the tinkle of a cow bell.

"This is a beautiful country——" Jonathan said suddenly.

"—where sheep may safely graze." She completed his thought, unexpectedly, delightfully. "Switzerland has a fine tradition of peace, of giving refuge to the unfortunate—I think perhaps because of the mountains. One feels very close to God in the mountains." She added, "And of course, the Red Cross was started by a Swiss."

Jonathan was staring at the passing scene, fascinated. He was thinking, I've been in Switzerland for six weeks, but I haven't been out of Lugano . . . how unenterprising all these energetic tourists would think that! But he had not wanted to go far afield, he had been very happy at the *albergo.*

"There's still snow on that ridge," he said in surprise.

Nicole nodded. "There is always a little snow on the caps of the highest mountains." She yawned involuntarily.

"You're tired," said Jonathan. "But never mind. We can go to sleep as soon as we board the French train."

Nicole smiled at him. "You're very kind, Jonathan. But I don't think I shall sleep tonight. I'm too full in here." She touched her breast lightly. "I feel as if I shall never sleep again!"

He did not argue with her, he thought that by the time midnight had come and they had transferred to their *wagon-lit* in the French train, Nicole would sleep. She was worn out, poor child.

She added thoughtfully, "I suppose I was very wrong to be rude to the detective. Père Angeli scolded me afterwards. He said that pride is a sin of the devil, that one must always be tender with the aged. . . . I daresay my grandmother thinks I am terrible——"

Jonathan realised what the admission must have cost her. He was able to reassure her with absolute sincerity. "She would not have written as she did, if she did not understand. I think Helen Stannisford will surprise you, Nicki. . . . She is a woman who has suffered too much through being gentle, because she allowed her husband to bully her. I think she only longs for you to understand that . . . though she is old-fashioned, and probably will not discuss Henry's character with you. She will think you are too young to understand."

"I am not a child," Nicki said quietly, and in the soft after-glow from the sunset she did not look a child any more, and for once Jonathan did not want to tease her. He said gently, "Age is comparative, don't you think? When one is a child, thirty seems old—incredibly old—and when one is in the seventies and rather delicate, probably twenty-two seems very young!"

Nicki laughed. It was the first time she had laughed since the train left Lugano. "In eight years I shall be thirty," she reminded him. "I think it is not the years that count but the age of one's heart." She added gravely, "I have been grown-up since I was twelve."

"In eight years I shall be forty-five, getting pompous and probably fat"—he sketched a caricature on the menu, pleased that the shadows had left her eyes—"and even more unpopular with my staff than I am now."

"Un—unpopular?" For once an English word failed to reach her. "What do you mean?"

"Not liked. A detestable person!" He grinned across the table at her. "My staff all think me a tyrant."

"But you are *not* detestable!" she cried vehemently, with a trace of the old laughing Nicki, her best behaviour forgotten, and several heads were turned in the dining-car, to smile at the girl. "You are wise and kind, and you laugh at the right things."

"Ah, but you have only known me on holiday," he answered with a trace of dry irony. "When I'm working I'm a very different person. Impatient. I have to work fast, and I can't afford inefficiency or bungling in the theatre staff."

"No. That is probably true." She looked at him candidly, remembering the night of the operation, when for a while he had forgotten her existence. "But that is understandable"—she thought that probably his patients did not find him either impatient or detestable—"when you have important work to do. But I'm glad I'm not one of your nurses!"

He grinned again, fleetingly. "So am I. I like you better as an artist. Now we'd better go back and get what rest we can until midnight."

In their comfortable compartment there was only one other passenger, an elderly man already dozing, so they did not talk any more. Night swiftly blotted out the magnificent mountain scenery, and after they had passed Lucerne the compartment lights were extinguished, leaving only the small blue bulbs that gave an eerie look to human faces. Nicole took off her hat and made herself comfortable in her corner, and Jonathan put a rug about her when she was asleep. She thought she would not sleep at all this night, and already she had dozed off, lulled by the soporific gentle rhythm of the train and the exhaustion of the day.

It had been an exhausting week altogether, Jonathan thought, going out into the lighted corridor for a last cigarette. Nicole's small face, asleep, touched him to an almost painful tenderness, and he hoped with all his heart that they were doing the right thing for this child, this little orphan—he and Uncle Steve and Aunt Bella and her grandmother—in dragging her back to England. She looked very innocent and defenceless, sunk into the corner seat, yet sleep was erasing the strain from her sensitive face. Remembering how they had agreed there was something unfair, almost indecent, in observing old Lucia fast asleep, Jonathan removed himself to the corridor and stared out at the twinkling lights that flashed past. What was it Lucia herself had said . . . "does the man not know that a person's soul looks from the eyes?"

Yet the surgeon, who had seen many unconscious faces, did not find Nicole's sleeping face lacking in expression; only like a child's, relaxed and trustful.

Lucia's portrait was hanging in the kitchen at the *albergo* now, and though she merely grunted and shrugged her old shoulders when anyone commented on the likeness, he knew she was immensely proud of it.

To his own surprise Jonathan found that leaving the *albergo* had been a wrench for him, too. Nothing like the agony it had been for Nicki, naturally, but still a wrench. As if he were leaving behind a little bit of himself, a Jonathan Grant who was on holiday, a released and carefree man. . . . Not given to sentimental analysis, he yet stood in the corridor of the gently swaying train for a long time, thinking about this emotion. Perhaps he had grown fond of the place and of Lucia and the Fionettis because from the first he had seen them through Nicole's eyes, and because they had very soon accepted him. Certainly this nostalgia was quite different from one's usual feeling in leaving a hotel and one's host at the end of a holiday. . . .

But if he felt the pull of Gandria as strongly as this, Nicki's heart must be very sore, he realised. She had enough pride not to break down, even at the end; she had been very brave. But she had not allowed them all to come and see her off at the station, as they had wanted. Emilio had wished to give his young cousin a proper Italian send-off, with tears and gifts of flowers and much shouting to and from the platform. . . . But Nicole had been adamant.

"Do you want to make a fool of me, making me weep in front of all the tourists who will be travelling?" she had demanded fiercely. "And Pietro can't come. He would be desolate if you all came without him. I will say *au revoir* to you all here, in my home, and thin k of you here until I return. Then it will not feel as if I'm going away for ever!"

They had agreed reluctantly, though in the end Emilio brought them over in *Pegasus*. Nicole shook hands with him on the jetty, and with Francesca who had been shopping in the town. "Take care of him, *carissima*," she told the girl in Italian, after hugging Emilio and kissing him on both cheeks, and Francesca had promised fervently, glowing with her happiness, so that the travellers went on their way knowing that Emilio's future was in good hands. There had been no more emotion as they made their way to the station. Their baggage had been brought across yesterday, and registered through to Victoria—a refinement of travelling that astonished Nicole.

"Do you mean to say we shan't see our things again until we arrive? Will they not get lost, and what about the *douanes*?" she had cried, gazing at his big suitcase and her strapped basket that contained most of her worldly goods, including some of the precious new clothes.

"They won't be lost, and we go through the Customs for these packages at Victoria." He showed her the registration receipts, smiling when she seemed unconvinced. "But you don't register your precious instruments!"

"No. They might get damaged."

"So might my basket," she argued, with feminine logic, though she finally relinquished her treasure. That basket had been a sore trial to Jonathan, he was glad to see the last of it for a while. It was a hideous piece of baggage, a large rectangular basket with a deep lid. The lid had handles for two straps to go round the whole contraption, which bulged when it was fully packed.   Nicole had dragged it proudly forth from the *albergo's* cupboard when he asked if she wanted to buy a suitcase. "Tia Maria gave it to me," she said. "It is better than any suitcase; it expands, it can hold everything.   Also, for the cost of transport, it is very light."

Jonathan had refrained from comment on the basket, to which he took an instant dislike. It was not only old-fashioned, it was archaic. It reminded him of one used by his nannie when he had been a very small boy. But he considered Nicki's feelings had been scratched sufficiently by the necessity of buying new clothes; he could not criticise her splendid basket. He had finally compromised by registering it in advance and buying her a small, light overnight bag for her travelling necessities—and called himself a snob.

Certainly, he thought now, if he was shy about that damned basket, he need not be shy about his travelling companion; Nicki was behaving like any other well-bred young girl travelling with an uncle——

He saw his own face, reflected in the window, grinning at him boyishly as he remembered the assistant in the store, and Nicki's teasing, "You're not old enough to be my father, nor even my uncle!"

"Only short by four or five years," he had retorted, smiling.   But he felt quite old enough to be her father. Except at those odd moments when she was very grown-up and wise beyond her years.

There had been trouble with Pietro. Bianca was delighted that Nicki was going to her rich grandmother. She anticipated all sorts of presents in the post, and imagined that she would be able to get round Francesca easier, especially during the first blithe months of her marriage to Emilio. But Pietro, irritable with the limitations of his convalescence, was not consoled easily.

"I do not want Nicki to go away," he said firmly.

"You will have the boat, *caro*, for your own," she had tried to console him.

"But he——" Pietro was not grateful to Jonathan for saving his life. At ten years old the present is all that matters, and though he liked the Englishman, it seemed to Pietro that Jonathan was the person now restricting his activities. He felt well and strong; it was silly to keep on these two fat nurses, to make him rest so much. "*—He says*

I must not row the boat, not for ages and ages! What is the use of having my own boat if I cannot use it?"

"Emilio will take you out in it, at first," Nicole suggested quickly. "And after, it will always be yours. That is something, isn't it?"

Pietro agreed, eyes bright, cheeks flushed. "I'm sorry, of course it is something. Always I have wanted a boat of my own. But I want to run, and row, and fish, and not lie here like an old man!"

Jonathan grinned. He understood enough Italian now to follow the little boy's disgusted remarks. He knew that it was only natural for Pietro to be disgruntled, a sign of returning strength; naturally the child could not understand what a narrow escape he had had, nor how blessed he was to have missed any permanent injury to the brain.

"Look here, old man, it is just *because* I want you to be able to do all those things soon that you must be patient a little longer," he said firmly. Pietro stared at him crossly. "And Dr. Adler agrees with me. You believe what Dr. Adler says, don't you?"

Suddenly the small brown face was irradiated with a smile that made it almost angelic. "He's all right. He knows about fishing and climbing trees, too. Once when he was a boy he fell out of a tree, stealing walnuts, and broke his leg——"

"Well, you broke your head, and that takes a bit longer to mend," Jonathan reminded him dryly, "and you've been sensible enough. Don't let Nicki go away worrying about you, thinking that as soon as her back is turned you will be up to tricks again."

"He has promised me to be good," Nicole said it in English and Italian to make sure. "And Pietro does not break his word."

"All the same, I do not want you to take Nicki away. Those nurses are a bore; she is the only person who has time to read to me," Pietro grumbled sullenly.

Jonathan was worried about the boy. He did not want to leave him so discontented; it might undo all their careful work. He said impulsively, "Pietro, we have good fishing in England, too, where I live. How would you like to come and stay at Combe Castleton later in the summer, before you go back to school?"

The question was sufficiently answered by the rapid change in the boy's expression. Behind him Jonathan heard a little indrawn gasp of breath from Nicki, and she spoke for both of them when she whirled round to him, hands outstretched, eyes shining. "Oh, Jonathan, do you think he could? But—would Grand'mère object?"

The small thin brown hand on the coverlet gripped Jonathan's convulsively, and he grew reckless. He said gaily, "If she does, Pietro can come and stay with me. That is not very far from Osterley House, and much nearer the sea."

"Thank you—thank you!" Pietro whispered in English, so that his friend could not possibly misunderstand all he felt. Nicole's eyes thanked him without words, and he knew that however this promise complicated things, however busy he might be when he got home, Pietro must come to Combe Castleton before the summer was over. As he got up he loomed large with mock severity. "Only if you behave yourself now," he warned gently, "and do exactly what Dr. Adler tells you."

"*Si, si!* Bianca will want to come too, but a girl is a nuisance when men want to go fishing."

"Bianca has not had to lie still for so long," Jonathan smiled down on the boy in a purely masculine conspiracy, "so you shall come alone this time. Next summer perhaps we can have Bianca, too."

Satisfied, already dreaming dreams, Pietro had lain back on his pillow and they had left him. Outside the door Nicki had asked nervously, "Is he not a little young, to travel alone?" and Jonathan had shaken his head. "He can be put in charge of one of the couriers; he is perfectly sensible, and I think the responsibility will do him good."

So in the end they had left everyone at the *albergo* reasonably happy, though there were tears in old Lucia's eyes as she stiffly embraced them, and Bianca cried copiously when she actually saw Nicki stepping into the motor-boat.

Nicole had no qualms about watching Jonathan asleep, later, when he returned to the carriage and composed himself in his corner opposite, and after a little while she woke up. In the dim blue light from the small bulbs everything looked strange, unreal, and the elderly man in the other corner was snoring in his sleep. It took Nicki, who had been dreaming of climbing San Salvatore in search of gentians, a few seconds to remember where she was. It must be late, for there was no chatter down the length of the train, and no lights shone through the dark night outside, yet it was not midnight or they would be drawing into Basle.

Nicole was concentrating on Jonathan, trying not to think about the Fionettis, about leaving the *albergo*. Everything was unreal in this strange blue light, and most of all the fact that she, Nicole Berenger, was actually at last on her way to England, to visit the house wherein she had vowed hotly never to set foot! Sometimes her sense of fairness told Nicki that she was doing the right thing, sometimes she almost hated Jonathan for having broken down the emotional barriers she had erected so carefully against her English grandmother. . . . But most of all, when the realisation of what she was doing flashed upon her, she was frightened.

Frightened of the unknown.

What did she know, after all, of her grandmother, except that she had allowed her own daughter to be treated very badly, and was now a regretful, frail old lady longing to make amends . . . ? Everything nice about Helen Stannisford had come to her from Jonathan and his Uncle Steve, and men were so easily taken in, especially nice men. . . .

Yet, looking at the firm, assured sleeping face opposite her, Nicole could not really believe that Jonathan was easily taken in by women's lies. Once upon a time, perhaps, but not now—— She wished he had treated her as a grown-up confidante, and told her about the woman who had made his mouth set in that firm line; he was sufficiently fond of her now to talk to her about so many things, but Nicole knew that he still thought of her as a child. How could she ever convince him, she thought despairingly, that she was a woman grown, capable of loving a man, of making him happy, of bearing his children, of comforting him when he needed comfort, of flying to him for succour when the roles were reversed? But perhaps he truly was content with his work; it was a very wonderful work to be doing in this troubled world.

She felt like a child now, alone in this dim, blue world with two sleeping men, while the train went swiftly right across Switzerland from the south-east corner to the north-west. Her beloved Switzerland, her adopted country. . . . Soon they would be at the frontier, and then in France. But after what had happened to her father in his own country, Nicole had no nostalgia for France. Clean, kind, friendly Switzerland was her home now. . . .

They had promised her she could go back to Lugano if she grew too home-sick, if the experiment at Osterley House failed; but it would never be the same again. In a few weeks Emilio would be married to his Francesca; they would not need her any more. Lucia in her great age, Bianca and Pietro in their childhood, lived wholly in the day and would soon forget her. Nicole realised for the first time in her life that she was indeed an orphan, without a home, without relatives, except this stranger who was her grandmother. She had been happy enough until Jonathan had come and exploded her fairy-tale. For a moment she almost hated him, she was so scared of the immediate future. She wondered if it would be possible to run away at Basle, to lose herself in the crowd when they changed trains, until she remembered that her basket had gone on ahead. That basket contained all her few treasures, she could not leave it abandoned at Victoria——

"Cheer up, Nicki, we'll soon be there," a deep voice said quietly, and Jonathan was leaning across the compartment to hold her trembling hands in his strong ones that were so firm and warm, so she was not alone after all.

"I was frightened," she admitted in a small voice. "I think it's this horrible blue light."

"I'll get you a hot drink at Basle; you'll feel better when you can go to bed properly."

The old man in the corner grunted, and Jonathan withdrew his hands unhurriedly, with a little reassuring pressure. "You can see the lights of the station now."

It was true, and all at once Nicole's fears diminished, and she busied herself putting on the absurd hat, ashamed to meet his quizzical regard. She had been telling herself that she was a woman grown, but always with Jonathan she behaved like a child! Yet she wished secretly he had not reserved *wagon-lits* for the next part of the journey. They would be shut up in separate boxes until daylight, and she would be alone again.

It was a ghostly business, changing trains at midnight, carried out swiftly, almost silently, except by a group of English tourists who made a great fuss about finding their couchettes; there was apparently some confusion over numbers, and strident middle-aged voices argued interminably in the quiet station, in atrocious French that had to be shouted for the benefit of apparently deaf officials.

"Silly cackling hens! Can't they see people are trying to sleep in both these trains?" Jonathan commented irritably. The Customs examination of their hand baggage was swift and perfunctory. "Now you see why it is sensible to register the big stuff right through," he added with a smile at Nicole. "It gives us time here for a drink. Come on."

She chuckled, completely restored to equability. Silly cackling hens was so apt a description of the fluttering, arguing, over-tired females on the platform outside. In the all-night buffet it was bright and warm, and their coffee and sandwiches arrived promptly. A young Swiss courier sat at their table, bolting coffee and yawning. He told them he was a university student who took on this job during the vacation to earn a bit extra. "But I had to meet a train at six this morning," he grinned engagingly, "and I feel as if I had not seen my bed for a week! Now for those——" and he used a word that was far more uncomplimentary than cackling hens, leaving Nicki and Jonathan convulsed.

"He is *bavard*, that one, but nice," she said, and he was conscious of a faint prickling feeling of jealousy. The young student's eyes had hardly left Nicole's face.

Jonathan pulled his thoughts up smartly. Nicole Berenger was an attractive girl, naturally people would stare at her; he was taking her out into the world, helping her towards a life in which she would take her place in society, equipped with the cash, the clothes, the grooming that was her right; from now on young men would certainly pursue her. He wasn't in love with the child himself; he must not be a miserable dog-in-the-manger. Yet somehow Jonathan felt that Nicole was his discovery, his little protégée, and he did heartily dislike that gleam in the young fellow's brown eyes.

"What's the matter, Jonathan?" She was looking at him with startled amusement. "You look as though you want to go and—and fight with someone!"

He grinned disarmingly. "Maybe I do. But there isn't time." He felt in his pocket and slipped a tablet into the remains of her drink. "That is to make you sleep on the train. I can't produce you looking a wreck."

"But we have a night in London?" she asked faintly. Their English train did not get to Victoria until four in the afternoon, and Jonathan had decreed that they stay in the capital overnight. He had wired reserving rooms at a quiet but good hotel in Park Lane.

Now he nodded. "Yes, but all these hours of travelling are tiring, little one. Drink that up like a good girl."

Their *wagon-lits* were already made up for the night, and they were not adjoining. The attendant accepted Jonathan's tip with smiling thanks and fussed a little over seeing that Nicole had everything she required—enough blankets, fresh water in the carafe, the promise of morning tea. It amused her that the man took her for an English girl, but she was too sleepy to startle him with a spate of French. Jonathan bade her good-night almost formally. "We will have breakfast in the dining-car, and lunch at Calais."

She was asleep almost before the attendant had closed the sleeping compartment and she had climbed into her night-wear. It was funny, going to sleep on a comfortable bunk in this little box, she thought dreamily, and blessed Jonathan for his tablet. She was more tired than she had realised. When she woke it was to find the bright morning sun streaming in at the window, and the flat landscape of northern France flashing past, and the attendant at her elbow with the promised cup of tea.

The rest of the journey seemed to Nicole to flash past like that landscape. The Channel steamer seemed enormous to her; it was the *Cote d'Azur*, a new French boat that carried the luxury passengers of the Golden Arrow as well as themselves, and it amused her to see what a fuss the attendants and stewards made over them for the short Channel crossing. The sea was sparkling brilliantly, and she leaned over the railing with Jonathan to catch her first glimpse of the cliffs of Folkestone, excited in spite of her forebodings, and inwardly delighted to hear the chatter of French tongues all about her.

"What are you so amused about?" he demanded once, pleased to note that the shadows had left her face.

She chuckled mischievously. "They think, because I am with you, that I am English," she whispered, with a backward glance at a group of stewards, "and they talk perhaps too freely about the passengers!"

She became more subdued when they embarked on the English train. Jonathan had pointed out the blue skies, the sunshine, the wheeling gulls of the port. "You see, it is not *always* raining in England!"

The hop fields of Kent appealed to her at once. "They are like vineyards!" she cried with pleasure. But the tea they had on the English train was served by men with sour faces who did not smile and bow when they were tipped, and all the French people seemed to have disappeared. The sight of her beloved basket in the Customs at Victoria cheered her as much as it depressed Jonathan, and then they were in the taxi, speeding through what seemed to Nicole the biggest city in the world. It was worse than the Paris she remembered as a child, noisier, more filled with people, and enormous red buses and cars—cars everywhere. She became silent and shy in the foyer of the hotel, feeling a gauche schoolgirl again under the hard stares of the receptionist and the commissionaire and the bell-boys, and when she discovered that Jonathan had booked her a room two floors away from his own she was almost panic-stricken.

"My little goose, you can always use the telephone if you want to talk to me. Uncle Steve and your grandmother would never forgive me if I compromised your—er—reputation," he told her in a dry, amused voice. It was the first time Nicole realised that she had a 'reputation' to compromise, and she could have laughed if she had not felt suddenly alone again, terribly alone in this enormous hotel, with its soft-carpeted passages and masses of flowers and its supercilious staff.

"Jonathan," she appealed to him suddenly, gently, "must we eat here? This place is so big?" She spoke in French and he was grateful for her tact, and answered in the same language.

"Of course we can eat elsewhere if you like. Go and have a bath, little one, and change into your black dress, and I will show you something of London. And Nicki——" He moved closer to her, oblivious of the waiting page dangling the key of her room from an impatient hand, forgetting even the amusement her basket had caused. "Don't let a hotel frighten you—or anything, ever! Promise?"

"I promise," she answered, much more bravely than she felt, and followed the page into the gilded lift.

Of course, he had been a fool to bring Nicole to a hotel like this, Jonathan thought savagely, as he changed into a dark suit after his bath. That bath, at the end of twenty-four hours' travelling, had been tremendously refreshing.

He smiled suddenly at his own reflection in the mirror of the wardrobe, hoping that at least Nicki had enjoyed the luxury of a private bathroom. The change in her way of life, the long journey, the fear of the unknown, were all confusing enough, without having to face unnecessary ordeals like this hotel . . . though at least he had spared her the Dorchester, he thought dryly.

It would have been better to book at one of the smaller, family hotels, but he knew so few of them, and he had wired this one with the mistaken idea that Nicki might like to experiment with a little luxury before meeting her grandmother. Jonathan's knowledge of London was limited to two extremes—the poverty of his student days and his mother's tiny flat in Bayswater, and Harley Street and this sort of hotel, where his secretary automatically made his reservations when he had to visit London. Here at least they knew him, and he wondered with genuine amusement what they were now thinking of his latest acquisition, Nicole and her basket. He had been tempted to send that basket straight through to Osterley House, once it was retrieved from the Customs, but the child's joy at seeing it again—and the possibility that she might need some of the contents—made him relent. It had come in the taxi, with his instrument case. Each to his own taste, he thought, and he thought in the French proverb. Nicole was improving his fairly-adequate French daily.

He wouldn't need French, though, for a long time, he realised, with the end-of-holiday depression resting on his spirits like a small cloud. It would be at least a year before he could take another vacation, if then——

The extraordinary peace of Lugano seemed very far away as he leaned out of the windows. The traffic down Park Lane was busy, as usual, and between the thick foliage of the plane trees he glimpsed lights dancing through the dusk in the Park, and the bright patches of colour that were flower beds, and the summer frocks of the strollers. He would not be able to show her the lights of London in any real sense, he thought regretfully; it was the end of June, and true darkness would not fall until well after midnight. But perhaps the long summer twilight would appeal to Nicole, used to the shorter evenings of Lugano. At least it was not raining. It was warm, and the pavements below gave up the hot, dusty smell that is essentially of the city.

In Combe Castleton the smell would be very different: a combination of sweet garden scents, the freshness from the moors, the salty tang of the sea. The fishing boats would be leaving harbour, perhaps, for their night's work, their riding lights twinkling like fireflies in the dusk.

Jonathan, who had loved the West Country so passionately as a boy, realised that he was seeing it now with fresh eyes—the eyes of a newcomer, Nicki's eyes, in his mind. He hoped it would present itself to Nicole tomorrow in sunshine, smiling and glowing with its own especial soft colours, so that Nicki too might learn to love it and be consoled for Lugano. . . . a little.

He glanced at his watch and telephoned through to her room. A very small voice said, "Yes . . . ?" on a rising inflection of curiosity and fear. He would never know what it had cost her to cross the big bedroom and pick up the telephone by the bed, for who could be telephoning her already in London? She thought perhaps it was some message from the management below, who seemed to know Jonathan. Everywhere he went he was treated with respect, waited upon with willing service; and not only, Nicole judged, because he gave good tips.

"Yes . . . ?" she whispered into the shiny white mouthpiece, her heart bumping noisily about.

"It's only me, you goose," Jonathan was laughing at her. He would be laughing a lot more if he could have heard her heart. "Did I startle you?"

"No, you only frightened me to death." Nicole grinned her *gamine* grin suddenly; it was good to hear his deep, familiar voice with a laugh in it. "I have had a bath—what a bath! So much hot water—and they put scented stuff in it, and the towels were *warm*!"

His chuckle consoled her for the way the chambermaid had looked at her, as if she were a native of Borneo, because she had not known how to manage the mixer-tap of shining chromium; because she had run about the big, tiled bathroom like a child, sniffing the bath salts, feeling the texture of the big, fluffy, warm towels on the electrically heated rail.

"Madame would like her gown pressed for this evening?" the girl had demanded, almost contemptuously.

"No, thank you, I am not dressing tonight; we are going to have dinner somewhere simple," Nicki had answered in her best grown-up manner, unconsciously using Jonathan's description, inwardly giggling because the girl could not pronounce *madame* properly, for all her airs and graces. Anyway, I am not a madame but a mademoiselle, Nicki had thought as she wallowed in the large bath of hot, scented water. It was very different from the zinc tub at home that they filled from Lucia's big copper kettles. *That* took two of them to carry it out and empty it afterwards.

Nicole could not know that one of the first things Jonathan had liked about her was her personal cleanliness; somehow, lacking all the much-advertised aids, she contrived always to be as fresh and sweetly scented as her own Swiss mountainsides. He did not think she needed the bath salts, but it amused him to consider her enjoying the unwonted luxuries of the hotel bathroom.

"Did *you* have the bath-perfume stuff?" she demanded now.

"No, just soap and water; but how good they were after all that dabbling in train wash-bowls!" he answered. "Now we'd better go and get something to eat. Will you meet me downstairs in the foyer in a few minutes?"

"Yes, I'm ready." She did not tell him she had been ready for a long time, ready and waiting, staring out over the park, in which lovers sprawled on the grass and the band was playing somewhere just out of sight. How could they lie on the grass, making love in front of all these hotels, with so many people walking past and the never-ending stream of cars and buses . . . ? Nicole wondered.

Jonathan waited for her to step out of the gilded lift, but she had chosen to walk down the stairs. Probably she was scared of managing the automatic lift by herself, he thought tenderly, and before they went out he took her across to the cage and showed her what all the push-buttons meant. He was struck again by her extraordinary mixture of worldly wisdom and complete innocence, when she turned her head away from the couples lying in the Park, and he saw that her cheeks were flushing rosily beneath their golden tan.

"That is disgusting," she said softly, "to hug and kiss in front of the whole world! Not even Emilio would do that!"

Jonathan acknowledged the truth of that by changing his mind and allowing the commissionaire to call a taxi for them. It was true; here, in sight of the windows of some of London's most expensive hotels, and the incessant stream of passing traffic and pedestrians, the sprawling couples lay. He had never given it a thought before, but as they drove off he said quietly, "You must understand, this is a city,

Nicole. Those people work all day in shops and offices and factories. The parks are their little bit of country——"

"Then they should go further away from the road, it is a big enough park! Or they should wait for the darkness," she retorted crossly.

"They might have to wait too long, at this time of the year it is not dark until ten," Jonathan grinned.

"I shall never understand the English!" Nicole said pensively. "Sometimes they are so reserved, so haughty! Especially one must not talk about love, or God. Surely God and love are the most important things in life, and afterwards babies and food and a roof over one's head?"

"Perhaps that is why we can't talk about them lightly. And don't forget you are half English," he answered slowly. In Lugano, in spite of her gypsyish ways, she had seemed to him very much Evelyn's daughter. He hoped she was not going to talk like a foreigner when she arrived at Combe Castleton. Yet he sympathised with the fastidiousness in her that disliked the display of emotion in the Park.

"All these taxis, and the hotel!" She turned towards him impulsively. "You will be ruined, Jonathan! Such expense—we could have walked, surely?"

He was touched and amused again by her change of mood. He knew the hotel had been a mistake; the only amends he could make now was to take her to a restaurant where she could feel at home, and by a lucky chance he had remembered Giovanni's in Soho. He had eaten many a cheap meal there during his student days, and hoped the place would still be there. So many of the smaller restaurants had changed hands since then, or disappeared altogether.

"I thought you might be tired."

"I am not at all tired!" Certainly she did not look as if she had been travelling for twenty-four hours. The black frock had been her one presentable gown before the shopping expedition. She kept it for special occasions and did not tell Jonathan that it had been made for her mother's funeral. It had a full skirt to her ankles, and since then she had cut out the neck and inserted a ruff of starched *broderie anglaise*, in which she wore the only bit of jewellery she possessed—a simple cameo brooch. The whole effect was simple and charming, and Jonathan—who had seen the black frock come out for church every Sunday in Lugano—had no qualms about telling her to wear it tonight. Lucia's parting gift to her had been a white lacy shawl, exquisitely soft and light, and she had draped it stole-wise over her shoulders tonight. Without bothering her head to read fashion articles, Nicole had struck the right note with sure instinct.

Giovanni's was still there, and Giovanni himself; the Italian looked very much older, with silver hair and a portly, almost distinguished, appearance. He still welcomed his clients personally, though it was a full minute before he recognised in Jonathan the thin, rangy medical student he used to feed very well for so little money.

"*Dio mio*! Mr. Gr-r-ant! How long it is since we have had the pleasure of your company!" Giovanni had lived in England so many years that he no longer embraced his English friends, but he did pump Jonathan's hands up and down excitedly, calling to his head waiter to give them the best table, the one in the corner by the old bottle-glass window. "Now you are the great surgeon you no longer come and wolf my *ravioli*," he murmured, with laughing reproach.

"Only because I am seldom in London. I live now in Devon," Jonathan explained, and introduced Nicole, who had been standing by with sparkling eyes, enraptured, as Jonathan had known she would be. As Giovanni bowed over her hand she murmured in Italian that she was delighted to meet an old friend of Mr. Grant's. Giovanni's face instantly lost its sophistication. He seized her hand and kissed her soundly on both cheeks, exclaiming like a blessing, "*Benvenuto, signorina! Da che parte dell' Italia viene?*"

He was so pleased to hear one of his patrons speaking his own language that he forgave her for being French and not Italian, for coming from Lugano and not further south, but he knew the Ticino canton well.

"Eet ees ver' beautiful, that country!" he used English in courtesy to Jonathan, and they were ushered to their seats, followed by the kindly or amused glances of other people dining in the small restaurant. Though it was only dusk, candles were lighted on the scrubbed wooden tables, stuck in bottles. There were flowers in glasses and little jars, and the place was warm with the smell of good cooking, the flowers, and a summer evening in the city. Nicole smiled at Jonathan in their little alcove by the bottle-glass window.

"You are kind!" she exclaimed softly. "To bring me here—this is like home. Here I don't feel foolishgauche

109

——" She gave a little mock-shudder. "Your grand hotel, I hate it!"

Looking at her in the flickering candle glow, Jonathan realised that she had changed already. She was a young woman, very good to look upon, with strikingly beautiful eyes. He smiled as she unfolded the clean napkin and stuck it, Continental-fashion, under her chin.

"I don't think you need feel foolish anywhere, Nicki. You're quite able to deal with anything that crops up. But here, we put our table napkins on our lap, so——"

She grinned at him, becoming instantly a child again. "*Here* we put it where I have put it"—she nodded towards several of the other diners—"but tomorrow I will do as you say. You must tell me everything, Jonathan—what do the Americans say? You must put me wise!"

The *ravioli* was excellent, better even than Lucia's, and the Chianti chilled to exactly the right temperature.

"To—your health and happiness, Mademoiselle Berenger," Jonathan toasted her lightly.

"*Votre santé, m'sieur*," she replied, but he was appalled to see that the tears stood in her eyes. She said simply, "I am terrified when I think of tomorrow, Jonathan. Can we not pretend, just for tonight, that we are friends without a care in the world, exploring London. . . . ?"

"But we *are* friends, and we will explore London, and to blazes with tomorrow!" he answered, falling in with her mood, and feeling an almost boyish excitement rising in him. "I, too, have to face the return to duty tomorrow. Let us enjoy this lovely evening the gods have sent us——"

"This lovely evening God has sent us," she corrected him gently, and for some hours Jonathan actually forgot the years between, and became a student again. Arm in arm they went into the warm, dusty streets, after thanking Giovanni for his good supper, and Jonathan showed her the hospital where he had trained, St. Cuthbert's.

"We were very hard-up in those days, my mother and I, and I would probably have failed my exams if Giovanni hadn't fed me so cheaply," he reminisced aloud.

Staring up at the great, grimy building, Nicole shuddered with no pretence at all. "I would not like to be ill there," she said definitely.

"Oh, it's not so bad inside, and you'd be lucky to get a bed there," he grinned, making a long arm. "They have a first-class staff, a waiting list so long, and a reputation that is known all over the civilised world!"

"Ah—yes. I remember now newspaper articles. I am afraid I am not what you would call civilised." Nicole sighed, and tucked her hand inside his arm again. She refused absolutely to remember who Jonathan was, to-night, because it seemed to remove him so far from her. Even in this dark suit, which he had never worn in Gandria, he looked different; the professional man, the famous surgeon . . . yet when he forgot the grim side of his recent experiences he looked so much happier.

Jonathan was shelving memories, too, as they strolled among the crowds on the warm pavements, pausing to look in shop windows, at the photographs outside theatres and cinemas, at the books still displayed in Charing Cross Road (how many times he had bought second-hand text-books at Foyles!), and the luscious fruit piled on the barrows in the side streets off Leicester Square.

It was years since he had had the time to wander like this, looking and listening to the chatter of a girl. And Fay had been so very different from Nicole; the only thing they had in common was the silken sheen of their fair hair. Fay had been brittle, hard and witty, even in the early days; her comments on the passing scene would have been critical; she was always grumbling because he could not afford to take her into one of the glittering restaurants or theatres . . . but he wanted to forget Fay. She seemed as unreal as a ghost tonight.

"Would you like to go to a theatre—we might still get into one of the late shows?" he asked suddenly.

Nicki shook her head. "Not tonight, thank you, Jonathan. . . . There is so much to see, and we have so little time!"

So little time. . . .

A few short hours to try and show this child something of the greatest city in the world. He was very content to wander round the West End and let her look at everything and everyone to her heart's content.

"Piccadilly"—he presented it to her with a little bow, ironically—"supposed to be the heart of the world!" And he bought her a spray of gardenias to fasten in the belt of her black frock.

The crowds and lights and noise bewildered her a little, but the shops in Regent Street were fascinating, though she did not linger by their windows for long. Jonathan was surprised to find she wanted to see the Houses of Parliament and St. Paul's, and Nelson's Column; she wanted to go into the Underground and take a bus ride.

"Once a courier, always a courier," he teased her, but she was undaunted. He promised her a quick sight-seeing tour by taxi in the morning; their train did not leave until noon. But they did see Trafalgar Square, Jonathan had to buy some cakes in Lyons to feed the pigeons, and Nicki cried out with the delight of a child when finally she coaxed them to come and feed from her hands.

"It is like Milan, only there are *thousands* of birds there! How huge this town is, Jonathan, and yet you have *les étalages*—what you call them—markets for the fruit——"

"Stalls."

"Fruit stalls, among your theatres, and ladies dressed so grandly! And the old women selling flowers—and pigeons! It is like home, that——"

Jonathan sat on the edge of one of the fountains and looked at the girl's puzzled face. "Yes, in all the great cities, you will find things like this. And slums just around the corner from the most expensive residential district. . . . I suppose it is because London grew so gradually." He smiled and drew her to her feet. "And do remember that this is your home, now, Nicki. You are half English, you know."

"I have no home, now," she said sombrely, but the shadows left her face as soon as she saw the river. It was not yet dark, but in the blue twilight the lights from the Embankment and the bridges were reflected in the swift-flowing water, and there were little ships of all shapes and sizes moored along the banks.

"Oh, I love water!"

"I'll take you further down tomorrow, to the Pool, and you will see everything from coal barges to ocean liners," he promised.

She dragged him into a dubious-looking milk bar in the Strand to have a Coca-cola, and flushed when a gang of skinheads looked her up and down. "I thought this was a café, it looks like such a nice place!" She sighed as they went out again into the night. "But the Coca-cola was delicious!"

Jonathan thought Coca-cola could never be delicious, but he was determined to let Nicole do anything she wished tonight, even to the ride on the Underground and the bus. It was late and they were both tired out and a trifle dishevelled when at last they got back to the hotel.

In the lift Nicki smiled up at him, satisfied. "Thank you, Jonathan. I think you do not like walking the pavements very much, but I have enjoyed myself!"

"I'm glad." He was thinking it was a mistake to be always in a hurry, to go everywhere in a metal and glass box on wheels that cut you off from the colour and smells and movement of humanity on the pavements. But she was a funny child, Nicki. . . . As they came across the foyer just now they could see the dancing in the hotel ballroom, hear the orchestra; most women would have regretted missing that, but when he had asked if she would like to dance she had shaken her head emphatically. "Among those—those icebergs? I'm not dressed for a ballroom, Jonathan!"

"I've enjoyed myself, too," he said now, suddenly, as the lift stopped at her floor and he opened the doors. "Good-night, God bless you, and sleep well, darling."

"*Et tu aussi*," she whispered, standing to watch the gilded cage carrying him away from her. The key in her hand seemed the key to another cage—a prison cell. Nicki grinned at herself at the absurdity of thinking the luxurious hotel bedroom a prison and bade a sleepy page good-night as she let herself in. The bedroom, in blue and gold, seemed enormous, the single bed big enough for a family, after the austerity of her room at the *albergo*, and she pulled a grimace at it. But she was tired, tired out at last, and she fell asleep in spite of the roar of traffic that never seemed to stop in London, and the unfamiliar, lonely room. The last thing she remembered was the sweet fragrance of the gardenias. Already their waxen petals were curling like brown paper at the edges, but she had put them in a glass of water on her bedside table. They reminded her of home, and Jonathan had given them to her.

CHAPTER FIVE

THE small smile quivered again at the corners of Nicole's sensitive mouth when Jonathan pointed out the White Horses of the Wiltshire downs, and for a few miles the sight of Somerset fields, so crammed with buttercups that they looked like cloth of gold, banished the look of strain from her face, but it soon returned.

"Nearly home. This is the West Country," Jonathan said when they had passed Salisbury. It was another clear, sunny day, and even after growing up in a place like Lugano, Nicki could hardly find anything to criticise in the English landscape that slid past the windows of their train. He was inwardly grateful for the weather; it was absurdly important that this child should come home to sunshine and warmth . . . and according to the weather reports a good June was going to be succeeded by a flaming July. It was the best summer England had known for several years.

They had lunched on the train soon after leaving Paddington, and Nicki had pulled a little face of dismay at the dingy purlieus of the station. But she had enjoyed every moment of their sight-seeing tour of the morning, taken this time in a taxi; she had stood breathless on the terrace of the House of Commons, listening to Big Ben striking across the fair stillness of the morning; she had peered into the Abbey and the Cathedral and St. Paul's; had her glimpse of the City and the Pool of London; and insisted on wandering across "the big market"—Covent Garden. The fruit shops interested her more than the Opera House, to his amusement; and behind Henrietta Street she had discovered a tiny, hidden-away, Continental church that delighted her beyond everything.

"It is *exactly* like the ones at home!" she whispered, kneeling before a medieval statue of the Madonna. And indeed, in this dark, soft peace, with the smell of flowers and incense faint on the air, and the only light the flickering of many tiny candles and the warm red glow of the Sanctuary lamp, Jonathan found it hard to believe they were only a few hundred yards from the roaring traffic of the Strand.

They had collected their luggage from the hotel and caught the train with only a few minutes to spare, breathless and laughing like two children as they sped up the platform in the wake of their impatient porter.

Then suddenly the holiday mood had deserted Nicole; she had remembered where they were going; that Jonathan, too, was returning to his proper place. In Combe Castleton he would not run down a platform hand in hand with her to catch a train, nor wander into cafés to drink a Coca-cola, nor lie in an old boat and let her row him out to look at the town's lights at night . . . The holiday was over for both of them.

"Tired?" he asked gently.

"A little." Now they were getting so near the end of their long journey she could not even say she was terrified. He would despise her completely if he knew how her knees were knocking together and the number of butterflies in her tummy. Yesterday evening he had laughed, he had made her promise never to be afraid of anything . . . but today was different. He would not even understand why she was afraid. So she sat silent for long periods, or answered his conversation politely when he pointed out objects of interest on their journey, and stared at the cloth-of-gold fields with unseeing eyes. She, who loved growing things and flowers so passionately! She had even kept last night's faded gardenias, wrapped in the new lace handkerchief Bianca had given her.

Jonathan had given her the corner seat facing the engine, and suddenly now the train ran out of a tunnel, and there in front of them was a curving bay, and the crooked grey and red roofs of an old town, and the sea.

"Combe Castleton," Jonathan said softly, and began to get their luggage together. Out of the corner of his eye he saw the look of delighted enchantment die out of the girl's face, to be replaced by a frozen expression that was almost sullen, but there was nothing he could do about it now. For Nicki this was zero hour. He could only grasp her arm firmly as the train stopped and give her a last swift, comforting smile before they were on the platform, shaking hands with his aunt and uncle.

"Welcome home, Nicole. Your grandmother asked us to meet you and bring you to Osterley House. Waites has brought your car, Jonathan."

The old-fashioned solicitor looked very formidable to Nicole as he arranged everything so deftly, taking it for granted that his arrangements would be acceptable. She shook hands with Mr. and Mrs. Grant politely, unaware that they were secretly relieved to see that she looked so presentable. The chauffeur came to take Jonathan's bags, touching his cap. "It's nice to see you back, and looking so well, sir."

"Thank you, Waites. Take care of this one, please—and I'll drive."

In the bustle of arrival—quite a lot of people had got off the train—only one painful fact arrived in Nicki's tired brain. They were going to take her away, these old people with their stiff, polite manners; Jonathan was to get into his car and drive off; leaving her at their mercy.

She whirled round to Jonathan, the one familiar person in this confusing new world, and clung to his arm, crying impetuously, "*You* come, Jonathan! Please come with me to my grandmother's, or I shall run away and go to a hotel!"

To the solicitor and his wife she looked like a beautiful, spoiled child, but in her panic she was oblivious of their surprised faces, even of the faintly disapproving expression Jonathan himself turned upon her. "Please!" she whispered, "Please come and help me, Jonathan!"

For an instant Jonathan could have shaken her. This was not his proud, laughing Nicole Berenger, this white-faced, trembling stranger! Though she had not seen it, he had noticed the light of approval in his uncle and aunt's eyes, until this—this childish exhibition.

Then he realised that he was looking at it all through his own eyes, not hers. Combe Castleton was his home, these were his familiar relations, even Waites was his uncle's chauffeur and had been with the family for years. To Nicki they were all strangers, stretching out hands to snatch her into a wholly unfamiliar world. Naturally she clung to the one person she knew. And after all, Jonathan thought dryly, I'm the one responsible for bringing her here.

He took her arm in his usual warm, friendly grip. "All right, *petite âme*. Waites can take my car back." It was his especial name for her—their secret joke—and it comforted her at once. Old Lucia, when she wanted to scold, always accused one of having a "little soul," and when he had translated it into French, Nicki had explained that "*âme*" also meant one's heart, the essence of one's personality. In Jonathan's mind it became also little wild goose. . . .

Aunt Bella took the girl's other arm and spoke with all the kindness of her heart. "*Of course* Jonathan can come with us; we should have thought of it, Steve—and Helen will be delighted."

"Knowing Jonathan, I imagined that he would want to get into his own quarters without delay," Stephen Grant said dryly, but Nicole was beginning to see the twinkle of kindly humour beneath his craggy manner. "And Helen has the whole tribe waiting to welcome this young lady— Joyce and Paul, and Nigel, of course. But come along, she will be waiting and anxious——" He bustled them gently to his waiting car, an ancient Daimler that could hold them all comfortably. In front of it, Nicki saw Waites

116

get into a long, low-slung black car and drive it off. She did not know it was a Jaguar, but she did recognise the grace and beauty of its expensive lines.

"You sit here, Nicole, beside me—Jon can keep his uncle company. I'll try and tell you about this town as we go up to Osterley House——" Aunt Bella was chatting away affably to try and take away the strained look on the girl's face. Nicole listened with one ear; the other one was listening to Jonathan while Stephen Grant drove them slowly and carefully out of the station drive. Jonathan was saying: "What on earth did Helen want to have those vultures for, so soon?" in a tone that told Nicki he did not care much for Joyce and Paul and Nigel, whoever they might be.

The car climbed through the pleasant old seaside town to the higher, residential district, with Aunt Bella chirping about various buildings of interest. "We live down in the town; in the days before cars it was handier for my husband to reach his office, and now, of course, Jonathan has the ground floor for his professional rooms——"

Nicki was very willing to listen to news of Jonathan. She was surprised at this item, though. "I thought he would live at the hospital?"

"Oh, no, dear. He is a *consultant*, not a resident member of the staff." Aunt Bella sighed, wondering how to explain the intricacies of the National Health Scheme piled on top of the intricacies of the old medical etiquette. "He has private patients also; he operates in several nursing homes. He is a *specialist*, you see——"

Nicole nodded eagerly. "I understand. Like Dr. Adler, of Zurich." And she told the interested woman all about Pietro's accident, and how Jonathan had performed the emergency operation.

"I saw something about it in the paper; not much. Dr. Cranford was very cross"—Aunt Bella smiled reminiscently—"because Jon had promised him to do no work at all. That was why Dr. Cranford forbade him to take his car abroad; he wanted him to *rest* completely."

"I think he has rested well," Nicki said softly, remembering the change in Jonathan, "except for that one night."

"Well, he is certainly looking very well, and so brown! But we are having a wonderful summer here for once, Nicole, so I hope you will not be too disappointed in England." She turned to look at the girl by her side and was struck by the soft glow on her face. Of course, they had been talking about Jonathan instead of looking at the views! The child was staring now at the back of his head, that well-shaped head with its thick, unruly brown hair, and Aunt Bella chuckled inwardly. If that was how the land lay, her favourite nephew might yet find the happiness she had always wanted for him. But Steve called her a sentimental old idiot whenever she dreamed dreams for him, pointing out that Jon got along very well without women hanging on to his coat-tails.

Osterley House was inland, away from the sea, in the residential district. It was a mansion, built in the Victorian era of the early industrial boom, and the Stannisford who built it had been lucky enough to own coal-bearing land in Wales. The architect who designed it had been unsure of his periods, with the result that it was an extraordinary hotch-potch of Victorian grey stone, pseudo-oriental cupolas, glass porches, and towers and portico trying to pretend they were Tudor. Jonathan had warned her that the house was hideous, and it was hideous.

Nicole stared at it with dismay. Going up the curving drive, gay with rhododendrons, she had been almost hopeful, but this huge, ugly, pretentious house, staring at her from its many flat and bowed windows, made her heart sink. The Albergo Fionetti was a palace of grace compared with Osterley House.

Stephen Grant pulled up sedately under the big portico, and as Jonathan jumped out to help them from the car, the big front door was solemnly opened by a manservant. The hall was as big as the foyer of the hotel, and seemed to be full of people, and Nicole felt an irresistible desire to giggle as Jonathan handed her up the steps. She knew, she could feel it through the hand he held so firmly under her elbow, that he felt the same. It was all so pompous, so ridiculously like an early Hollywood film of the long-exiled princess returning to her father's castle. . . .

Only her father's castle had been a Paris *atelier* on the fifth floor of an old ruined house in Montmartre, she remembered suddenly, and did not want to giggle any more. The next few moments were a flurry of introductions, after Jonathan had led her up to the white-haired little lady in a wheelchair.

"My darling, it is lovely to have you home!" Helen Stannisford whispered, holding her hand in one that trembled, and Nicole dropped the demure curtsey that was the due of old people. But she did not curtsey to Joyce, that hard-faced, middle-aged woman who stared at the girl while she shook hands indolently, or to Paul, who was apparently an uncle on her grandfather's side, nor to Nigel, her cousin. Though Nigel, with his fair, boyish head and laughing eyes, seemed the most human of the lot. At least he smiled at her as though he was glad to meet her.

"Thank you, Jonathan, for bringing her home safely." Helen was too moved to notice the danger signals. This child *was* so like Evelyn it seemed impossible that she would not at once feel the love that surged in the old, weak heart. Helen had succumbed reluctantly to Joyce's suggestion that they should be at Osterley House when Nicole arrived.

"It will help the awkward beginnings, make the child feel she has a family after all, and I can help her choose some decent clothes," Joyce had insisted. Helen had never been able to withstand the strong wills of her husband's family, but she was longing now to have Nicole to herself.

Apparently there were servants to greet too, and as they were briefly introduced, Nicki made the mistake of starting to shake hands with them also. Simpkin, the butler, stepped back from the proffered hand with pained reproach on his face; and the girl merely nodded to the others. To Mrs. Moore, the housekeeper; to Paget, the parlourmaid; and Coles, her grandmother's personal maid who was to look after her also for the present; to Flora, the head housemaid.

While his uncle and aunt chatted casually with the family, Jonathan stood in the shadows watching Nicole going through this perfectly ridiculous ordeal. The return of the prodigal granddaughter! He guessed that Joyce, who was introducing the staff crisply, with the air of the-woman-in-possession, had stage-managed the whole thing.

And there, sitting rather desolately on one of the black-and-white marble squares of the hall, was Nicole's precious basket and her travelling bag. Coles picked them up as if they might bite her. Jonathan wished they could. For the first time he felt affection for the horrible basket.

"This is all the baggage? If Mademoiselle will give me the keys I will unpack for her."

Nicole wondered why servants referred to one always in the third person. And why these so very English women tried to sound as if they were French. . . . She said abruptly, "That is all the baggage and there are no keys. I will unpack it myself, thank you."

"Let Coles show you your room, dear. I expect you will want to freshen up after your journey. Then we will have sherry in the little drawing-room. Do not bother to dress for dinner, tonight," Helen said quietly.

The staff had melted away, having given Nicole what Jonathan privately called the "once-over" beneath their mask of old family retainer. Joyce had taken her husband and son over to the group around Helen's chair, and Nicole was obediently starting up the stairs in the wake of Coles's stiff back. Jonathan felt a longing to call her back, to grab the horrible basket from the supercilious maid's hand, to run away with Nicki from the whole fantastic, Victorian situation. . . . Poor child, he'd had no idea he was letting her in for anything like this.

He wished that he could have had a private word with her, to reassure her. Helen alone would be all right; she was obviously extremely happy to have Nicole at last under her roof. . . . But what a crashing mistake to have allowed Joyce and her family to muscle in on the reunion! To Jonathan the staff was unimportant either way; he could not imagine himself in Nicole's shoes enough to understand the intense humiliation a young girl could suffer through tiny things. . . .

Suddenly she turned and ran down the stairs again, and put her arms up to give him a quick hug, kissing him on both cheeks. "I'd forgotten to say thank you, Jonathan— for bringing me safely home!" she said, in a passable imitation of her grandmother, and only Jonathan heard the heartache and the mockery beneath her tone.

"It'll be all right, later, when the two of you are alone," he answered in a very quiet voice, and she ran away up the stairs without waiting to argue, afraid that she would burst into tears in front of them all, afraid that she would run away.

Probably, she thought, as she looked round the comfortable bedroom, when Coles had departed, I *shall* run away . . . but not too soon, not soon enough to give *Grand'mère* a shock. . . .

Her grandmother was nice. No one could have guessed what a shock the tiny, silver-haired woman had given Nicole. This was how her mother would have looked, if she had lived to grow old. . . .

"Very touching!" Joyce commented acidly. "You seem to have made quite an impression on the child, Jonathan."

He was conscious of the group by the wheel-chair surveying him after the little scene. Aunt Bella smilingly, Uncle Steve frowningly, young Nigel grinning openly.

For once Helen stood up to her relations. She said firmly, "I owe a great deal to Jonathan for—everything. Naturally Nicole feels strange here, and he has been kind to her——"

"Not very difficult; she's a pretty girl," Joyce commented. "But at that age they always prefer an older man. It's a father complex or something. Nicki thinks she can trust you, I daresay, Jonathan."

Jonathan would have liked to murder the woman. Instead, he managed to smile, and addressed himself entirely to Helen. "Nicki is tired and a little confused, Mrs. Stannisford. She has always lived simply——"

Simply—he thought with self-contempt; the child has lived like a gypsy, like a happy little gypsy. . . .

"My dear Jonathan, *we* live simply enough these days!" Helen argued gently, oblivious of the irony in his eyes. To her, the great house, half permanently closed up, and a staff of six servants, was indeed living simply. "Won't you come and have a sherry, if you won't dine with us?" she added.

"Thank you, but I'm afraid I must go. Dr. Cranford is coming in this evening to see me." Jonathan made his exit almost brusquely, feeling that he would stifle if he stayed in the museum-like atmosphere of Osterley House another minute.

"What an impatient man he is," Joyce murmured, as Simpkins passed round the tray of drinks.

"He wants to get back into harness, I expect," Stephen Grant answered absently. He was worried. Worried and annoyed. What on earth had Helen been thinking of to let Joyce and her gang get into the house before the child herself? he wondered. And after a few minutes' casual conversation he and his wife went away also. The car was still in the portico, so Jonathan must have walked.

As soon as the family was alone Joyce turned to her son. "Yes, Nicole is very pretty. Just like Evelyn at her age."

Helen's face lit up; she did not see the ironical wink that passed between mother and son. Paul was fiddling with the piano; he was passionately fond of music, and this Bechstein—never used nowadays—was better than anything he had left in his own home. The Steinway had been sold long ago, of course. He was wondering if Helen would consider giving him the piano, if Nicole did not play. . . . Paul Stannisford was not very interested in the family reunion. He left all the intriguing to his wife and son.

"If she doesn't play, I shall have someone up to give Nicole lessons, Paul." Helen interrupted his thoughts all unaware, her faded blue eyes shining with happy plans for her grandchild. "Or perhaps you would give her lessons? It's so nice to hear that piano being used again——"

She left unspoken the fact they all realised, that the Bechstein had not been played since Evelyn ran away from home; though it had been regularly tuned.

There goes my hope of this piano, Paul thought, without much regret. He had given up feeling much about anything. The iron will of his brother, Henry, nearly old enough to be his father, and then his wife's equally strong selfishness, had knocked most of Paul's dreams into dust. He answered lazily, "Nigel could teach her, I daresay. He's a better pianist than I am, Helen. Far better."

"I say, Dad, that's not the same thing as giving *lessons*," Nigel protested hotly, ignoring his mother's frown. "Nicole may only be at the five-finger-exercise stage!"

Helen tapped the arm of her wheel-chair absently. Sometimes her dislike of her husband's family led her to the brink of open discourtesy, until she remembered Henry's wishes. After a lifetime of obedience to an autocrat she found it difficult to realise that he was dead, that now she had control of a vast fortune, that she could do as she liked.

"All the better if she has never touched a piano," Paul was arguing with his son, without heat. His passionate love of music was about all the boy would inherit from him, and he knew all about Nigel's bitter disappointment that there had not been enough money for his training as a concert pianist. For years they had tried to wangle the money out of Henry, but he had regarded all forms of creative art as so much waste of time, particularly in his own family.

Now there was a faint hope that Helen might be persuaded to advance enough money for Nigel to give up his job and take up music seriously, if it was not too late. Henry, though he had been too mean to lend his brother a fiver, had made no secret of the fact that Nigel would be his heir, after he had cut Evelyn out of his will. He had thoroughly enjoyed, Paul thought, as he played a Chopin

Nocturne softly, keeping them all dangling on their expectations. . . . And now Joyce was all het-up because Nicole had come back to her mother's home and might get the whole fortune. If he had not been too lazy to worry overmuch about anything, it would have amused Paul; Joyce, with her extravagant ways and social ambitions, deserved a little of her own medicine. . . .

Joyce was frowning still at her son, who stood by the open french windows staring down the garden. The garden was by far the best part of Osterley House . . . formal, enclosed by old stone walls, it had a graciousness that was sadly lacking in the bumptious building. Nigel said sulkily, "All right, I'll give Nicole lessons if you like, Aunt Helen," because he felt his mother's eyes boring into his back, "but I won't go on with them unless she wants to learn."

"Thank you, Nigel dear."

Helen liked her young nephew the best of them all, though she secretly deplored the way Joyce had brought up her son; she also thought it a pity that Henry had told them about his will. It gave her an uncomfortable feeling when they were in the house. In spite of their good clothes, she always felt as if they were professional beggars. She never let them go away without a handsome present, but she suspected that the cheque did not last long. Joyce's clothes and bridge debts ran away with most of Paul's modest salary, and Nigel ran a sports car which he surely could not afford. . . .

Nevertheless, perhaps it was as well that she had a presentable young man to take Nicole about.

"She must have dancing lessons, also, and some riding," Helen planned aloud.

Cinderella comes to the ball, Joyce Stannisford thought bitterly. The girl was going to have the whole box of tricks. She was also deeply thankful Nigel was here—they lived in Exeter and he could easily come over every week-end—and that her son was presentable. She said with a little laugh, "At least you can teach her to dance and to ride, Nigel."

Nicole came in quietly in time to hear that. She looked very charming in her black frock, though there was none of last night's animation in her pale face. Her eyes were a brilliant blue under their dark lashes—those dark lashes that were such a contrast with her fair hair—and she held her small head very proudly.

"Cousin Nigel need not trouble himself to teach me

anything," she said distinctly. "I have come to visit my *grand'mère,* not to go dancing and riding."

Nigel swung round from his contemplation of the garden and coloured slightly. "I say, I'll be only too pleased to take you around, Nicole."

As he said it he realised it was true. The girl looked different from any of his girl friends, but it was a charming difference.

"*Cousin Nigel*—how sweet you are!" Joyce laughed softly in a way that did not match her hard face. "It sounds like something out of *Jane Eyre.*"

Nicole faced her. From the first moment it was clear that they would be enemies, herself and this woman. She said quietly, "In my country we still address our relatives so," and obeyed her grandmother's smiling invitation to come and sit beside her.

"Have a sherry, Nicole—or do you prefer something with gin in it?" Paul wandered over to the tray of drinks, amiably intent on keeping the peace. He was kind, in a weak wort of way, she decided, and to please him she accepted the sherry. Helen sat with her hands on the girl's, content to watch her. It was like having Evelyn back, and yet not quite the same. Though she spoke English without a trace of accent, there was something of French grace in the way Nicole moved, the way she draped her skirt over her feet as she sank on the stool, sometimes in the way she arranged her sentences.

"Now that you are here, we must see that you enjoy yourself, my dear." Helen smiled into the frosty blue eyes and received a sudden, dazzling smile in return. She was proud, this child, but she was loving too. Nicole could not resist the hungry gaze of her grandmother's eyes, though she was tully aware that the others resented her. Except perhaps Nigel. "You're so young, you have had such a hard lite—it's only right that you should learn to play a little now."

A shadow crossed the sensitive young face. It was only Helen's age and obvious frailty that protected her from the scorn in Nicki's mind. *What about my mother . . . did she have much chance to enjoy her youth . . . ?* She wanted to shout at them, to tell them to keep their beastly patronage. But with her instinctive wisdom she knew that it was true what Jonathan had told her, that it had not been Helen's fault. I don't wonder my mother ran away from it all, she thought suddenly, hating the house, hating everything.

The dinner was dreadful. It seemed to go on and on for ever, with the family making polite conversation because the servants were in the room all the time. Nicole thought the soup tasteless; she did not care for the salmon, and the salad dressing was not comparable with one she could mix herself; and the elaborate sweet was not half so good as Lucia's *Torta alla Crema* which she made for special occasions. Simpkins' solemn face as he directed Paget through the courses by a look or a gesture made Nicole want to giggle. She felt terribly homesick for the laughter and chatter that would be going on round the ancient oak table at the Albergo Fionetti, where Emilio would be recounting amusing anecdotes from his day's tours, and Bianca discussing her day at school with her plump arms sprawled on the table, and Lucia would be scolding gently. And over all the peace of sunset on Lake Lugano and the rich smell of good cooking from the kitchen beyond. . . .

And Jonathan . . . but she would not think of Jonathan just now, it hurt too much. She had rushed to the window of her big, sombre bedroom upstairs as soon as Coles had left her, in time to see him striding away down the drive. Something about his walk had conveyed to her his feeling of anger; she knew he was upset about something. Perhaps she had been wrong to run up to him and kiss him goodbye like that, perhaps she had made a fool of him in front of his uncle and aunt, in front of these supercilious cousins. . . . He had looked angry, too, on the platform, when she had begged him to come with her to Osterley House. Only for an instant, but he had never looked at her like that before. Yesterday had been heavenly; only yesterday evening they had been having such fun (if it had been Jonathan who was to take her riding and dancing, how she would have enjoyed it. Only, of course, he would be far too busy). And this morning, rushing round the sights of London in their taxi. . . .

It seemed incredible that forty-eight hours ago they had been having dinner on the Basle Express.

A much better dinner than this, too, Nicole added to herself practically, though I expect all these sour-faced old servants swindle Grand'mère every day over the housekeeping. . . .

In the drawing-room afterwards it was a little better; they could talk more freely, but Nicole answered all their questions guardedly, conscious that there was some unexplained antagonism between Joyce and herself. Helen retired early, and asked Nicole to wheel her to her bedroom, which was a sort of boudoir on the ground floor, but in the far wing.

"It is easier for them to look after me here, and I am not supposed to climb stairs," she explained when they were alone in the boudoir, a pleasant room decorated in rose-du-Barry and gold. "I have what Dr. Cranford calls a tired heart." She smiled suddenly at the child who was so like Evelyn. "It may go on for years or just suddenly stop."

"Oh, no," Nicole answered promptly, from conviction and not tact. "Now that my grandfather has gone and left you in peace, I think you will live for many years, very happy."

"Dear, let us discuss this now, and then forget it—come and sit close to me." Helen was painfully conscious of the pride in the young face.

Nicole obeyed, because she had been taught always to obey older people, but she stuck her small chin in the air. "I can never forget my grandfather's wickedness," she said clearly and quietly, "because my mother died of a broken heart. Not only because of the way they treated my father, but because after his death she wanted to bring me home, here, to you. And you never answered her letter."

"I—I only saw that letter after my husband died." Helen found the words difficult to bring out, even now. But her love for Evelyn compelled her to be honest. "You must not call your grandfather wicked, dearest. He was just according to his lights. He was keeping his promise that your mother would never enter this house again if she—— He did not want her to marry your father, you see. Of course, all this is very old-fashioned to you, but he was an old-fashioned man."

"And you wonder that *I* did not want to enter this house!" Nicki jumped to her feet, the words bursting from her until she saw Helen's rose-leaf complexion go grey, and the sinister shadow round the pale lips. Then she took her grandmother's hand and held it to her for a moment. "I am sorry, Grand'mère; if you wish we will never speak of it again. I am glad to know you did not receive the letter——"

"It is best to try and forget the past. I will try and make the future happier for you, dearest, and it will make *me* much happier if you enjoy yourself. . . . Your mother would wish you to have everything, would she not?"

Nicole smiled.

"Maman gave me everything, *everything*! I did not need dancing and riding lessons and pretty clothes."

Helen closed her eyes against the pain that was not wholly physical. How like Evelyn Nicole had sounded just now! She opened her eyes and smiled to show that she was not as ill as she felt and said gently, "Nevertheless, I think she would be pleased to see you enjoying yourself, Nicole. So let Nigel take you about when he is free, and let Joyce help you choose some new clothes. Mr. Grant is going to open a bank account for you tomorrow—no, I insist, it will save you running to me for every penny. Now ring the bell for Coles, dear, and I will go to bed."

When her grandmother said "Mr. Grant," Nicki's heart jumped, but it was the uncle, of course, not Jonathan. And her grandmother was obviously a sick woman, with whom one could not argue. Though what she would do with a bank account of her own, perhaps with as much as fifty pounds to spend again, Nicki hadn't the faintest idea. All the same, it obviously pleased Grand'mère to give her things, and to please an old, sick woman Nicki would take presents, dress herself up like a fashion-plate, and dance all night with that dreamy young man, Nigel.

There was just time to kiss the soft, pale cheek and wish her good-night before Coles came, cool and efficient and somehow reproachful to Nicki, though she did not address the girl directly.

"You've stayed up too long, madam," she told her mistress as she helped her out of the chair. "We've only just got over that bad attack, only just got rid of the nurses."

Nicole was to learn that Coles always used the royal "we" concerning her mistress, to whom she was devoted in a grim, possessive fashion. She left the room feeling guilty, though not sure of the reason.

Nicki's future was the subject of a great deal of speculation that evening: among the Stannisfords, in the servants' hall, and in the Grants' house down in the town. When Jonathan had seen Dr. Cranford off he went to have a nightcap with his uncle, and to his amazement Stephen Grant was perturbed about his friendship with Nicole, instead of being delighted that he had persuaded the girl to come home.

"Uncle Steve, I'm very fond of you, but I don't like you as a lawyer. What's on your mind?" he demanded bluntly.

"I—er—oh, dammit, Jonathan! Bella says—I mean,

that child is obviously very attached to you, and I don't want Helen to think we're fortune-hunting."

Jonathan stared at him, his whisky forgotten, between amusement and exasperation. "Well, we are friends, very good friends. What did you expect? You make me almost sorry I persuaded her to come—and surely the Stannisford fortune isn't as large as all that?"

"About a quarter of a million, to be shared between Nicole and Nigel, if all goes well," Stephen answered dryly, "and even with death duties, that's not to be sneezed at, Jonathan."

Jonathan drained his whisky, and something in his expression made his uncle add, "My dear boy, don't think I'm interfering just for the sake of interfering. I don't think it would be betraying a confidence if I told you—Helen is hoping that Nicole and Nigel will marry. She hasn't made a fresh will yet, though I've done my best to persuade her. I think she's still—er—still under Henry's thumb to some extent."

"Do you mean to say she's going to try and match-make for Nicki—after what happened to Evelyn?" Jonathan cried, and saw his uncle shrug helplessly.

"I'm only a solicitor; I can only carry out my client's wishes."

"Well, I think it's damnable. I wish I'd left the girl where she was." Jonathan put down his glass steadily, but he was conscious of a deep, hurtful anger rising in him. He paused in the doorway and flung over his shoulder, with a set face, "And you needn't worry. Tell your friend Helen I am not after her granddaughter's fortune. When I marry, it will certainly not be for money."

Bella, hurrying down the hall, saw Jonathan's face, though he stared past her with unseeing eyes, and she went into her husband's study breathlessly. "Now you've upset him, Steve—whatever have you been saying? The poor darling looks like he did when that dreadful girl married that American."

"I've only been trying to—do my duty," her husband answered heavily. "I wish Henry had taken his wretched money with him!"

Nicole left her grandmother's room feeling lonely and bewildered. That woman Coles had succeeded in making her feel as if she should not have come here at all, upsetting a frail old lady with a weak heart. . . . Yet she had come entirely because Jonathan and his uncle's letter had persuaded her, not because she wanted to get round an old woman to get a share of the Stannisford money. Probably Coles and all the servants despised her, thinking as her aunt and uncle did, that she was after what she could get. . . .

Alone in the passageway Nicole's face flushed rosily with hurt pride. She had allowed herself to be caught in a trap—to please Grand'mère she would have to be gracious, to accept at least some clothes, some pleasures . . . and all of them would be thinking that was what she had come for. All of them, except Jonathan and perhaps his relations. . . . *They* knew, she thought, with a faint return of her old humour, what a job it had been to get her to come at all! But she felt in a wretchedly lonely position. It would be possible, she thought, to love Helen Stannisford; to show that tired old woman that she was forgiven for her husband's beastliness. But it would be difficult to show her any affection while those others were always watching, criticising, speculating. Nicole had no illusions about Joyce, especially. There was a snake for you——

To her annoyance, Nigel was lounging in the hall, waiting for her. He caught the expression on her face and held out his hand with a disarming smile. "Don't be cross with me, Cousin Nicole! Let me show you the garden, it's the best part of this mausoleum."

She had to smile at the change in him, the way he teasingly said "Cousin Nicole," yet with niceness too. He was the most human of these new relations of hers, yet she did not wholly trust him. She thought he was probably under his mother's thumb. She said quietly, "It's late, and I'm tired. I was going to bed."

He glanced at an old grandfather clock. "It's only ten—and a gorgeous evening. Come on, Nicole, I must talk to you, and I'm only here for the week-end."

Reluctantly she allowed him to lead her through the folding doors into the conservatory and out into the garden, but as soon as they were outside she drew in a deep breath of the warm evening air, scented with roses and stocks and mignonette, and cried impulsively, "You're right—this is much the best part of this place!"

He was tall, but not as tall as Jonathan, and his good looks were more obvious. He moved with a certain grace by her side as they walked down the grass path between the roses, and he talked casually to put her at her ease. She was a funny little thing, old-fashioned one moment and blunt the next. Pretty . . . ? Well, perhaps not pretty; but there was an undeniable charm about the girl, and the way she moved, and on the rare occasions when she forgot to be dignified and chuckled, she was delightful. Nicole Berenger. . . . Nigel had been intrigued, greatly intrigued, about her. A little while ago, when he'd heard that Jonathan Grant was bringing the child home after all he'd mentally kissed good-bye to his hopes of the Stannisford money. Then his mother crudely, and Aunt Helen more subtly, had hinted that there was plenty for both of them if he played his cards cleverly. Nicole intrigued him more now that she was actually here. She might have been so much worse, he acknowledged in the privacy of his own mind.

"These roses are Crabtree's pride and joy; they're at their best now," he was telling her. "Isn't it funny, the way gardeners' names so often go with their jobs? Crabtree! It describes him, too. Do you know, he will not allow even Aunt Helen to pick the flowers, until he has shown her the ones available for the house?"

Nicole chuckled. She thought of her own efforts with the wilderness behind the *albergo*; there was never enough time to do all she wanted to do there. She sympathised with Crabtree; if he could make a garden like this, enclosed between the soft grey walls that shone like silver in the twilight, he had a right to be autocratic.

"What are you laughing at?" Nigel demanded, opening a wrought-iron gate for her at the top of some brick steps that led down into the sunken garden, with miniature conifers growing about a lily pool.

"Oh, this is beautiful! How could anyone build a house like that in a place like this?" Nicole exclaimed, and he touched her arm to indicate a seat by the pool. Her skin beneath his fingers was warm and firm; even in this light it looked golden. Sitting by the pool she looked just right—a fairy child in a fairy world. I could fall in love with her, Nigel thought, and was conscious of a grim amusement at the idea. How many of them would believe that? Least of all his mother. . . .

As if coming back from her wonderment, Nicole said practically, "I was laughing because—rich people have so little freedom! My—the friends I have been living with—they are poor and hard-working, but they are so free, they have everything!"

"What do they have?" Nigel asked curiously.

Her face, bent a little towards the lily pool, had a little smile on it. The sky was still softly lighted from the afterglow of the magnificent sunset, and it seemed reflected on the face of this young girl. Nigel discovered that there was some elemental wisdom in her simplicity, that she went straight to the heart of things, without sentiment and without the blindness of social prejudices. Her small, thin brown hands made a gesture that seemed to embrace all the world, all beauty and love and happiness. She said simply, "They have faith, they know that whatever happens, nothing can separate them from the love of God. They are blessed, too, with sunshine and the mountains and the lake. It is very beautiful, in Lugano."

It was as if she was talking to herself. Nigel felt a momentary discomfort. He argued more to comfort himself than to convince her. "It's not much fun being poor in this climate, believe me. And I bet your friends could use a little money as well as the rest of us."

She thought of Emilio and the motor-boat, and the publicity over Pietro's operation, and laughed softly. "Oh, yes, they can use money! But they are not prisoners to it like rich people are—you see, my grandmother can afford a gardener, but she cannot pick her own flowers! And I think her servants cheat her in the house. That was a poorly-cooked dinner. At Emilio's inn we would have served a better meal with half as many things in it."

"Phew! You *are* going to be popular with Mrs. Moore and the cook." Nigel grinned, swinging round on the seat to look at her again, to offer his cigarette case. "You don't smoke?" he demanded incredulously when she shook her head.

"Sometimes. I don't like it very much, and after only one cigarette one's hair smells of smoke," she answered absently, and he wondered who had told her that her hair smelled of smoke. . . . How little they all knew of this girl.

"Look here, Nicole, I don't want you to think I'm responsible for the set-up here," he began almost brusquely, and at the change in his tone she liked him better. Now, at last, he was speaking the truth.

"Set-up?" she queried, puzzled.

He grinned again briefly. "The layout, the family arrangements—our being here to welcome you, and all that."

"But you are relations; you have the right to be here," she answered, still a little puzzled, "only I think that your mother does not like me. Perhaps she thinks—perhaps they all think—I have come to get what I can of the money?" She asked it as a question, so flatly that Nigel was nonplussed.

She added quietly, with immense dignity, "I do not want the money. Any of it. It could have helped my mother and my father once, if it had been given with love, but I do not need it."

If anyone else had said those words Nigel would have laughed aloud. All he said, almost reverently, was, "Well, we need it all right."

Nicole smiled faintly. "Then take it. I came only because—because Jonathan said Grand'mère was old and sick, and needed to make her peace with me because of what my grandfather did to my parents."

The man beside her crushed out the butt of his cigarette and was silent for a while. He was thirty-two, and since he had been a boy of twelve his mother had impressed upon him that the Stannisford money was the most important thing in the world. And here was this girl—this child—tossing it into his lap as carelessly as if it were one of old Crabtree's roses. He had always considered the family feud ridiculous—blatantly unfair to Evelyn—but the prospect of inheriting a quarter of a million pounds was not ridiculous. Even the moneylenders had been generous on the strength of the will . . . until Henry's death. Now, knowing that Helen Stannisford could leave the lot to a cats' home if she wished, they were drawing in their horns. Nigel's affairs were pretty sticky just now.

He said almost roughly, "Don't you realise how much there will be? Over two hundred thousand pounds, if that means anything to you——"

She tried to work it out in francs or lire and failed. It did not mean anything to her. She said again, "Rich people are always worrying, they are slaves to their money. I don't want to be a slave. I think you're foolish if you're willing to give up your freedom for this—you're young and healthy and nice-looking, you can earn your living."

"Thank you," he answered dryly, but he knew she was not being ironical. She literally had no idea what it cost to live, to have a bit of fun, to run a car. . . . He added grimly, "I have a job of sorts. I work in an office in

Exeter. Uncle Henry saw to that—though I wanted to be a pianist."

Nicole turned to him impetuously. "There are are, already you are a slave, not doing what you want!"

"Well, I've been a slave for so many years now, I'd hate to think I wouldn't get the stuff in the end," Nigel admitted with rare honesty. "And I'm heavily in debt. Don't you see, now you've come back, Helen may leave the lot to you? *That's* why my revered mama doesn't love you!"

"Oh. . . ."

It was a very small word, full of understanding. Nigel went on, a little embarrassed in the face of her child-like honesty, to explain the terms of his uncle's will; that will that had been so unfair to Nicole's mother.

"There's plenty for both of us," he concluded a trifle shamefacedly, "though of course you're entitled to the lot."

"But I've told you, I don't want any money!" Nicole shrugged, with a hint of exasperation. "I'm only here for a visit. In a while I shall go away."

"It doesn't matter where you go, Aunt Helen can still leave you the money. Probably she will, anyway, to wipe out the past—— My only hope is for her to realise that we get on well together, you and I. Then she may compromise and split it between us."

"Oh," Nicki said again, with a different inflection. It was growing dark now and she could not see his face, but she felt the effort it had cost him to be honest. She liked him much, much better than she had thought she would. She was also sorry for him, in a way that would have made his ears burn if he could have read her mind.

"If we go about together," he added awkwardly, "and Aunt Helen is pleased . . . if she thinks—well, it will do no harm if she thinks——"

"That we're going to be married?" she demanded, amused.

"Oh, we needn't commit ourselves," he answered hastily, and Nicki jumped up from the seat, still laughing.

"Your debts must be very heavy."

"They are." He stood close to her, rueful, yet relieved that they knew where they stood. "And you will be friends, Nicole? After all, it will only make Aunt Helen happy——"

I have to do such a lot to make Grand'mère happy, she thought suddenly; I have to buy clothes I do not want, and behave like a young lady, and pretend I am liking very much this cousin. . . . Yet it was what her mother would have wished, she felt certain, allowing Helen to die happier. Besides, it was rather fun; it appealed to a mischievous streak in her nature. Also she appreciated the position of the man standing so close, waiting.

"I think if you have waited so long for your fortune," she said definitely, "you should have it." She did not add what was in her heart: that she thought he was making a bad bargain with life. "And of course I'll be friends. I can't promise more."

"Thank you, Nicole, that's all I want."

She moved beside him up the long, smooth grass path with the unselfconscious grace of a wild creature. She did not know that she had shocked Nigel tonight, by her simple creed that was the antithesis of his own sophisticated one, and he had no idea that she was pitying him from the bottom of her heart; pitying a boy whose dreams had been torn from him through the spite of an old man. For to Nicki the integrity of the artist, though she did not use those words, was far more valuable than any amount of money in the bank. And somehow she knew that Nigel, and perhaps his father before him also, could have been an artist with music if he had been left free to choose. . . .

Nevertheless she was grateful to him for being frank. It cleared the air and she did not feel so bewildered, so lonely, so full of dread for tomorrow. This new life was only a game, a sort of game, after all. She gave a tiny skip that was wholly childish, chuckling, "Now I have two friends. You and Jonathan. I shall tell him tomorrow."

"For heaven's sake don't!" Nigel answered, more sharply than he intended. "He doesn't approve of any of us; he's a smug devil. I think he despises us all—Mother and Father and me. It's all right for *him* to be superior, sitting at the top of his profession!"

"Jonathan isn't—smug," she said hotly, "and he has worked hard to get where he is; he is a wonderful surgeon!"

Nigel laughed shortly. "Quite your hero, isn't he? But I wouldn't get too fond of him, if I were you. You're a nice kid, Nicole, but Jonathan has no use for women. It'd be a pity if he broke your heart as well as all the others."

With her hand on the door that led indoors from the conservatory, Nicole swung round to look at her cousin.

She did not like his tone when he spoke of Jonathan; yet tonight he had been honest about his own affairs. What, after all, did she know of Jonathan's life in Combe Castleton, both professional and private? She had only known him on holiday, recovering from an illness. Yet it hurt her inexplicably to hear him spoken of in that casual fashion.

"What do you mean?" she demanded bluntly. "Jonathan doesn't seem the sort of man to enjoy breaking hearts!"

Nigel laughed shortly. "He does it, all the same. He's quite a lion here, you know, and in Harley Street circles. Women throw themselves at his feet, and old Jonathan just smiles and passes on."

He saw the unbelieving expression in her eyes. Until now he had been half teasing, but he thought suddenly that it would be a nice mess if she fell in love with Grant seriously. Aunt Helen would probably be delighted . . . the nephew of her oldest friend and all that. And then he *could* kiss his share of the money good-bye. . . .

"I don't believe you!" Nicki cried softly. "Jonathan is never cruel!"

"I didn't say he was." Nigel felt uncomfortable again. This child was disconcerting. "A man can't help being attractive to women, you know, any more than a woman can help being beautiful. To do him justice, Jonathan avoids all social life when he can—but naturally he can't live entirely like a hermit."

"Why should he want to live like a hermit?" she demanded suddenly. This conservatory was stifling her, the scent of the flowers was overwhelming; not fresh and sweet, like the rose garden outside. She could feel the pounding of her own heart, and was afraid of losing her temper. "He is young and kind, he likes his work—and life—and people! *Why* should he want to live like a hermit, Nigel?"

She felt she had to know. There was something in Jonathan's life that was the key to his almost bitter absorption in his work, that lay behind his teasing irony.

Her cousin shrugged, narrowing his eyes as he looked at her. "I believe you're in love with him, Nicole! If you are, I advise you not to wear your heart on your sleeve. Don't show him what you feel"—he grinned suddenly—"partly because it would finish my prospects with Aunt Helen, but partly because you'd only get hurt, my dear. Jonathan, for all his kindness, does not trust women. I told you, he has no use for them——"

"But why, *why?*" Nicole demanded again, appearing to disregard his advice about wearing her heart on her sleeve. She had no trace of coquette in her, she could no more pretend she did not love Jonathan than she could say she had forgotten her parents . . . but until this moment she had not realised the strength of her love, nor had she any hopes that it would be reciprocated.

Yet, perversely, her cousin's high-handed opinions roused her obstinacy. She defended Jonathan swiftly. "Someone has hurt him," she said thoughtfully, with conviction, "some woman. He's not like that, Jonathan; I tell you, he likes *p eople*, Nigel. . . ."

Nigel laughed shortly. "Then you've seen a different side of him from the good ladies who pursue him so desperately for their daughters and friends!" He added, lighting a fresh cigarette, "I believe he was jilted once. He was engaged to a smashing blonde who married a rich American instead—that was in the days before he made his name, of course."

"Aah. . . ." It was a tiny sigh on the perfumed air of the conservatory. I would like to kill her, the beast, Nicole thought passionately. She wished with all her heart that Jonathan was not a rich and successful surgeon pursued by women, that he had come to Lugano while he was still a struggling young doctor. . . . *She* would have given him love and life and laughter, and in those days he would not have thought of her as a child to be teased and petted and looked after. . . .

Her cousin touched her shoulder lightly. "Don't pay too much attention to that old story, my sweet. If Jonathan had wanted to salve his pride he could have married some very attractive women. I honestly think he prefers his freedom, and that the old scar over Fay has healed long ago. Maybe he finds it very useful. I think he's a born bachelor."

"Maybe." Nicole did not agree with him, but she was learning rapidly. "Anyway, he is my very good friend, Nigel—and I promise not to embarrass him by—by wearing my heart on my sleeve!"

"Good girl," he answered approvingly. "Remember that for the present, anyway. I'm the interesting male in your young life!"

She chuckled. "You make it sound very unromantic!"

"Well, if you want it with soft lights and sweet music, you'd better let me take you to the Milburs' dance to-morrow," Nigel grinned down at her. "Very county. Old friends of Aunt Helen's and all that—sent the invitation as soon as they knew you were coming." He looked at her closely, suddenly, "You'll have to run the gamut of all the old biddies—the dowagers—but, lord, you'll give 'em a shock, Nicole! Do you know you're a very pretty girl?"

"No, I'm not pretty." She shook her head definitely. "And I don't want to impress these old ladies! Besides, I have nothing to wear."

"Ah, now I know you're human!" Nigel was suddenly delighted with her. "I was beginning to wonder if you were an angel! Let Mother choose a frock for you tomorrow—she has decent taste, you know. And if she thinks you're going with me she'll find something just right."

Nicole could not think of anything she would like less than to go to a private dance that was "county"; to run the gamut of a lot of elderly women who knew the story of her mother's runaway marriage, who would be curious and critical; to wear a gown chosen for her by Nigel's mother, that woman with the cold, unsmiling eyes. . . . She would rather, oh, infinitely rather, have gone out with Jonathan in one of the little boats she had glimpsed down in the harbour. But perhaps here at home he would not have time to go out with her in rowing-boats. . . .

"Aunt Helen will be pleased if you come," Nigel urged. He was, suddenly, inexplicably eager to take her to this dance. It was not the sort of dance he could have taken any of his girl friends to, but Helen Stannisford's grand-daughter would be accepted without question. It would be amusing to see how she behaved herself with the old biddies, how she danced——

"Please, Nicole. It will be a good way of breaking the ice, and Fourways is a lovely old house, a Tudor manor. You'll be interested in that, anyway."

"Yes, I will come, thank you," she answered at last in her quaint, old-fashioned way. "Good-night, Cousin Nigel."

"Good-night, Cousin Nicole." He was laughing down at her as he opened the door for her. "Sleep well, for tomorrow you go to the ball!"

She would not sleep well, she thought, in that dreary bedroom with its heavy Victorian furniture looming over her; but she was tired out with all the experiences of the past three days, and she was asleep before she had time to think it all over, as she had intended.

CHAPTER SIX

NICOLE awoke in a panic, to a strange room in a strange house. She had a terrible sensation of loss; she had lost Emilio and Bianca and Pietro, and the *albergo* and her old rowing-boat, and every dear familiar thing she had ever known. She had even lost her friend, Jonathan, she thought wistfully, remembering Nigel's careless confidences. Yesterday Jonathan had gone away, back to his own place, leaving her with all these strangers. . . . Even Jonathan had deserted her. And she had almost promised her grandmother to fall in with all the old lady's plans for her future life—she had quite promised Nigel to go to this big dance tonight in the old manor house. . . .

Panic spread as she lay in the big bed, a small, desolate figure, feeling horribly alone in a world she did not very much care for.

She had not danced very much. Only sometimes with Emilio or one of the insistent tourists at the lake-side cafés . . . and a formal private function might be a very different affair.

A gentle knock on her bedroom door heralded the arrival of a young maid in a pink cotton uniform with her tray of morning tea. She was a pretty girl and Nicole instinctively smiled at her. "Thank you; good morning! What is your name?"

"I'm Annie, Miss Nicole. I 'ope you 'ad a good night after your journey?" The girl was busy drawing back the heavy curtains, which Nicki had thrust aside last night without arranging them properly. She was a pretty girl, bright-faced, and often smiled. Nicki sat up in the big bed that was not as comfortable as it looked, clasping her hands round her knees. Already the sight of someone as young as herself, someone with a friendly smile, made her feel better.

"Breakfast is at nine," Annie vouchsafed shyly, "and Miss Coles gave me a message from Madam for you—she does not come in for breakfast, but she would like you to go to the boudoir when you've 'ad yours."

Annie was breathless with the length of her message,

and added with a run, "And i'm to run your bath for you, miss, when you're ready."

There was not a bathroom to every bedroom at Osterley House, like the hotel, but Nicole had already discovered that there were three: one downstairs for her grandmother only, one on this floor, and one at the top of the house for the staff. She smiled at Annie. "I can run my own bath, thank you—and this is all the breakfast I shall want!" She dealt with the tea, the biscuits and butter. "At home we have coffee and rolls and perhaps fruit. I cannot eat your bacon and eggs in the morning!"

Annie laughed naturally. It was the first time she had seen the new arrival, and Coles and Mrs. Moore had been ever so catty about her luggage, and even Mr. Simpkins had unbent enough to tell them how Madam's granddaughter had tried to shake hands when the staff was introduced to her. "Foreign, that's what she is," the butler had said darkly. "Foreigners are all the same—kiss you on both cheeks one minute, stab you in the back the next!"

Jealous old fogies, Annie thought contemptuously, looking at the face of the girl in the bed. Afraid of changes being made, below-stairs, probably! A few changes might be a good thing, when you come to think of the way Coles and Mrs. Moore, Cook and Simpkins ran the place as if they owned it! And she for one liked the look of Nicole, foreigner or no foreigner.

"I'll tell Mrs. Moore you won't want no breakfast downstairs," she said breathlessly, "and, Miss Nicole, it is nice to 'ave you 'ome! It's *nice* to 'ave someone young about the 'ouse, whatever the old tabbies say!"

With which fervent declaration Annie blushed furiously and almost ran out of the bedroom. Nicki thought it was the first real welcome she had had, except of course her grandmother's, and wished Annie could know how it had cheered her up.

"Good morning, dearest. I'm afraid I'm very lazy, I only get up for lunch," Helen greeted her when Nicole, bathed and wearing a clean linen frock, rather shyly entered the boudoir. "I need not ask if you slept well, you look radiant. Joyce tells me you have quite a programme today—the bank and shopping, and the Milburs' ball tonight. You will like that, child." She smilingly indicated a chaise-longue near the window. "Sit down and let me look at you. You *are* so like Evelyn, my dear—it gives me such happiness to be able to say that."

"Yes, I am like my mother," Nicole said sedately, but she smiled back at Helen. One could not grudge those hungry old eyes their fill.

Helen was pleased that she had made friends with Nigel. "He is a nice boy, but I'm afraid his mother has made him a little extravagant. You will be good for him, Nicole."

Nicki was amused at the idea. Besides, Nigel was a man, not a boy. Only a few years younger than Jonathan, eleven years older than Emilio . . . yet perhaps he was one of those persons who never grow up. Poor Nigel, who could perhaps have been a great artist if he had not been brought up on expectations!

"I am sorry for him," she said expectedly. "I think he might have been a good pianist if my grandfather had not promised him all that money. It is not good for very young people to be promised a fortune without having to work for it."

"Well. . ." Helen was astonished at the child's directness. In her world the subject of inheritances was skirted round with delicacy. She sighed. Henry's money seemed to have done more harm than good, one way and another.

"I do not want you to alter your will, to leave me anything at all." Nicole got up to speak more emphatically, though her tone was respectfully gentle. "I want you to understand that, Grand'mère." She glanced at the luxurious boudoir with a small sigh, felt for the pockets of her slacks that were not there, planted her small feet well apart and clasped her hands behind her back. For an instant she reminded Helen not of Evelyn but of Henry.

"I don't think I could stay with you," Nicki continued firmly, "if all the time we are all thinking about the money, even if we don't talk about it. I can earn my living, I have good friends in Lugano, I don't want the money that might have helped my mother and father. It's bad money."

"Don't say that, child. Money is good or bad according to how one uses it . . ." Helen argued faintly. "But I am glad to know what is in your mind. We will not let the wretched stuff come between *us*, anyway. And I do want you to spend your allowance freely while you are staying here—that at least you can do to please me!"

"I can spend it on anything—anyone—I like?" Nicole asked childishly.

"Exactly how you like," Helen agreed. It was wonderful to have Evelyn's daughter here at last. Wonderful that she had so quickly made friends with Nigel. Perhaps, she thought wistfully, the money would in the end come to them together—and that would satisfy even Henry. There was something straight and strong in this girl that would help Nigel's weakness, and perhaps even Joyce would stop interfering then. . . .

"Thank you, Grand'mère." Nicki stooped and kissed the old cheek softly. "I think you are very kind."

Helen laughed. "Come and show yourself to me when you are dressed this evening," she commanded gently.

"Using the Daimler always makes me feel like minor royalty," Joyce said when Parkinson had ushered them into the car's roomy interior and ensconced himself safely behind the glass partition. Joyce was being affable; she was pleased with the news Nigel had broken at breakfast, and she had complimented her son on being a fast worker. She had not noticed the faint expression of disgust that passed across his face as she spoke. Now she was intent on making friends with Nicole; they might as well make the best of a bad situation. Joyce was suddenly intensely grateful that she had a son, a good-looking, unmarried son, to hook this poor-little-rich-girl. She was sick and tired of being the poor relation, the hanger-on at Osterley House.

"What is minor royalty?" Nicki asked curiously. She was a little amused herself by the way Parkinson put them into the car.

Joyce laughed shortly. "Oh, you know—not the reigning ones, but the cousins and aunts and poor relations." She added without meaning to, "It's years since we had a car of our own."

"I would not want a car, but I would like a boat," Nicole said thoughtfully, as the big car swept gently down towards the harbour. She added quickly, "I would like first to go to Mr. Grant's house, please, Mrs. Stannisford."

"Oh, call me Joyce!" Joyce answered impatiently. "It makes me feel less of a museum piece. We are meeting Mr. Grant at the bank; there's no need to call at his house."

"But I want to see Jonathan," Nicole stated definitely.

Joyce glanced at her curiously. Nigel had not broken any confidences about Nicole's feelings for Jonathan Grant, but yesterday Joyce had not been blind to the girl's sudden affectionate leave-taking in the hall. *That* would be a highly unpleasant and unnecessary complication, she thought. She took a patronising tone. "My dear, I expect you've seen a lot of Jonathan on holiday, but he will be up to his eyes in work, appointments and things, today. He is rather an important person in the medical world, you know. I wouldn't bother him today if I were you."

"There is something I want to see him about," Nicole repeated firmly. Her face did not reveal the hurt of Joyce's words, the very plain warning. As if she did not know she must not make a nuisance of herself to Jonathan! But she wanted so desperately to see him, if only for a moment, to reassure herself that he was still her dear friend, the Jonathan she had known in Lugano, not a stranger . . . the stranger these people were presenting to her as Jonathan Grant.

With a shrug Joyce picked up the speaking-tube and redirected the chauffeur. If the stupid child could not take a hint, maybe it was best to let her make a fool of herself. Jonathan was not the sort of man to welcome interruptions during working hours.

The Georgian house, with its white pillars, appealed to Nicki a great deal more than Osterley House. The step was snowy white, the brasses gleaming on the dark green door, and there was a small discreet plate with Jonathan's name on it, and a row of initials that meant nothing to Nicole. Her heart was thudding ridiculously as she pressed the bell.

A maid in a very neat uniform answered the door and ushered her into the waiting-room. "I am a friend of Mr. Grant's, not a patient," Nicki said eagerly. The girl only smiled at her.

"I'll tell Miss Denbigh. She is the receptionist," she said, and left Nicki among the glossy magazines in the Adam room that was now given over to Jonathan's patients. She looked round at its cool elegance, sniffed the faint smell of polish, and wanted to giggle. There was something very un-Jonathan about this room, even if it was much nicer than the rooms up at the other house . . . something cool and formal that kept one at a distance. . . .

Miss Denbigh swished in, a middle-aged woman with a clever face, well groomed and capable. One guessed that beneath the starched coat she wore a well-cut suit. She smiled at Nicole, but the smile did not reach her eyes.

"Miss Berenger? Good morning. The maid said you are a personal friend of Mr. Grant's, but I'm afraid he does not receive friends here at this hour." She glanced pointedly at her wrist-watch. "He has two doctors with him now; I can't interrupt him—but, of course, if you have an appointment you could wait——"

"I have no appointment," Nicki admitted quietly, her heart heavy within her. Through those heavy folding doors, somewhere, was Jonathan. Jonathan talking about cases with doctors . . . and she had blundered into his consulting rooms like a fool. Her small face was flaming as she made her escape, after thanking the cool Miss Denbigh. What a woman! She was like a dragon protecting her employer from foolish females . . . perhaps that was why Jonathan had her, Nicki thought ruefully.

"My dear! How nice to see you again."

She had almost run into Aunt Bella coming through the hall, an Aunt Bella wearing a gardening apron, trailing raffia, and carrying a big basket of flowers. "Isn't it a heavenly day? Do come and see my garden. Have you been in to see Jonathan?"

"I—I was very stupid to come at this hour." Nicki flushed again vividly and Aunt Bella wanted to hold the slender figure in her arms, to comfort the woebegone child. "Miss Denbigh said he was busy with doctors."

"Oh, Jonathan wouldn't interrupt a consultation to see the Queen!" Bella laughed consolingly. "But I expect he will be so sorry to have missed you, all the same. Could you come and have dinner with us tonight, dear?"

Steve would be cross with her, she thought, but she couldn't help it. If Jonathan were fond of this child—this adorable child—it would do him all the good in the world, and no family match-making should be allowed to spoil it all. . . .

"Thank you, but I have to go to a grand affair—a ball." Nicole grinned her *gamine* grin suddenly, ruefully. "Mrs. Joyce Stannisford is waiting outside now, to take me shopping. But—oh, I would much rather come and have dinner with you! Thank you."

"Run along, then, my dear." Aunt Bella put her arm round the girl's slim shoulders and gave her a little hug. "And don't forget, you are always welcome here. Some other evening, perhaps, when you are free."

When the front door had closed behind her, Aunt Bella went out to the little cloakroom where she always did the flowers, indignant with her menfolk. Even Helen was allowing her family to interfere again with this sweet child.

A grand affair . . . a ball. That could only be the Milburs' dance for Frances's twenty-first birthday. Bella pulled a little face as she arranged the roses carefully. There was an invitation for Jonathan among the pile of personal letters upstairs; she had seen the crest on the back of the envelope. Jonathan had promised to lunch at home today; she would tackle him about it when they were alone and peaceful.

Jonathan himself was not thinking of anything or anyone but the work that had been piling up against his return, until he drove to pay his duty-call on the matron of the nursing home where some of his private patients would be sent.

He presented himself at Matron's office, smiling. She was an elderly woman, kind and capable, and an old friend.

"I've come to show you I'm as good as new, and rarin' to go on the new job," he grinned.

"Why, Jonathan Grant! Let me have a good look at you. You look wonderfully brown and fit—twenty years younger! Come and have some coffee and tell me all about your holiday."

But it was not his holiday they talked about at any length, it was shop. It was always shop one talked with doctors and nurses in the end, he thought ruefully, as he ran down the steps to his car. Obeying an impulse, he stopped on the way home at a shop that sold radio sets and records, and asked rather haughtily for a song about a wild goose.

"'*The Wild Goose Cries*'?" The girl smiled up at him. "That's quite an old record, sir, but it's making a comeback. I'll see if we have one left in stock."

Aunt Bella had an old portable record player somewhere, he remembered. Feeling like a guilty schoolboy, he carried his record into the house, routed out the machine and set it in motion. It was quite absurd, probably Nicole did not even know the tune; yet it was hers, inescapably hers. . . .

He beat time to the haunting tune with his pipe, staring down at the pleasant small garden that was Bella's pride and joy. *Wild goose, brother goose, which is best? A wandering foot or a heart at rest . . . ?*

But would her heart be at rest, even if they persuaded her never to wander again? Would she be happy, his wild and wise little goose, in the conventional atmosphere of the old town, among the old fogies? Would she even be happy if they succeeded in marrying her off to Nigel?

He simply could not imagine Nicole having any time for Nigel Stannisford or his parents, and he was aware of a bitter storm brewing in his own breast. Damn old Henry and his money! Nicole had said she could never be bought . . . but had he not helped to bait this golden trap for her?

"Jonathan! I wondered who on earth could be playing the gramophone—how nice to hear it again, dear." Aunt Bella stood in the doorway, surprised and delighted, her kindly face beaming. "What a queer tune—yet somehow beautiful."

"You darling." Jonathan grinned as he stopped the gramophone, came across and gave her a hug. "Most aunts would have said, oh, something inane. I heard a Negro sergeant always singing that thing in Vietnam and somehow it got under my skin. I think the wild goose was as responsible for my taking a holiday as old Cranford."

"Then I shall love it, too," his aunt replied placidly, "because that holiday has changed you, Jonathan. You're much more human."

He raised one heavy eyebrow at her quizzically. "Was I such a monster before?"

She considered him smilingly. "Not a monster exactly, but there's something wrong when a man forgets how to play, and you were too wrapped up in your work, dear. No man should immerse himself entirely in his job, however important it is and when you came back it wasn't only the wound in your leg that was wrong—that ghastly war had embittered you—but come and eat your lunch or Bessie will give notice."

Stephen Grant was lunching at his club, so there were only the two of them. When justice had been done to Bessie's excellent soufflé, Aunt Bella told him about Nicole's visit. "I ran into the poor child in the hall; your horrid Miss Denbigh had just snubbed her—one could see it in her face."

"Oh, blast. I'm sorry, Aunt Bella, but I had no idea Nicki would think of coming here this morning." He was furious with Denbigh, but he added justly, "Miss Denbigh was only doing her duty, of course. She has strict orders— she didn't know that Nicki is different——"

Bella knew that he was talking chiefly to himself, but

she was delighted to know that, even to Jonathan, Nicole Berenger was different.

"And Nicole, of course, did not know that you would be at work so soon," she said softly. "I *do* like that child, Jonathan. I'm sorry she has to go into Joyce's clutches."

He shrugged his broad shoulders and changed the subject with decision. It was dangerous ground, discussing Nicki with Aunt Bella. The dear, sentimental creature would have him married to the girl in her imagination, and after what Uncle Steve had revealed last night, that was out of the question. Even if she loved him enough, he could not do her out of more than a hundred thousand pounds. He was comfortably off himself, but he had nothing comparable with that fortune to offer her. He wished sometimes that he had left her at the *albergo*, in peace, to work out her own destiny . . . yet even that wish could be selfish, he told himself; it was Nicki's right to have this fortune if she chose.

After lunch Aunt Bella casually produced the sheaf of invitations that had accumulated during Jonathan's absence. "Here's one to the Milburs' ball, dear—Frances's twenty-first, you know—Lavinia would be pleased if you went." .

"What a hope! My dear Aunt—a twenty-first dance should be crammed with trendy young things!" Jonathan looked at his watch. "And probably the hospital will keep me too late to change into glad rags this evening."

"Don't let them," Bella answered calmly. "If you are not careful, Jonathan, they'll have you back in your treadmill within a week—eating, drinking, sleeping surgery! Now this thing of the Milburs' is something you *should* go to—everyone will be there. Frances herself adores you. Besides, you'll be some support for Nicole."

"*Nicole?*" He glared at her. "What has Nicki to do with this affair? What are you up to, Aunt Bella?"

"Nothing, my dear. I had nothing whatever to do with it, I assure you! I know that Helen told Lavinia when Nicole would be arriving, and Lavinia said something about it being in time for Nigel to bring her to the ball. And today Nicole said she had to go to a 'grand' dance . which she seemed to dread a little, so—obviously——"

Nicki. Nicki at Fourways, that lovely old manor house; Nicki, shy, wild little Nicki among all those old snobs, Lady Lavinia being patronisingly sweet to her because she was Helen's granddaughter. . . . Nicki, who was actually a trifle older than Frances, yet who seemed so much younger. Poor little Nicki, they hadn't wasted any time in pushing her into her appointed niche!

"I think that was what she wanted to tell you, dear," Aunt Bella said smoothly. "I'm afraid there isn't time to answer the invitation properly, but I did half promise Lavinia that you would be there. There is always a shortage of young men at a dance nowadays."

"The hell you did!" Jonathan grinned at her wickedly. "When you knew perfectly well that I loathe these full-dress affairs."

Aunt Bella smiled placidly. "I think you'd be a comfort to Nicole," she repeated gently, "and, after all, you are her sort of guardian, aren't you? I mean, you brought her here, and your friendship will be a lot safer for her than young Nigel's——"

It was on the tip of Jonathan's tongue to tell her that her husband was plotting to make Nicki young Nigel's wife, but all he said was, "We'll see what time I get home." Driving furiously up the hill to the hospital, he thought of Nicki as he had first seen her, in old faded jeans and a ragged shirt, and his heart was sore.

"Helen, that woman of yours gives me the shivers!" Stephen Grant smiled as he stooped for a moment, clasping the hands of his old friend.

"Coles?" Helen laughed softly. "Poor Coles! She tries to keep me alive by wrapping me in cotton-wool, Steve. When one considers that she will gain by my death, that is really rather altruistic of her!"

"Oh, I think she's fond of you, in her way. But it's high time we drew up your new will, Helen, if I may say so —the one you made on Henry's death was nothing but a copy of his, after all."

"I know. I was too upset to think very clearly. Nicole is at the hairdresser's, Steve—that is why I sent for you this afternoon."

The tall, silver-haired laywer looked down at her with quizzical despair. "So you had to see her first. What do you think of your granddaughter now you've got her, Helen?"

Helen looked up at him with happy eyes, and he was struck by the renewed youth in her face. She clasped her small hands over the arms of her wheel-chair. "Need you ask? She *is* so like Evelyn, Steve! And not only in looks. She has Eve's loving heart and generosity. . . ."

"I understand that her father was a decent chap, too," Steve contributed dryly. "Well, now we can get down to business. I'll make notes of your wishes, and we'll submit the draft to you within the next few days."

Helen laughed softly. "I thought you had retired, Steve."

An answering smile twitched at the corners of his mouth, and she realised afresh what a distinguished-looking man Stephen Grant was . . . Bella had been lucky. She put the thought firmly behind her, as disloyal to Henry. Poor Henry, whose temper had cut himself off from so many of life's joys. . . .

"I have retired, except for a very few affairs I like to keep in my own hands. Old clients and old friends, like yourself, Helen. Otherwise golf and chess and Bella's beloved garden make up my whole life."

"Well, I'm afraid you are not going to approve of my new will, either, Steve"—the old lady leaned forward a little—"so I wondered if you would rather send some other member of the firm to take the notes?"

She remembered the silver revolving pencil in his hand so well. She could see, even with her eyes shut, Steve's precise movements as he wrote with it, and the beautiful copperplate that evolved. What he called rough notes were never rough scribbles. . . .

"Oh, Helen——" There was a hint of exasperation in his tone. "My dear, I do hope you're not going to—to prolong that old folly of Henry's! I know you won't hear a word against him, but surely enough harm has been done——"

"Yes, enough harm has been done." She spoke almost absent-mindedly. Steve could have shaken her if she had not been so frail. Yet today there was a new resolution about her, some quality he could not place, and there was nothing absent-minded about her when she spoke again, and her faded blue eyes looked directly into his.

"Steve, whether you approve or disapprove of my new will, I want you to know that Nicole does not wish for a great deal of money." Her smile was suddenly reminiscent. "She made herself quite clear on that point this morning."

Stephen shrugged impatiently. "Nicole is a young girl who's probably never had twopence to bless herself with! How can she possibly know whether or not she wants the responsibility of a great fortune?" he demanded irascibly.

Helen sighed. "I think Nicole is wise. Wiser than you, wiser than me, wiser than Henry. Perhaps *because* she has had so little she knows what is really valuable in life. You must leave this to me, Steve. If you are not prepared to draw up the will, I'll get some other firm to do it."

He stared at her. This was a new Helen. A Helen he had not encountered for many, many years. That child Nicole seemed to have bewitched them all, brought something fresh and strong-willed into their lives. Jonathan was subtly changed; Bella was already absurdly fond of the girl; and now Helen.

"Very well." He spoke more heavily than he realised. "You know perfectly well that a lawyer must carry out his client's wishes, my dear—whatever his private opinion of them!"

"Turn round, darling, so I can see better."

Slowly, obediently, Nicole pirouetted in front of her grandmother's chair in the boudoir. All day she had been docile, obedient—ever since that moment of bitter disappointment at not being allowed to see Jonathan. She had managed to compose herself before joining Joyce again in the car; Aunt Bella's kindness had been like a warm fire over the sudden frozen gulf that separated her from Jonathan. And she had no intention of revealing her feelings to the observant Joyce.

"He was busy, of course. Jonathan's time is very valuable, you know," Joyce had observed with some satisfaction.

"I saw Mrs. Grant," Nicole had answered sedately, "and that was very nice. She has invited me to dinner."

The shrewd old busybody, Joyce thought vindictively. Of course she's in the know about Helen's will. . . .

That anyone could take a sudden liking to the little orphan beside her, without regard to her being a possible heiress, did not occur to Joyce. After a lifetime's work on that old brute, Henry, and later on Helen, she thought it would be the last word in unfairness if Paul and Nigel were to see the money slip through their fingers now, almost at the last moment. Helen could not live much longer; Dr. Cranford had been severe in his warnings.

Mr. Grant had been waiting for them at the bank. He had detached Nicole from Joyce with a suave tact that left the older woman in an adjoining office while they proceeded to the manager's sanctum. He felt it incumbent on him to give the child a word of warning when they were alone for a moment.

"Mrs. Stannisford senior has instructed me to place five hundred pounds in your account here, Nicole. You are to spend it how you please; it is a personal allowance. But there is no necessity to tell—er—any other members of the family the figure——"

"Five hundred pounds! But I shall never want to spend as much as that, Mr. Grant!"

He was touched to see that the girl was genuinely shocked by her grandmother's generosity, though he was also afraid her ignorance of money would lead to foolish extravagances—it certainly would if Joyce directed the spending.

"I'm afraid you will have to take the gift, it's all arranged," he answered dryly, wondering how long it would be before Nicole learned to spend money like water, and there was no time for further private conversation. The manager joined them, welcoming Nicole as gravely as if he had heard nothing of her family history, and she was initiated into the mysteries of a cheque book and quarterly bank statements. Her specimen signatures were written with a small defiant flourish because her hand was trembling.

Nicole Berenger. . . . She wrote it proudly, her father's name. It was absurd, of course, but she need not spend the five hundred pounds. She would buy a dress for this ball tonight, and whatever they thought necessary for her wardrobe . . . but nothing else. To be paid five hundred pounds for doing nothing! She had never in her life had an allowance; she did not know whether it had to last a year, or a lifetime, and she was too shy to ask Mr. Grant. He was so like an older Jonathan, yet there was some legal severity in him that was not in Jonathan. She could not take Mr. Grant's hand as they came out on the steps of the bank, looking down the main street of the town to the glittering blue of the harbour, and cry, "Oh, but this place is beautiful! Let's go and find a little boat!" as she would have done with Jonathan.

They had insisted on her writing a cheque for twenty pounds so that she would have some cash on her. The clothes could be paid for by cheque. The crisp new notes were in her handbag now, the handbag she had chosen with Jonathan in Lugano a week ago. It felt like a year ago.

"Well, my dear, I'll leave you to your shopping orgy."
Mr. Grant shook hands with the two women, adding dryly,
"Don't spend it all today," and he went down to his own
car waiting a few yards up the street.

"Stuffy old man!" Joyce settled herself comfortably
back in the Daimler. "I wonder why being a lawyer always
puts red ink instead of blood in a man's veins!"

"I think he is a kind and honourable man," Nicole answered in the old-fashioned manner that exasperated Joyce.
"I like him. Please, Joyce—before we go to the shops—
may we drive round the harbour? I want to look at the
water."

Lord, she's like a child! Joyce thought impatiently, but
she gave the order to Parkinson. She did not want to
antagonise the girl if she was going to be friendly with
Nigel, but she thought the long detour by the harbour road
a complete waste of time.

Nicole was oblivious of everything but the sea, a sea
that reflected an azure summer sky, with dozens of small
boats bobbing on the white-capped waves. This was no
grey and dingy land, as she had always thought of England.
There was colour here—soft, entrancing colour—and the
movement of the light breeze on the water, and the sea-
gulls crying overhead, enchanted her. She forgot the new
responsibility of her bank account; she forgot the shopping ahead; she forgot even the heartache over Jonathan
last night.

"Oh, I would like to take out one of the little boats!"
she cried ecstatically.

"My dear child, there's no time today. We'll be lucky if
we find you a suitable frock ready-made for tonight,"
Joyce replied tartly, and the ecstasy faded from Nicole's
small face like a light being switched off.

"Of course, I'm sorry," she said humbly. For the rest of
the morning she submitted .atiently to the endless shopping, the trying-on, the seemingly inane conversations between Joyce and the saleswomen. These women were not
like the girls in the Lugano shops, with laughter in their
eyes and the knowledge that a woman in love wants to look
her best. They were elderly, for the most part, obsequious
to the name of Stannisford, and deferring to Joyce's opinion.

"The young lady is very slim—very small."

She found herself wanting to giggle. The large, old-fashioned stores contained nothing that would satisfy Joyce.

"White is too obviously *ingénue*," she complained.

They found what she wanted in a small exclusive shop in an arcade overlooking the harbour. And Nicole, when she saw herself gowned in the misty sea-blues and sea-greens of silk chiffon, had to admit Joyce's taste. A halter of sequins in the same colours disguised the thinness of her collarbones, and matched the flowers sprayed over the full skirt. Her golden skin rose out of the frock that was light as sea foam, and she was glad she had swum and sunbathed so often at Lugano, so that there were no ugly patches in her tan.

"You're a lucky girl to have skin like that," Joyce conceded grudgingly. "I think this will do."

"It's very pretty." Suddenly Nicole was shy of looking at herself transformed in the long mirrors. She wished that it was Jonathan taking her to the ball and not Nigel. Jonathan had never seen her look like this. . . . She pulled her thoughts up sharply. He loved her as his little friend, he thought of her as a child, affectionately. She had not really needed Nigel's warning not to throw herself at him as a woman. . . .

"Now for some lingerie, and shoes. I've made an appointment for the hairdresser this afternoon." Joyce was practical; she was pleased that she had dug out such a frock for Nicole in this one-eyed town. It might have been created especially for the girl—and she was not easy to dress, with that unusual colouring and that queer, almost boyish slenderness. There was certainly nothing boyish about her in that gown. . . .

"Thank you, Joyce—for taking so much trouble," Nicole had said at the end of the long morning, feeling churlish because she would so much rather have been out in one of the little boats. She chuckled inside herself, remembering Mr. Grant's caution. It had been all in vain. Joyce had, of course, seen her writing the cheques, and noted her careful sums. The evening dress alone had cost something terrible; the memory of it froze her now as she turned for her grandmother's inspection. The hairdresser, in the salon in one of the big hotels, had done her hair differently, too; the soft fair curls were done in demure Victorian ringlets. And Joyce had helped her to make up; a process which for Nicole usually consisted of dabbing her nose with powder when she remembered it. "Very little

I think—just a touch of eye-shadow and lipstick." Joyce had been almost softened by the results of her handiwork. The girl certainly paid for dressing and grooming. If Nigel had to get married, she would rather have this quaint child for a daughter-in-law than one of his usual girl friends.

"There. Run along and show yourself to Helen," she had said, almost kindly, and hoped that Helen would appreciate the trouble she had taken.

"This gown cost thirty-five guineas, Grand'mère," Nicole said tremulously. She had already thanked her for the allowance, but she felt this was a ridiculous price for one frock. It would have kept them all in food at the *albergo* for a month. "I think I shall not need any more evening dresses."

"Nicole, you must spend your allowance just as you please—and don't worry me with the price of each article! Helen smiled to soften the admonition. "You look charming, darling—charming. Now bring me the box on that chair."

She selected the antique silver and sapphire set of necklace and ear-rings, and made Nicole stoop so that she could fasten them herself. "Those are perfect with that frock. You must keep them, darling, with my love. I always meant Evelyn to have them."

There was nothing to be done against this blackmail of love, Nicki decided, as she kissed her grandmother impetuously and ran down the passage to the waiting Nigel. When he saw her his eyes brightened and he took a step forward. "Nicole! You look like a princess! I told you Mother is clever about clothes."

Nicole privately thought his mother was clever about a lot of things, but she could not help being excited. Grand'-mère had stared at her entranced, and no man had ever looked at her as Nigel had just now. On the long drive through the warm summer evening she could not help enjoying her new grandeur, though she reminded herself quizzically that Nigel's admiration was not for herself alone. She represented to him a great fortune.

"You all make me feel like Cinderella," she said laughingly.

"But you won't have to return at midnight," Nigel grinned.

The old manor house delighted her, as they had promised it would. It was all, to Nicki, like a fairy-tale, with the Milburs receiving their guests in the great Tudor hall, the gallery festooned with flowers and creepers, and the orchestra playing in the ballroom beyond. Lady Lavinia was charming to her, and Frances accepted her shy birthday wishes gaily.

"Phew! Thank goodness that's over—now we can dance," Nigel said. Nicole wished she had not to dance; she wanted to hide herself away up on the gallery and watch this party. She wanted to explore this lovely old mansion. But as the evening wore on and she found dancing with Nigel much easier than she had expected, and other men looked at her with that expression of open admiration in their eyes, she found herself being a little intoxicated by it all. It was, after all, fun . . . to be young, and dancing; to have men look at you as if you were a woman and not a child; to be wearing the most exquisite frock you had ever possessed. . . .

If only Jonathan were here, it would be perfect, her unruly heart whispered. As if in answer, she heard Nigel's voice laughingly close to her ear.

"What did I tell you about Jonathan? Look at the way young Fran is adoring him! With her mother's full approval, too, I bet."

Jonathan was there. Across the ballroom she saw him, dancing with Frances Milbur. And Frances was gazing up at him with the entranced look of a woman in love, a woman careless of what anyone else might see or think.

In the same instant, as if drawn across the crowded room by their thoughts, Jonathan's eyes met Nicki's, and widened a little in surprise, and smiled suddenly before he stooped slightly to answer some remark of his partner's. And Nicki longed for the earth to open and swallow her up; she thought he was laughing at her. Laughing about the transformed Cinderella with that girl—Frances—a girl of her own age, who was so very, very different from Nicole Berenger. A girl who was utterly at home in this lovely house, among these people; a girl who was more beautiful, more sophisticated, than she could ever hope to be.

Jonathan was stunned. A less civilised man would have had his mouth hanging open, his eyes on stalks. He had expected changes in Nicole . . . their little shopping expedition in Lugano had opened his eyes to her possibilities . . . and of course she would have to be dressed up for a show like this ball. He had not expected such a complete transformation. It wasn't only the dress, though

154

that made her look enchanting; it was the poise of the girl, the way she seemed so happy dancing with her cousin. With that stuffed shirt, Nigel Stannisford.

It gave him a queer, cold feeling down his spine, in spite of the warmth in the ballroom, the fragrance and soft lights, the music and the girl he held in his arms. Only this afternoon he had been thinking of Nicki as she had been on his arrival at Lugano—that slim, shabby, boyish little gypsy . . . and now in a few short hours they had turned her into a lovely young woman. He was not oblivious of the other male eyes glancing at Nicole, lingering on her radiant face.

And he had come here to give her moral support!

Fortunately he managed to smile across at Nicki, fortunately his face did not give away his thoughts.

"What are you looking so pleased about?" Frances demanded.

He stooped a little to reply, transferring the smile he had managed to produce for Nicki to Fran. She was taller than Nicki, a very different type; one would never think of Frances as a sweet, wild child. . . .

He pulled his thoughts up abruptly, wishing he had not come. Aunt Bella had been right off the mark this time. Except, of course, that Frances and her mother were pleased; he could not very well avoid the realisation that Fran was falling in love with him—or thought she was—and Lady Lavinia had practically given her public blessing to the idea. Jonathan was sorry for Frances, who was missing a lot of fun with her own young set to dance with him—but she had almost demanded it, and it was her party——

"I was thinking what a magnificent show you're putting on tonight, young Fran—nice party. I haven't seen Fourways look like this since I was at school."

"If you're trying to remind me that you're old enough to remember me in my cradle, forget it, Jonathan!" The Honourable Frances laughed up at him knowingly.

"But I *did*," he assured her with mock gravity. "I was a schoolboy, admittedly, but the last time I came to a party here you were three years old—a little horror!"

"Poor old man, I'm glad you can still dance," she teased him gaily, but she was seething inwardly. For the rest of the evening she would try different tactics, dance with the younger men, make him jealous. "I'm glad you are enjoying it, anyway," she added lightly. "We were

155

afraid you'd be stuffy as usual and not come, and that would have *ruined* my evening!"

"My dear child"—he laughed shortly, feeling a hypocrite and a humbug because he was trying to be avuncular with Fran, whereas Nicki—a year older than Fran—did not make him feel at all like an uncle—"*nothing* can spoil one's twenty-first!"

Frances was no fool, though she was willing to be foolish over one particular man. She had seen the tenderness in his eyes when he smiled across at Nicole Berenger. She remembered suddenly that he had brought her back from Switzerland. She glanced up at him shrewdly. "There's something fascinating about your little friend, Nicole," she ventured thoughtfully. "Mother was quite taken with her, and, of course, Nigel is head-over-heels already."

"Is he?" Jonathan was dryly non-committal.

"Oh, Nig knows which side his bread is buttered, I daresay, but Nicole is a girl any man could fall for, isn't she? Your dear aunt and uncle didn't tell us you were bringing home a raving beauty!" Fran tried again, casually.

He laughed shortly. "Because I hadn't described her as a raving beauty, I expect. She's only a child, Fran——"

"Oh, you're infuriating!" Frances gave him a little shake as the music ended and he handed her over to her next partner. She suspected him of posing a little in his attitude towards young girls; he was not as old as all that. Yet the fact remained that he had not married . . . and Fran had no intention of throwing herself away for any lost love. She would keep one or two men in reserve, just in case. . . . Only a child, indeed!

It was at the buffet supper that Jonathan came over to speak to Nicole. Until then they seemed to have been separated by an ocean of shining parquet floor, by an army of people. Nigel greeted him before moving away to speak to some of his other friends. Nicole and Jonathan were left standing by the laden buffet, decorated with flowers and garlands of greenery and tender ferns. In the ballroom beyond the orchestra still played—the last tune before the supper interval. There was a gay crowd at the buffet; the colours of the women's dresses set off by the sombre black-and-white of the men, and much laughter and snatches of conversation. Frances was the centre of a laughing group at the far end of the table. For a brief moment Jonathan and Nicole might have been alone, as it is possible to be alone in a crowd.

"Well?" He dropped the little word at her, the lines round his eyes deep with laughter and something else she could not fathom. "You look different, Nicki—like a fairy-tale princess or something. Quite a stranger."

She flushed a little beneath the skilful make-up. "So do you." There was a tiny, half-defiant gasp in her low voice. "I've never seen you in this *grandeur* before! Now you look like Jonathan Grant, the famous surgeon . . . the so successful surgeon. And I thought you said once you did not like dances, parties!"

Somehow she had turned the tables on him. He could not guess that she thought he looked heartbreakingly distinguished in his evening clothes, yet removed still further from her; that she was bitterly disappointed because he was laughing at her, instead of praising her lovely dress.

He said ruefully, "Aunt Bella made me come tonight, Nicki. She had the mistaken idea that you might need a friend among all these strangers. That you might even be—scared."

So he had come to look after her . . . not merely to dance with Frances, who obviously adored him. Nicki's blue eyes were shining like the Swiss gentians as she looked up at him; her tender mouth smiled a little, suddenly. "Oh, but I *was* terrified! How kind of Aunt Bella, how kind of you, Jonathan. I thought you had gone away and left me to my fate."

Incredibly, there were tears in her eyes. As he passed her the champagne cup their hands touched for an instant, and he knew that she had not changed. Under the hubbub all round them he said quickly, "I'll never do that, Nicki. I'll always be your friend. I want you to understand that, if they try and force you to do anything you don't want to do. Anything at all. Will you remember that?"

It was as much as he dared say. She trusted him, she had always trusted him, so completely. Yet he could not encourage her to throw away a fortune for his sake. If she chose Nigel and great wealth, that was that; but the choice must be hers, freely made. He would not stand by and see her being forced into anything.

"I'll remember." She blinked back the tears. "It seems such a long time since yesterday, Jonathan! And this morning your Miss Denbigh made me feel like a worm."

He grinned suddenly. "Come and see the garden, that's the place for worms. Let's get out of this."

The grounds of Fourways were magnificent, the smooth

velvet turf of the terrace was guarded by high elms. Lanterns were hung in the trees and among the flowering shrubs, and the night was warm and scented. From the edge of the terrace the house was gloriously illuminated, and from the open french windows of the ballroom a great swathe of golden light made the grass look like a glowing emerald.

"Old England at her best," Jonathan said quietly, when they had turned at the sloping edge of the terrace. Most of the guests outside were strolling near the house. Here in the shadows they were quite alone. Jonathan, standing beside her, seemed very tall, very dark; as he had said, they were suddenly like strangers.

"It's beautiful, like something out of a book," she agreed softly, "but too grand for me. I wouldn't like to live always in a mansion, Jonathan."

He glanced at her smilingly. "You haven't done so badly tonight, Nicki. You look magnificent. I didn't know you could dance."

At last he had praised her, though "magnificent" was not the adjective she longed to hear. She was suddenly absurdly happy. "No, we never went to any of the cafés on the lake, did we? Because Pietro was ill. . . . I hope he is not missing me too much, *il poverillo*."

She said naively, "It is easy to dance with Nigel. He is very good."

He's had plenty of practice, Jonathan wanted to snarl, but grinned instead. "Well you can dance the next one with me, and suffer for my sins."

"To please Aunt Bella?" she asked with shrewd mischief.

"To please Aunt Bella," he agreed gravely, adding quietly, "And don't fret your heart out over Pietro, little one. We'll have him over soon."

"Oh, you haven't forgotten," she cried happily, and the music started again, dragging them indoors. But waltzing with Jonathan was very different from dancing with Nigel. Then she had been just a young girl wearing her first pretty dress, a little intoxicated by the music, the atmosphere of gaiety, the novelty of power. In Jonathan's arms she forgot the rest of the world entirely; they were like one person. . . .

"Why," she said in sudden surprise, "you can dance even better than Nigel, your leg is not stiff any more!"

"Don't talk," he commanded abruptly. "Let yourself go—just let your feet listen to the music."

She was very willing not to talk. It was all she asked, she thought childishly, to dance like this with Jonathan. If only they could go on like this for ever, until he forgot the woman who had spoiled his life; until he forgot that she, Nicole, was in his eyes a silly child. . . .

She did not feel a silly child any more. That much, at least, Joyce's careful shopping and Nigel's admiration had done for her. And with Jonathan's strong but gentle hold of her body she knew she was a woman, and a woman in love. He must be very blind or very bitter, she thought, not to realise the strength of her love, holding her close like this.

"Thank you, Nicki." The music had stopped; he was leading her back to Nigel, who was waiting with a quizzical expression on his lazy, good-natured face. "I'm leaving now, I have to operate in the morning. I'm afraid we shan't see much of each other for a while, but you can always get hold of me through Aunt Bella. And if Joyce and young Nigel bother you——" He broke off abruptly, though they were still half the length of the ballroom away from her waiting escort.

"Don't worry about Nigel, I like him. I'm sorry for him. I think my grandfather treated him abominably," Nicole said softly, to Jonathan's amazement. He had not expected Nicki to be sorry for Nigel. Anything but that. She added with quaint dignity, "And I will not bother you at your rooms again."

CHAPTER SEVEN

For Nicole it was a long, tedious month that followed the Milburs' ball. Jonathan had been right . . . they saw nothing of each other. It was true that, during his absence in Vietnam and his long vacation, work had piled up for him—professional consultations, treatments, operations, and conferences. But Nicki thought he could have made time to see her, if only for a few moments, if he had wanted to . . . and she was determined not to contact him through Aunt Bella again unless there was some real crisis in her life.

She wrote regularly to all of them at the *albergo*, making light of her loneliness and boredom, describing in some

159

detail for their entertainment the house of her grandmother, the new clothes she had been given, the grand ball that had been her entrance to local society. But she did not emphasise the cost of her new status; she laughed at it, so that they could laugh at it too.

There are so many things a young lady must not do here, she wrote to Emilio, smiling as she wrote, though her heart was heavy. *There is a harbour full of little boats, but I cannot go and row myself about the sea wearing the clothes I have always worn; it upsets Grand'mère to see me looking like a ragamuffin, she says, but I think she is frightened of what the servants will think! I must go down in a pretty summer frock, and hire an old boatman to take me out—ME!*

She did not write that she was bored, bored, bored with living in a house that was staid and fusty with Victorian stuffiness; with having no work to do, and no one of her own age to play with, except perhaps Nigel at the weekends. She went exploring the old town alone, always ending up by the harbour, and wrote careful descriptions in her letters. She was looking forward passionately to having Pietro for a visit. Helen had indulged her by consenting to the little boy's coming. Nicole hardly realised herself how much she missed the children, and having the responsibility of their welfare; the scoldings of Lucia and the laughing teasing of Emilio. She watched the post eagerly for the flimsy air-mail envelopes bringing her news of Gandria, but they were few and far between. Emilio, though he enjoyed her letters, was lazy about replying to them. Old Lucia could not write, though she sent Nicole many loving messages and admonitions. Nicki had to reply on Bianca's careless scribbles for her news, and Pietro's large, childish writing was most faithful of all. Pietro was looking forward to his trip to England as passionately as Nicki herself, though she knew it was chiefly so that he would have something to brag about when he went back to school.

Osterley House, after the dramatic impact of her arrival and the Milburs' dance, had settled down again into its slow, precise routine that revolved round a frail old lady, And though she had developed a real affection for Helen, Nicki's young vital strength had no outlet in that direction. She was for ever guarding her impulsive tongue so as not to upset her grandmother. She was for ever having to do things she did not really want to do.

"They are making a robot of you, Nicki Berenger!" she told her reflection savagely one day. She was wearing jodhpurs and brogues polished like chestnuts; a well-fitting jacket that had been tailored for her by Nigel's own tailor. *Correct wear for young English lady going riding. . . .*

The rebellion of years made her resent being turned into a young lady, the habits of her free life at the *albergo* made all these new restrictions irksome. In a quiet way she was being sent to school again . . . and there were so many little things to learn! Yet even as she stared so savagely at herself in the mirror she knew she looked nice in riding clothes, in the beautifully tailored things. And in spite of herself she felt drawn to so many English customs; already she loved the coast, the harbour, the rolling hills and the moorland above—her English blood felt suddenly, wonderfully at home. Everywhere except at Osterley House, a fact she tried hard to hide from Helen in case it hurt the old lady's feelings. If only—if she could have lived in one of the fishermen's cottages down by the wharf, or even in one of the small moorland farms! There were days during that hot July when Nicole—used to the much greater heat of Lugano—felt she would stifle.

There was a riding school beyond the town, on the road up to the moor, and almost every week-end Nigel drove her up for her riding lesson. Nicole had never had much to do with horses beyond taking apples and sugar to the line of patient carriage-hacks that waited by the lake-side in Lugano to take tourists for drives. At first she was frightened, the mount they gave her at the school seemed enormous, but she was too proud to confess her fear to Nigel and the riding master, and after a few lessons she conquered it. She grew attached to old Prince, who was docile in spite of his size, and quickly learned how to control him.

"You should come up several times during the week," Nigel told her, "then in a short time you'll be able to ride with me over the moor."

Mr. Bates, the riding master, was an Australian. He taught her to have a good seat by riding bareback at first, with only a single rein. "Get the feel of your horse, make yourself part of him, learn to control him as much with your knees as with the rein," he advised patiently. He was a big, loosely knit man still brown from many Australian summers, and he looked clumsy until he sat a horse. He liked Nicole because she was different from the average run of his pupils; he understood all about her first fears though she never mentioned them, and he admired her because she laughed and picked herself up quickly when she took her first toss, jumping.

"Get right back on again," Mr. Bates grinned encouragingly, "and make him take that hurdle feeling that you're cemented to his back!"

"Do I *have* to jump?" Nicki pleaded, but there was laughter in her eyes as she rubbed her aching behind. She knew that the fall had been her fault, and not Prince's.

"Certainly you have to jump." Mr. Bates led her mount up to her. "This is a hunting county. By Christmas you'll be taking fences with the best of 'em."

"I shall *never* hunt," Nicki proclaimed stubbornly. "I should hate it. But I suppose I must learn to jump——" She thought, by Christmas I may not be here. . . .

There had been no time limit laid down for her visit. She had made it plain that it *was* only a visit, that she should be free to go away when she chose. Yet in her heart she knew that she would not find the hardness to leave her grandmother very easily.

She threw off her sombre thoughts as she remounted. In July Christmas seemed a long way off, and there was Pietro's visit coming closer and closer. Pietro, she thought, would love to learn to ride . . . she could pay for his lessons out of her allowance.

One day when she and Nigel were riding down from the moor, her face flushed and laughing from her first good gallop, her curls blown by the wind, Jonathan passed them in his car. He did not stop; he was on his way to an urgent call at a lonely farmhouse, and Nicole had not even seen him. But for days he carried about with him the vision of her laughing, radiant face as she turned to say something to her cousin; her easy seat on the big horse, her obvious enjoyment. He knew nothing of the many painful lessons that had preceded that day, the back-ache and the fears, or that Nicki had something to be triumphant about because both Nigel and Mr. Bates had complimented her, and she no longer had any fear of Prince. She could control him, or any horse, and there was something wonderfully exhilarating about a gallop across the moor. For a little while she had been free. . . .

"You're only pint-size, but you have good muscles," Mr. Bates had teased her.

Jonathan remembered only the look on the girl's face, her laughing ease, the cut of her riding clothes. So the experiment of turning his little wild goose into a young lady of fashion, with all suitable accomplishments, was succeeding. . . .

He called himself a dog-in-the-manger because he was not pleased at her success. Then, slowing to take the rutted driveway to the farm, he saw the other doctor waiting for him and forgot Nicki completely.

The daily riding lessons were fun, Nicki decided. She and Nigel had struck up a friendship that was cheerful without being intimate. He was surprised to find her good company, amusing and undemanding, yet wise in her quaint manner; and Nicki, while she never talked to him as naturally as she had done to Jonathan, was still sorry for him. His mother dominated his life, and the time he spent with Nicole enabled him to escape into comparative freedom.

"If I ever do get hold of any cash, I shall live in America," he confessed one day. "I'm sick to death of Mother's moaning and the office. Would you like to live there, Nicki?"

"Is this a proposal?" she smiled. She knew Nigel well enough to tease him now. Lucia would have called him a wet fish to let his mother dominate his life, but Nicole was beginning to understand how it had come about. A boy of twelve could be so easily influenced . . . why, he had been only two years older than Pietro when her grandfather had started talking to him about the money he would inherit one day. . . .

"No." He grinned at her. "I'm waiting until you grow up, darling, before I propose." He added in a different tone, "I doubt if I shall ever marry. After Aunt Helen's tragedy and the way my parents have conducted their married life, I've lost faith in—permanent contracts."

She started talking of something else. Marriage described as a permanent contract sounded horrible to her, but she could understand well enough that any ideals Nigel had possessed had been well and truly killed. She was fervently grateful, then, for the happy memories left her by her own parents . . . perhaps the best legacy any parents can leave.

The riding took up an hour or so from each long summer day, and Nicole insisted upon swimming. No one was going to keep her away from the water. Helen objected gently to her going alone to the crowded beaches.

"It is holiday time, my dear. I'm afraid even Combe

Castleton gets crowded with trippers at this time of the year."

Nicole had laughed. "But I like people, Grand'mère! And I am used to tourists. After all, they kept me for many years."

She had dropped a brick again. Always when she talked with her grandmother, it was Evelyn they talked about. Helen wanted to hear every anecdote about her daughter that Nicole could rake up from her memory; and the girl so loved her mother that it was easy to remember. But always, always, there were the rocks sticking up perilously from the sea of memory. . . .

Nicki was beginning to understand her grandmother. From many little bits of information she had made a whole picture of Henry Stannisford, and disliked him more and more. But Helen had had to live him him for nearly half a century. She had had no choice, according to her strict upbringing, but in order to endure her husband's harshness she had had to build a little world of her own, away from realities. Helen was a gentle, tired, sad woman, but in some ways she was younger than Nicole, and in many ways more narrow and conventional. One did not betray one's husband; one did not speak ill of the dead. Though she was Edwardian, Helen was in heart and mind a rigid Victorian; she had kept herself as she had kept Osterley House, a century behind the times.

She did not encourage Nicole to chatter of the Fionettis, who had befriended Evelyn when her own father would not help her. She did not like to be reminded that her granddaughter had earned her living by painting bad pictures and taking parties of tourists round Lake Lugano.

"I would like you to take one of the servants with you, Nicole, if you must go to the beach," she said a little distantly.

Inwardly Nicki groaned, thinking of Coles and Mrs. Moore and the rest of the staff. Parkinson might be the best of a bad bunch, but she could not take Parkinson away from the car in case her grandmother wished to go for one of her rare drives. . . . "Let me take Annie, then," she begged suddenly. "Annie is a dear!"

Helen frowned again slightly. "Very well. But don't let her become familiar with you, Nicole."

Annie was young. The only person in the whole of Osterley House who really liked Nicki, who laughed rather shyly at her jokes. Annie was delighted to accompany

Miss Nicole on her daily expedition to the beach, whenever it was warm enough; but Annie, born and brought up by the sea, did not swim. She sat sedately in a deck-chair and minded the towels, and looked like an anxious terrier when her young mistress swam too far out. After the swim the two girls sat together for a while in the sunshine, drinking coffee or eating ice-cream from the kiosk, and Nicki would try to draw her out.

"Have you ever been in love, Annie?"

"What, me, miss? Oh, no, Miss Nicole. Mum 'ad eleven kids and that don't give us much time for falling in love, like."

Nicole laughed. She tried to get Annie to talk about her home, and her brothers and sisters, but the girl was too shy. She would only come out of her shell to laugh at one of Nicki's little jokes, or admire her clothes, or the new way she was doing her hair. And when Nicki got into conversation, as she invariably did, with other people on the crowded beach, Annie would suggest respectfully that it was time to go home.

"Mrs. Moore's that cross if we're late for lunch, miss—" or tea, as the case might be. Inwardly amused and a little exasperated, Nicole knew that even young Annie had been sent as a sort of watchdog to see that she made no undesirable acquaintances. It made her feel more trapped than ever.

There was a small cliff railway to the town beach. Because it reminded Nicki of the Swiss funiculars, she loved it. But Annie resented the packed, swaying crowd of humanity that used it during the holiday season. And Nicole learned the odd fact that English servants are even more snobbish than their employers. Coles snubbed her by implying that she tired her grandmother unnecessarily, Mrs. Moore snubbed her when she tried to take an interest in the housekeeping, and her one and only visit to the kitchen to see Cook had been a complete failure.

"There's other prettier beaches along the coast," Annie vouchsafed one day, "where there's not such a mob, Miss Nicole."

"But I don't mind the crowd," Nicki argued firmly, and it was true. She liked seeing the families sitting on the sand, the children enjoying themselves, the young people sun-bathing on their brief holidays, the swimmers. She did not explain to Annie that she knew about those other, smaller, prettier beaches because Jonathan had told her about them, or that she was still absurdly hoping he would take her to them one day.

Riding and swimming, while the weather lasted, were fun; but there still seemed to Nicki an endless day to fill in. And at the end of July the weather broke in a thunderstorm and lashing rain. Her grandmother had a slight relapse and had to stay in bed. Nicki had made friends with Dr. Cranford, who made regular weekly visits to the house, but on this visit his face was graver than usual. The heart specialist had left when he spoke to Nicki.

"There is nothing to worry about immediately," he told the suddenly frightened girl, "but it is essential that your grandmother should have no shocks, no extra strain whatever. I'm afraid a young boy about the house would be very unwise, at the moment——"

"But Pietro is such a sensible child!" she cried with real dismay. "All the time he would be out of doors, with me!"

Dr. Cranford glanced out of the study window at the teeming rain. "I'm afraid our weather is not reliable, Miss Berenger—and an active ten-year old can make a lot of havoc in a quiet, elderly household like this. I advise you to postpone his visit."

Disappointment tore at her heart like a burning pain. In that moment she hated Osterley House fiercely. But it was no use explaining to the doctor that to postpone Pietro's visit would break the child's heart . . . he must go back to school in the autumn, and three or four months' delay to a little boy would seem like a lifetime.

In a sort of frozen sadness she went slowly along to the boudoir. Coles answered her gentle knock on the door and whispered unnecessarily, "Madame is resting, Miss Nicole; it would be best not to disturb her."

The whole dark, looming house seemed like a cage about Nicki, shutting her in, stifling her. She rushed up to her bedroom and threw on a raincoat she had brought from Lugano, a shabby old thing she had never worn before in England. She pulled a hat ferociously over her hair and ran down the stairs and out of the horrible house. She just remembered not to slam the heavy front door behind her, in case it woke Helen. She ran and ran, heedless of the deluge about her, down the drive among the sodden rhododendrons, down the hill past the cathedral close that she loved, without a glance in its direction. Down, on into the town, running as if the devils of Osterley House were at her heels, to Jonathan. He was the only person who could help her now, who could save a boy's heart from breaking; Jonathan had promised Pietro . . . today he would have to see her. She would find him somehow, if she had to go to the hospital, if she had to wait until midnight. . . .

"Please, I must see Jonathan," she told Aunt Bella when she came to the door. It was Bessie's afternoon off, and she had been getting the tea ready.

"My dear, of course you shall—he's upstairs in his study, the first door on the left"—Bella smiled kindly at the distraught child—"but do take those wet things off first."

She was talking to space. Nicole had rushed up the stairs, a small, dripping whirlwind. She opened the door without knocking; it was no use knocking when he had the radio on so loudly in there. But it was not a radio, it was a portable record player. Jonathan was stretched in a low chair beside it, smoking his pipe, an odd expression on his face as he listened to the queer, haunting tune. Nicki paused on the threshold, her anxiety forgotten for a moment in her surprise.

"*I must go where the wild goose cries. . . . Wild goose, brother goose, which is best? A wandering foot or a heart at rest . . . ?*"

"*Jonathan!*" She was hardly aware that she cried aloud, until he jumped up and stopped the turntable and smiled at her. He had looked like a man in love, a man dreaming of his love. . . .

"That's your tune, Nicki . . . you're a little wild goose, you know." He spoke like a man coming out of a dream, accepting her presence there without surprise, until he saw her face properly and her sodden clothes. "Darling! Whatever's the matter—what have they been doing to you?" In two strides he had come to her and folded her close, and she laid her face against him and wept with long, shuddering sobs.

The only other time Nicki had wept in his presence, in his arms, had been the night of Pietro's operation. Those had been very different tears, tears of relief and joy. The long, shuddering sobs that shook her small body now dismayed Jonathan terribly; he had been buoying himself up recently with the knowledge that the child was obviously adapting herself to life at Osterley House very well. He had told himself that he had been a fool to imagine she would

be different from any other girl of her age, suddenly pre
sented with a comfortable life and the prospect of being
able to buy almost anything she desired within a few years.
He had resolutely turned his back on his memories of
Nicki, young and proud, yet so very wise, when she had
first confided her family history to him, when she had so
practically and yet so idealistically confided her philosophy
of life.

Yet, when he had a little leisure, like this free afternoon,
he found himself remembering. And playing that absurd
record. It haunted him, anyway; he thought that playing it
over and over might exorcise that wretched tune. . . .

And now Nicki had come to him, very dear and like
her old self in the shabby raincoat, with the water dripping
off her on to his study carpet. He let her cry out the first
storm, holding her firmly in his arms and making the
small, inarticulate sounds of comfort that one gives to
children in trouble. Then, very gently, he stripped off the
soaking raincoat and took the hat from her head. "I'll put
the electric fire on, darling, and dry you off—and myself.
Look at my shirt!"

A wan smile rewarded the tiny joke. Hope—ridiculous, impossible hope—was surging in Jonathan's heart.
He put her into a low chair in front of the fire, sat on the
floor and took her hands between his own, smiling because
she had had to use both his handkerchiefs to mop herself up
with, and ended by blowing her small nose like a trumpet.
His Nicki had always blown her nose in a most unladylike
way.

"Now, little one, let's have it. I thought you were
getting on so well at Osterley House—according to Uncle
Steve, Helen adores you and only wants to lay the world at
your feet, and your cousin Nigel has fallen nicely into line
with all her plans——"

"I *hate* it there!" Nicki almost shouted contemptuously,
"I am so bored I could jump over a cliff! Grand'mère is all
right, but she doesn't understand anything; she lives in a
world that has been dead for a hundred years."

Jonathan smiled involuntarily. Nicki always hit the
nail on the head so neatly. "Yet she loves you, I think." He
reminded her gently, "She likes giving you things."

Nicole nodded slowly. "Yes. And to please her I have
to—to pretend *I* like being given things. *I*—Nicole
Berenger!"

He laid his fingers lightly across her lips. "Come off your soap-box, darling. I know—we all know—that you're an independent little hussy. That you're accepting everything to please an old lady who cannot live very long. But you can't tell me that you haven't enjoyed wearing pretty clothes—going to dances with Nigel—and riding. I saw you out riding once, Nicki—and you looked very happy."

She nodded. "Of course I like my new pretty clothes!" She thought shyly, *Because I hoped you would see me looking nice.* . . . "But even you don't understand. To please Grand'mère I have to lead such a dull life—you wouldn't believe how dull. I am not even allowed to go swimming alone, I have to take Annie, one of the maids, down to the beach with me every time!"

Remembering Lugano he could understand her irritation with the perpetual small restrictions of life at Osterley House.

"But you have sense, Nicki. It will not be for ever. And if it gets too cramped you can leave——"

"Oh, no. I came because I thought that, too. But Dr. Cranford is always warning me that Grand'mère must not be upset in any way—how can I escape when I know that it would be a bad shock for her?" Nicki spoke with a sad finality that was new to her. "And I do not want to wish her dead, that would be terrible. But yesterday she was not so well, and now they will not have Pietro . . ." The tears welled into her eyes again suddenly, and she brushed them away with the back of her hand impatiently. "Dr. Cranford talked about him this morning as if he was an ordinary, stupid little boy who will make a great upset in the house! Jonathan, I can't bear to stay there if they break Pietro's heart! Every week he has written to me, counting the days——"

"And you've been counting the days, too, my poor poppet," he answered, smiling, "but that's nothing to worry about, Nicki. We'll have Pietro here. Aunt Bella adores children."

"Oh—oh, Jonathan, *could* you?"

Like a child she looked up at him, trustingly, the fury and the grief suddenly wiped from her tear-stained face. He nodded and spoke cheerfully, though his heart sank a little. If this was all. . . . He was conscious that he had had an ignoble hope that somehow Nigel had antagonised Nicki. But she had not come to him on her own behalf, only on Pietro's. Or chiefly because of Pietro.

"He will have a much better holiday with Aunt Bella," he added casually, and could not help the thought, *And we will see more of you, my darling.* . . . "She understands children."

"I think your Aunt Bella understands everyone," Nicki said shakily, with the laughter coming through her tears like spring sunshine breaking through the clouds. Then her face fell again. "But you have your consulting rooms here, Jonathan—this is a professional house—perhaps Pietro will be a nuisance here, also?"

Jonathan grinned. "Not a chance—Miss Denbigh would see to that! But I have a better idea—I have a boat, you know."

"No, you never told me." Her eyes were bright as stars. "Oh, Jonathan! Why have you not let me use your boat all this long time?"

"Because I keep her down the coast, and I imagined your grandmother would not let you go out alone in a small boat"—and because I had no intention of letting Nigel take you out in *Bluebird*, his honest mind added—"and because it's different from the lake here, Nicki. We have currents and tides and rocks along this coast—can you sail?"

She nodded vehemently. "Of course I can sail, and I know about navigation. Will you let me take Pietro out in your boat?"

He smiled. "Yes, on condition you take me as well. I get a little free time, you know—the evenings are light enough now, and the week-ends. But what I wanted to tell you was that I have a cottage in Cobbler's Bay—Aunt Bella was thinking of having a month there, anyway. She could take Bessie; my uncle never wants to leave this house if he can help it—and Pietro can stay with her there."

"And I can go there every day! Oh, Jonathan, thank you, thank you so much!" She jumped up and held out her hands to pull him up from the floor. "Let us go and ask Aunt Bella now—please—then I won't have to write and put Pietro off . . . he has been looking forward to coming here for so long!"

"I'll be glad to see him again," Jonathan contributed dryly. "I have a professional interest in his cranium!"

"Dr. Adler has given permission; he is very pleased with him."

Aunt Bella looked up when they entered the kitchen, laughing, and her eyes were kind.

"Thank goodness you've come down—I've been tactfully waiting to make the tea and I'm parched! You made a nice little series of puddles all the way up my stairs, young Nicki. Now come and tell me what it's all about."

While she brewed the tea and they carried trays upstairs, they poured out the story of Pietro's possible disappointment.

"Of course we'll have him, and we'll have him at Vine Cottage," Aunt Bella promised placidly. "It's just the place for a boy who likes messing about in boats." She turned to Nicole. "I never had a son, dear, but I helped to bring up three nephews, so your cousin will be quite safe with me. I know what boys like to eat, too."

"Thank you—*thank* you, Aunt Bella!" Nicki cried, gibing the plump little woman the kiss of gratitude she would have liked to offer Jonathan. He sat a little away from the women, letting them settle final details, aching with the question he could not ask Nicki . . . the question about Nigel. He knew that this coming holiday for Aunt Bella and Pietro would be a bitter-sweet interlude for himself. Cobbler's Bay was delightful, an old fishing hamlet that was too small to take in many holiday-makers, and Vine Cottage—he must get Vine Cottage in order at once. If he paid old Creehan enough of a bonus the men could be working there tomorrow——

His thoughts took a practical turn, and he excused himself to telephone the builder. Though Nicki would only be visiting Vine Cottage every day for a few weeks, he would have it ready for her down to the last detail. . . . He would make it as much like the *albergo* as he could, and perhaps a happy time there with Pietro would cure her homesickness for Lugano, and be an escape from the conventional life of Osterley House.

His poor little wild goose had been trapped indeed, by her pity for an old sick woman. But he could look further ahead than a girl of her age, and he knew that before long she would probably be able to lead any life she chose; she would be able to buy herself a dozen Vine Cottages and a mansion or two into the bargain.

That blasted money! he thought wearily, when he had spoken to the builder, who had promised to put the interior work in hand immediately. "And the outside colour-wash, doctor, if the saints stop this downpour before the week is out!"

The discreet promise of a handsome bonus for time saved had worked wonders. Money again. Jonathan was thankful he had enough to procure this little pleasure for Nicki . . . but what he had would be mere chickenfeed against the Stannisford thousands.

He would have to be very, very careful not to influence a grateful child like Nicki during Pietro's visit. . . . He, at least, would avoid emotional blackmail at all costs.

CHAPTER EIGHT

AUNT BELLA entered into the arrangements for Pietro's holiday with complete enjoyment. Having a boy of ten again would bring back the happiness of Jonathan's school holidays, and without fuss or bustle she attended to many details in the week that followed.

Stephen Grant, as they had predicted, preferred to stay in his own home. But he had no objection to his wife deserting him for a month or so. "Leave me Thomas and I shall be quite comfortable—probably spend my evenings at the club. I never was much use in cottages, or on the water," he said with a twinkle in his eye. "But no match-making, my dear."

"Match-making?" Aunt Bella was all innocence. "I leave that nonsense to silly old things like Helen, dearest."

Stephen had not mentioned the matter of Helen's will again to any member of his household. Helen had particularly asked him not to confide in Bella.

"Bella always *disliked* Henry so much, Steve," she said on a small sigh.

"Perhaps because she was always very fond of you," Steve retorted.

But Helen had a way of side-stepping arguments. She said softly, "Bella would be furious with me about this will, but I think I know what Nicole wants——"

"What Nicole wants at twenty-two may not be what she will want at forty-two." Stephen Grant had made a last effort to get the new will drafted on what he considered a just basis. "And after all, the money is hers, by right, Helen, without any strings attached to it."

"If it comes to that," the old lady argued with sur-

172

prising obstinacy, "Henry had a right to do what he liked with his own money. It was not entailed."

Now Stephen Grant was a little perturbed about this project of a holiday for the young Italian boy. Jonathan would surely spend most of his admittedly small free time with them at Vine Cottage, and Nicole would certainly be there every day. He hoped Bella was not planning anything foolish. He trusted Jonathan and Jonathan's pride completely, but he did not trust Nature, and young people could very easily fall in love in romantic, rustic surroundings. Stephen Grant was not a hard man, but he had the legal mind and its attitude towards the responsibilities of great fortunes.

He was also much too fond of his nephew to want him to get badly hurt, and he found it difficult to believe that any young girl could withstand the temptation offered by enormous wealth and power.

Aunt Bella even found time to go and talk to Helen, who had not been enthusiastic about the cottage project. "Nicole is a little inclined to behave in a bohemian fashion now," she complained gently. "This cottage idea will make her worse."

"You let her off the leash now and then, my dear," Bella patted her friend's hand, "or we shall have her running away altogether."

Nigel was inclined to sulk, too. "You won't have any time for me at week-ends, Nicki. I've never seen you so excited—anyone would think this little Wop was a real relation of yours!"

"But he is. He's more of a cousin to me than you are," Nicki flamed, "and he is not a Wop!"

Nigel apologised so humbly that she allowed him to accompany her to Folkestone to meet Pietro.

"*Carissimo*, but you have grown! At least four inches," she exclaimed, as the boy ran down the gangway of the steamer and flung himself into her arms, with much kissing on both cheeks.

"I grew a lot in bed," he boasted, "and Dr. Adler says I can do almost anything now. Who is that pale man with you? He looks like a *gigolo*."

She flushed and drew away a little. Pietro had been speaking in Italian, but Nigel had heard the word *gigolo* and he looked furious. Nicki said firmly, "Here we must speak English; it is rude to talk when others cannot

173

understand . . . and this is my cousin, Nigel Stannisford. Say how do you do to him properly."

"You're still talking Italian!" Pietro grinned like a monkey, but he held out his hand stiffly to Nigel. "How do you do. I also am Nicki's cousin. My name is Pietro Fionetti."

Nigel shook hands, but he wanted to spank the cheeky-looking child. However, the journey to London was filled with Nicole's loving questions about all at the *albergo* and Pietro's excited descriptions of his travelling adventures. He insisted on delving into his shabby fibre suitcase then and there to exhibit his treasures—the new clothes Emilio had bought for him with Nicole's present of money, the photograph of the wedding group when his brother married Francesca last week, the special cake Lucia had baked for Nicki.

"It has been dull without you," he broke into Italian again, involuntarily, "but when I go back it will be better. Francesca makes everything very nice."

Nicki suffered a tiny pang. Already he was talking of going back, already Francesca had taken her place at the *albergo* . . . but of course she had. Nicki told herself firmly not to be a fool, to be glad they had Francesca.

Nigel was not good at talking to children. He squirmed inwardly with embarrassment when people passing their carriage raised amused eyebrows at the mess on the seat. He thought the Italian wedding-group ghastly, and the rich cake in its cardboard box a sticky mess. He was glad when they finally got into the train for Combe Castleton. If this wiry little brown-skinned boy with his excited chatter and gestures was a sample of Nicole's beloved friends, she could keep them.

He dusted a crumb of *Torta alla Crema* carefully from his immaculately creased trousers, unconscious of Nicki's amused glance.

Nicole insisted that Pietro should be presented to her grandmother before going on to the cottage. Helen was kind to the boy, though she winced when his strident young voice rang excitedly through the boudoir.

"I am sorry that you cannot stay here as we planned, Pietro," she said gently, "but as you see, I am not very well and I have to rest a great deal."

"Me, too, when I hurt my head"—the boy grinned and touched his scalp where the thick dark hair had grown over the scar—"I had to rest for a long, long time. Too long. But now I don't have to rest any more, only not to fall on my head again. And I am happee to stay in a little house by the sea—I have not seen the sea before yesterday."

"Well, I hope you have a nice holiday." Helen dismissed him with a box of candy, looking wistfully at Nicole, whose face was glowing as she had never seen it glow before. "I shall not see you again until Monday, I suppose, dear?"

Joyce and Paul and Nigel were spending the week-end at Osterley House to keep Helen company, as Joyce said pointedly, while Nicole played sailors at the beach cottage. To them it was like old times, having Helen to themselves; but Helen knew that for her it would never be the same again. She would miss Nicole if only for a few days. . . . "Have a good time with your little friend, dearest," she whispered as if to make amends for her selfishness in wanting to keep the girl by her side . . . what was it Bella had said? *I should let her off the leash now and then or we shall have her running away altogether. . . .*

Well, she would not see much of Nicole for the next month, but she would put up with that if it made the child happy, if she lost the restless, rebellious look that sometimes crossed her sensitive face. Helen knew that Nicki was grateful, she wanted to bind the girl by ties of love and gratitude.

"Thank you, Grand'mère—for everything!" she whispered back, impulsively, stooping to kiss the soft cheek on the pillows. After all, Grand'mère had paid for this holiday for Pietro, for the new clothes and the journey anyway. Jonathan was providing everything else.

He came after dinner to fetch them, and the Stannisfords were mildly supercilious when the little Italian boy flung himself wildly at the surgeon.

"*Caro mio* Jonathan! I am here at last! I have been good, have I not? No more holes in my coconut!"

That was their own little joke. Jonathan rumpled the thick dark hair with gentle fingers. "Very good. For that you shall sail my boat, *Bluebird*."

"Ooh! What a car!" Pietro exclaimed joyously as they went out on the porch. His look begged Jonathan to let him sit in front, and Jonathan glanced at Nicki, who nodded.

"Of course. He will want to see how everything works."

She sat behind them, deeply contented. It was heavenly to be leaving behind the musty gloom of Osterley House, if only for a week-end (it had been Aunt Bella's idea that Nicki and Jonathan should spend the first week-end at the cottage, to make Pietro feel at home), and during the next month she would be at Cobbler's Bay every day. There was a bus service from Combe Castleton. And with Aunt Bella to see that she did not get into mischief, there was no need for any excort from Osterley House.

For the first time since her arrival Nicole felt free. It was like old times, sitting in the back of the car listening to Pietro's careful English that broke every now and then into Italian, to Jonathan's deep-toned replies. There was a smile in his voice today as if he, too, had temporarily escaped from the routine of his ordinary life.

He answered, patiently, all the boy's questions about everything they passed: the cathedral, the town, the harbour, and the little fishing hamlet for which they were bound, further along the coast. As soon as they were within sight of the sea Pietro fell silent, glueing his nose to the car window, rapt with this new joy. Even the weather had been kind to them; the August day had been long and bright, and now there was the soft summer twilight over everything; the red cliffs with their emerald crowns, the coves and beaches far below, the ships swinging gently to their anchors.

Nicole had not seen Vine Cottage. She thought that it had been rented for Aunt Bella's holiday; she did not know that Jonathan had only recently bought it, in a fit of recklessness, when the old owner died; she did not know that it had just been redecorated throughout. She only knew that it was delightful, that she loved it from the moment Jonathan pointed down the lane at the long, low, thatched cottage. The lane wound past Vine Cottage to other small houses, only a handful of them, and then down to the cove that sheltered half a dozen fishing smacks and a few private boats drawn up on the sandy beach. Cobbler's Bay was not large enough to attract the tourist steamers that invaded the larger beaches, it still belonged to the local inhabitants. From the front windows of Vine Cottage they could look down to the bay, from the back there were the rolling hill pastures, some golden with grain, some already harvested and ploughed.

Aunt Bella was on the doorstep waiting for them when she heard the car. She threw a smile towards Nicki and

Jonathan, but her eyes and her outstretched arms were for the boy, who stood shyly for an instant before running to her. Already Pietro realised that in England one does not make too free with kisses, with embraces; one shakes hands stiffly, with silly how do you do saying . . . but here at last was the beaming face, the open arms, the deep bosom which he had missed so sorely since his mother's death. Aunt Bella and Pietro disappeared into the cottage, and Jonathan grinned as they put the car away in the small garage.

"I don't think you'll have to worry about him, Nicki."

"I am not worrying about him." Nicole stood on the cobbled mossy path, staring entranced at the cottage. It had been newly washed in warm, glowing apricot; the creepers that gave it its name had been carefully tied back to the walls again. The windows were leaded, the thatch curved above them like smiling eyebrows; and they were all wide open, with white curtains blowing in the soft breeze. Hollyhocks leaned negligently against the cottage, and the garden was a tangle of overgrown roses and lavender bushes. It reminded Nicki a little of the *albergo*, as Jonathan had intended it should, only the house was not dilapidated. *I can tidy the garden*, she thought joyously, *when we are not in the boat; the days are so long at this season*.

And now, for a whole week-end, Jonathan was with them . . . her cup was full and running over.

"I am too happy to worry about anyone!" she cried, thrusting her hands into the slanting pockets of her linen frock with the old familiar gesture.

"You like it?" he asked unnecessarily, blinded by the smile she turned on him.

"Oh, Jonathan—so much! This is a home, not a museum. I think people have been happy here . . . but it's not a cottage, it's a house."

"It was two cottages I—er—they knocked two cottages into one," he explained rather lamely. "It's often done. It has only four bedrooms now, and a sleeping porch."

"Please—show me everything," she commanded, and he realised what she had been missing during her stay at Osterley House, apart from the freedom of her life in Lugano. There, she had been to all intents and purposes the mistress of the house; at her grandmother's she was a mere visitor in an over-staffed household. He was suddenly thankful that Bessie was such a nice person, she and Bella would not resent Nicole taking her share of the household chores at Vine Cottage.

He held out his hand to her. "Come and see everything, then," he bade her with a smile that held tenderness. This was his Nicki, his little wild goose, and everything he had had done to Vine Cottage had been done for her, though he knew she would only be there during Pietro's holiday. Nevertheless, the game of make-believe was infinitely worth while; he could pretend at least for a few weeks that this was their home. . . .

Her enjoyment of everything more than repaid his anxious thought, the money he had spent. Through the open french windows at the back of the living room they could see Pietro and Aunt Bella exploring the orchard; the contents of the boy's case were strewn on the floor, where he had been showing his treasures to his new friend.

"Sst! The untidy one! He will be spoiled." With a graceful gesture Nicki sank to her knees, collecting the oddments, rapidly, deftly. "Where does he sleep, please?"

Jonathan, suddenly amused by the little touch of maternal fussing, showed her the boy's bedroom, her own, Bessie's, and his aunt's. To her worried question he answered that he would use the sleeping porch, which was quite comfortable at this time of the year.

Nicki was in love with everything. Most of all with Jonathan, who had made this happiness possible. She had no experience of renting cottages in the English seaside villages, but this one struck her as unusual. It had period furniture, and glazed chintzes, and a few ornaments that were obviously good. Aunt Bella had probably brought the linen and arranged the flowers, yet——

"This house belongs to a friend of yours?" she demanded bluntly. "It is too good for ordinary summer tenants, I think."

Jonathan was looking down over the bay. "It belongs to me," he said casually. He longed to turn and tell her, *It is yours, my darling, if you want it* . . . but how could he bribe her, guileless and inexperienced as she was at present, with a cottage that happened to take her fancy because it reminded her of the place where she had spent her girlhood? In a few years, he reminded himself bitterly, she will be able to buy herself all the cottages and yachts she wants. And a husband or two into the bargain.

"*Jonathan!*" She came to him and planted herself so that he had to turn and meet her incredulous gaze. "You

178

mean—all this is *yours*? And yet you live in the town? There's a bathroom, and electric light, even a telephone," she added accusingly, glancing out through the open door at the landing. "You could easily live here, and still do your work in the town."

"I suppose I could." He answered her meekly, so that she was immediately suspicious. "But I only bought it three weeks ago. The old chap that owned it had a couple of boats; he looked after *Bluebird* for me as well. When he died it seemed sensible to buy the place when I had the chance."

"But you will live here, one day?" she argued, almost pleadingly. "Such a house is a home, Jonathan. It doesn't like to be left empty."

"Perhaps I will, one day." He was casual, dry, seemingly indifferent. He gave her no clue to his longing to take her in his arms and kiss her until she cried for mercy, to make her a free gift of Vine Cottage and himself and all that he possessed. "And now we'd better take Pietro down to the beach before it gets too dark to see the steps."

That first week-end went too swiftly for Nicole in her happiness. It was like old times, being with Jonathan and Pietro on the water. *Bluebird* was only a sailing dinghy, and Nicki soon mastered her, learning of the currents and rocks and tides. Pietro was in his seventh heaven, and because he already loved Tia Bella he was not even unduly naughty, he consented to rest occasionally. Aunt Bella and Bessie were happy, too; preoccupied with the comfort of the menfolk, and the fun of making a new home, if only a temporary one.

Aunt Bella had secret hopes that it might become a permanent home for her beloved Jonathan, but she was too tactful to press the matter. Meanwhile she and Bessie bottled the fruit from the small orchard and set it in neat, shining rows in the larder.

"It will give you something to fall back on, when you have an odd week-end here," she told Jonathan when he teased her about it.

The only bitter taste in Nicki's rediscovered happiness and freedom was that Jonathan never made love to her; he was just as he had been at the *albergo*: friendly, loving, teasing, but never sentimental. And yet instinctively Nicki knew that he had rushed through the decorations of Vine Cottage to please her. Everything had been done to give her joy, except the one thing she wanted most. She had spoken to Jonathan himself and her grandmother so frankly about the Stannisford money that it never occurred to her that she was the heiress to a vast estate.

During the first week of Pietro's holiday she slept at Osterley House, dutifully visiting her grandmother in the mornings and evenings, trying to tell the old lady of their doings down at Cobbler's Bay without hurting her feelings. But each day when Parkinson drove her down to the bus stop she felt like a prisoner released. All the week she looked forward passionately to seeing Jonathan again, though she had to hide her feelings from everyone.

But their second week-end was ruined for Nicki when Jonathan broke the news that he had to fly to America to attend a very special conference on nerve surgery.

"But—but your work—the hospital?" Nicki faltered, stammering in the sudden pain of her disappointment. Four week-ends was so little to ask of life, and she was going to lose two of them.

"The hospital wants me to go," he answered cheerfully, "and I wouldn't miss this for anything. Addison and McDiad are going to be there—this branch is very closely allied to my work, Nicki. I'm sorry to miss the rest of Pietro's holiday, but it can't be helped."

And me . . . what about me . . . ? her sore heart demanded, but there was no answer to the question. She did not know that his cheerfulness disguised relief, because these hours with her at Cobbler's Bay were becoming dangerously precious to Jonathan.

Perhaps Nigel was right, she thought sadly. Perhaps he was the sort of man who would never love again, would never be able to trust a woman again, or perhaps he was still in love with the woman who had run away from him to marry an American. Perhaps—and her sore heart jolted rebelliously at the thought—he would even see her while he was in the United States. Perhaps that was why he was so cheerful about going.

CHAPTER NINE

WHEN JONATHON got back from America Nicole had gone. His aunt and uncle were obviously disturbed about the whole thing, as well as Helen's sudden death.

"I came as soon as I could, after getting your cable,"

Jonathan said, lighting his pipe. "Now let's hear exactly what did happen."

Stephen Grant cleared his throat. Then, remembering that it was only Jonathan, he spoke in his normal voice. "Helen died suddenly last week, as I cabled you. Just didn't wake up from her afternoon nap, the way Dr. Cranford hoped it would happen——"

"A nice way to die, since we all have to go through the unpleasant business," Aunt Bella contributed dryly. "I hope I go in my sleep, dear."

"I hope you won't have to think about dying for years yet, Bella," her husband replied brusquely, forgetting that he, Bella and Helen were all of the same generation. It was upsetting enough seeing all one's old friends going, without this further anxiety about Nicole.

"Was Nicki—frightened?" Jonathan asked quietly.

"No—no, I don't think so. They sent for Dr. Cranford, of course, at once. Coles and Mrs. Moore are both sensible women, not given to hysterics. Nicole was down at the cottage, and a little later Parkinson went down with the car to fetch her home."

Home, thought Jonathan, with quick compassion—that dreary Victorian barracks with a lot of antagonistic servants, and an old lady lying dead in it. Poor Nicki! But somehow, after all she had been through as a child in France, he did not think she would have run away from death.

"Were none of her loving relatives available to break the news to her?" he demanded ironically.

"No, thank God. Poor old Helen died in peace."

Bella said gently, "I saw her afterwards. She looked wonderfully young and happy, Jon."

He nodded. He was familiar with death. He knew how it could erase the marks of an unhappy life from tired features. His pity was all for the living. "Nicole . . .?" he reminded his uncle, who seemed heavy with thought.

"Nicole behaved very well. Dr. Cranford was very kind to the child, naturally. She stayed for the funeral, and Joyce and her family came to Osterley House, and Bella brought Pietro back here so that they could be close together." Stephen sighed suddenly. "I'm afraid it was the will that sent her away. She just packed up everything, saying she would take Pietro back to Lugano, and would not leave me any forwarding address. She said she would get in touch through the bank, later."

Jonathan could imagine it all. The dreary sadness up at the big house on the hill, the crocodile tears of Joyce and her family. Nicki running away from it all, if only for a little while, escaping to the people she knew and loved best in the world . . . and he had been away when she most needed a friend here in England.

"No message for me?" he asked, too casually.

Stephen shook his head. "She seemed to be running away from something."

Aunt Bella looked up from her knitting. "She left a parcel for you, Jon. It's up in your study."

It meant nothing to him then. It was probably something of his she had borrowed from Vine Cottage. Uncle Steve was saying heavily, "I couldn't stop her, of course. She is over twenty-one, and in the unusual circumstances quite her own mistress."

"She is probably running away from the responsibility of too much money," Jonathan contributed grimly.

"But she isn't—she doesn't inherit," Stephen argued worriedly, "though I think the will is unjust. I wanted her to contest it; there is a legal prejudice against these family feud wills nowadays, we might have upset it easily."

Jonathan raised his head. "Tell me about the will," he said, in an odd, stifled voice.

Steve shrugged. "Helen said she was only carrying out Henry's wishes, and that Nicole herself did not want a fortune. Still, how can a girl of that age decide what she wants?"

"Nicole is very wise, for any age," Jonathan said almost to himself, and Bella smiled into her knitting. "Tell me the terms of the will, Uncle Steve. They're not confidential any more, surely."

"Of course not. I read it to them all, after the funeral." He coughed with embarrassment, remembering the occasion, and Jonathan could imagine it. Joyce, with her hard, eager eyes, Paul fiddling with something, Nigel waiting to hear his fate, and Nicki——

"Nicole didn't want to come, but I insisted." Stephen smiled suddenly. "She said she knew all about the will, her grandmother had shown her the draft." He went on in his quiet, dry voice to tell Jonathan about the terms. One half of Helen's whole estate went to Nigel; several thousand pounds to various servants; the residue to Nicole if she married Nigel. If she did not wish to marry her cousin she inherited five thousand pounds only, the rest went to medical research.

There was a small silence in the comfortable room. Bella's knitting needles clicked busily until she said, "I still think that was an iniquitous will, Steve. You should have refused to draw it up."

Her husband sighed. "Helen said she would put it in the hands of another firm if I refused."

Jonathan got up restlessly, prowling about the room. At last he got out the question, "Is she going to marry Nigel?" And it seemed to him as if the whole universe was waiting for the answer.

Stephen Grant frowned. "I don't know. I can't understand them at all. Nicole laughed when I asked her, and told me to ask Nigel. Nigel said there had never been any question of marriage between them. Of course, he has plenty without, now—but Nicole would be in a very different position if she married her cousin."

Aunt Bella made a noise like a small snort. "A beastly and horrible position, Steve. He's not good enough for her."

Jonathan left the room suddenly and strode along the passage to his study, looking for the parcel Nicki had left for him. It might contain some sort of clue to the abominable puzzle.

It was there on his desk, a big, flat package. Before he had undone the string Jonathan knew what it was. The painting of the *albergo*, which Nicki had said she wanted to add some finishing touches to before he had it. Staring at it, he felt it might mean everything—or nothing. It might merely mean that she was never coming back——

He picked up the light case he had not yet unpacked and put his head round the door of the living room. He grinned at his uncle and aunt as they looked round to him. "I'm going to Lugano. The hospital doesn't expect me for five days; I can do if it I fly. 'Bye."

Stephen Grant looked more perplexed than ever, but Bella's expression as she knitted was suddenly like a young girl's, full of sweet mischief.

Lugano looked very much as it had done four months ago, except that the leaves of the chestnut trees were turning colour already, and there was no Nicki greeting him casually at the *debarcadero centrale*. . . . The noonday sun glazed the surface of the lake to spun glass, and the imperturbable mountains looked down on the traveller as if to reassure him that the tumult of his heart was unnecessary. This time he hired one of the small motor-boats to take him to Gandria, and ordered the boatman to wait. Now that Francesca was installed as Emilio's bride he did not know whether he would be welcome to stay or not.

There was no sign of life on the front steps. The green shutters of the inn were closed against the noonday heat. Jonathan ran up the worn old stone steps lightly as a boy, but his heart was full of doubts. Nicki might have left already . . . might have started on the troubadour, wandering life she had always planned for herself. The untidy garden was quiet, too, and deserted. Only the neat rows of vines were heavy with grapes. Emilio would probably be having his usual picnic lunch between trips somewhere on the shores of the lake, the children might be back at school. . . . He walked quietly into the familiar kitchen, and old Lucia looked up from her rocking-chair and screamed softly as if she had seen a ghost.

"*Dio mio!* Jonathan!"

He crossed the kitchen to take her hands, smiling as he pushed her back into the chair. Francesca came running to see what the commotion was about, and exclaimed and smiled when she saw who it was. "Jonathan—*benvenuto*!"

"Nicki . . . ?" he asked tentatively, when he had greeted her.

Francesca smiled broadly, shrugged, opened her hands in a helpless gesture, and fired a broadside of questions at old Lucia. Then at last she turned to Jonathan and explained in halting English, "Always she is out. Lucia say she gone today to the grave of her mother, the cemetery of Morcoté."

"Thanks." He had turned and gone round the garden way back to the steps before the women had finished explaining to him how to get to Morcoté. He knew, Nicole had taken him there. He knew exactly where the graves were in the hillside cemetery, the graves of Evelyn and Maria Fionetti.

The boatman raised eyebrows at the new direction, shrugged, and set his engine going. It was a hot time of the day to be cruising from one end of the lake to the other, and his boat had no cover, but this *Inglesi* would probably repay him for his discomfort and his trouble. They were all mad, anyway.

"There are more than four hundred steps to climb, *signore*," he warned cheerfully as he drew alongside the jetty at Morcoté.

"I know. Wait for me, please." Jonathan threw him a twenty-franc note, more than twice his fare, and the man grinned.

"Si, si, signore!"

The four hundred steps took a lot of climbing, but Jonathan was in better condition than he had been in May. He took them steadily, in blocks, resting now and then to get his breath, and at last he came out past the old stone church and the many marble statues of angels and cherubs who guarded the dead in this peaceful place. At this hour there were no other visitors, and he found Nicole kneeling between her graves in the deep shadow of an ancient cypress tree, putting fresh flowers in the vases.

He came to her quietly over the soft turf, but because he did not want to startle her he coughed, once, and she looked up instantly. Her lips formed his name, but no sound issued from them. It seemed to Nicki, here in this peaceful garden of rest, that a miracle had come to pass for her. She had hoped Jonathan would write to her, but that he would come, so soon, like this, she had not even dreamed.

Kneeling there with the flowers strewn about her on the grass, a spray of roses in her hand, she looked to him like one of the younger angels poised among the graves. It did not seem an odd place for them to have met again. They smiled, as if they had met after a long, long time of separation; and because she was so impeded with her flowers and vases he dropped to his knees in front of her, and kissed her forehead.

"Thank God you're still here," he said prosaically. "I thought you might have started on your travels."

Nicki smiled again. She could find no words for him, unless she betrayed all she was feeling. She only said, childishly, "You climbed four hundred steps to find me?"

"Yes." As she seemed stunned he took the roses from her and put them in one of the vases. "Nicki, I came to ask you something. Do you want to marry Nigel?"

She shook her head emphatically. "No."

"Not even for a hundred thousand pounds, Nicki? It's a hell of a lot of money."

"Not even for a million!" she chuckled suddenly. "Five

185

thousand pounds is enough to do a lot of travelling, Jonathan."

"Yes. . . . Which is it to be, Nicki—a wandering foot or a heart at rest?"

She did not answer for a moment. She finished arranging her flowers and placed them gently on the graves to right and to left. Then, softly, not looking at him, she whispered, "There is only one place my heart can be at rest, Jonathan. . . . I have tried to tell you so many times."

"Nicki—my very dear, dearest little wild goose, will you marry me?" he asked steadily.

It seemed as if all the sleeping dead on this steep hillside above the azure lake were listening for a girl's answer. Jonathan added shyly, "It's an odd place to propose, my darling, but I can't wait any longer. Do you still want to wander round the world, or will you come and stay with me, always——"

"At Vine Cottage?" she whispered, and her eyes were shining like the lake far below them. Like the azure canopy of sky above their heads.

"At Vine Cottage, except when I have to go away, then you'll have to come with me." He added, putting a hand to tilt her face towards him, "I've loved you a long time, Nicki, but I thought you were going to be horribly rich——"

"Oh, Jonathan! I have loved you always, I think—and I'm horribly rich. I have five thousand pounds, and Vine Cottage, and you."

The kiss they exchanged was very gentle, very reverent, not unbefitting to the place where they knelt. Their passion would come later. As they got up at last, Nicki said softly, "I think this is a wonderful place to plight our troth—for who will be more pleased about us than my mother and Tia Maria?" And before they began the long, slow descent of the steps they left a loving glance with the two women who slept side by side.

When Nicki saw the hired boat she chuckled. "Such extravagance! I was going to go home with Emilio, his next trip. Shall we tell them at the *albergo*, Jonathan, or not?"

"Of course we'll tell them," he boasted boyishly. "We'll tell the whole world! And tomorrow, my darling, we'll be flying—*home*."

THE END

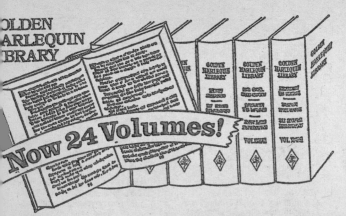

Harlequin readers will be delighted! We've collected seventy two of your all-time favourite Harlequin Romance novels to present to you in an attractive new way. It's the Golden Harlequin Library.

Each volume contains three complete, unabridged Harlequin Romance novels, most of which have not been available since the original printing. Each volume is exquisitely bound in a fine quality rich gold hardcover with royal blue imprint. And each volume is priced at an unbelievable $1.75. That's right! Handsome, hardcover library editions at the price of paperbacks!

This very special collection of 24 volumes (there'll be more!) of classic Harlequin Romances would be a distinctive addition to your library. And imagine what a delightful gift they'd make for any Harlequin reader!

Start your collection now. See reverse of this page for full details.

H
GHL 3?

FREE!

Harlequin Romance Catalogue

Here is a wonderful opportunity to read many of the Harlequin Romances you may have missed.

The HARLEQUIN ROMANCE CATALOGUE lists hundreds of titles which possibly are no longer available at your local bookseller. To receive your copy, just fill out the coupon below, mail it to us, and we'll rush your catalogue to you!

Following this page you'll find a sampling of a few of the Harlequin Romances listed in the catalogue. Should you wish to order any of these immediately, kindly check the titles desired and mail with coupon.

F

FC 372

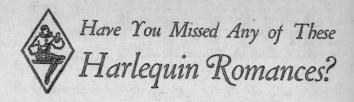

Have You Missed Any of These Harlequin Romances?

All books listed are 50c. Please use the handy order coupon.
C

Have You Missed Any of These
Harlequin Romances?

All books listed are 50c.   Please use the handy order coupon.

D

Have You Missed Any of These Harlequin Romances?

- [ ] 1100 THE BROKEN WING
  Mary Burchell
- [ ] 1103 HEART OF GOLD
  Marjorie Moore
- [ ] 1031 FLOWERING DESERT
  Elizabeth Hoy
- [ ] 1138 LOVING IS GIVING
  Mary Burchell
- [ ] 1146 THE IMPERFECT SECRETARY
  Marjorie Lewty
- [ ] 1149 A NIGHTINGALE IN THE
  SYCAMORE   J. Beaufort
- [ ] 1164 MEADOWSWEET
  Margaret Malcolm
- [ ] 1165 WARD OF LUCIFER
  Mary Burchell
- [ ] 1167 DEAR BARBARIAN
  Janice Gray
- [ ] 1168 ROSE IN THE BUD
  Susan Barrie
- [ ] 1171 THE WINGS OF MEMORY
  Eleanor Farnes
- [ ] 1173 RED AS A ROSE
  Hilary Wilde
- [ ] 1181 DANGEROUS LOVE
  Jane Beaufort
- [ ] 1182 GOLDEN APPLE ISLAND
  Jane Arbor
- [ ] 1184 THE HOUSE OF OLIVER
  Jean S. Macleod
- [ ] 1213 THE MOONFLOWER
  Jean S. Macleod
- [ ] 1242 NEW DOCTOR AT NORTHMOOR
  Anne Durham
- [ ] 1307 A CHANCE TO WIN
  Margaret Rome
- [ ] 1308 A MIST IN GLEN TORRAN
  Amanda Doyle
- [ ] 1310 TAWNY ARE THE LEAVES
  Wynne May
- [ ] 1311 THE MARRIAGE WHEEL
  Susan Barrie
- [ ] 1312 PEPPERCORN HARVEST
  Ivy Ferrari
- [ ] 1314 SUMMER ISLAND
  Jean S. Macleod
- [ ] 1315 WHERE THE KOWHAI BLOOMS
  Mary Moore
- [ ] 1316 CAN THIS BE LOVE ?
  Margaret Malcolm

- [ ] 1317 BELOVED SPARROW
  Henrietta Reid
- [ ] 1318 PALACE OF THE PEACOCKS
  Violet Winspear
- [ ] 1319 BRITTLE BONDAGE
  Rosalind Brett
- [ ] 1320 SPANISH LACE
  Joyce Dingwell
- [ ] 1322 WIND THROUGH THE
  VINEYARDS   J. Armstrong
- [ ] 1324 QUEEN OF HEARTS
  Sara Seale
- [ ] 1325 NO SOONER LOVED
  Pauline Garner
- [ ] 1326 MEET ON MY GROUND
  Essie Summers
- [ ] 1327 MORE THAN GOLD
  Hilda Pressley
- [ ] 1328 A WIND SIGHING
  Catherine Airlie
- [ ] 1330 A HOME FOR JOY
  Mary Burchell
- [ ] 1331 HOTEL BELVEDERE
  Iris Danbury
- [ ] 1332 DON'T WALK ALONE
  Jane Donelly
- [ ] 1333 KEEPER OF THE HEART
  Gwen Westwood
- [ ] 1334 THE DAMASK ROSE
  Isobel Chace
- [ ] 1335 THE RED CLIFFS
  Eleanor Farnes
- [ ] 1336 THE CYPRESS GARDEN
  Jane Arbor
- [ ] 1338 SEA OF ZANJ   Roumelia Lane
- [ ] 1339 SLAVE OF THE WIND
  Jean S. Macleod
- [ ] 1341 FIRE IS FOR SHARING
  Doris E. Smith
- [ ] 1342 THE FEEL OF SILK
  Joyce Dingwell
- [ ] 1344 THE DANGEROUS DELIGHT
  Violet Winspear
- [ ] 1352 THE MOUNTAIN OF STARS
  Catherine Airlie
- [ ] 1357 RIPPLES IN THE LAKE
  Mary Coates
- [ ] 1393 HEALER OF HEARTS
  Katrina Britt

All books listed are 50c.   Please use the handy order coupon.
B